A CLOUD'S LIFE

A.L. SMITH

ISBN: 978-1-4834-4182-5 (sc)
ISBN: 978-1-4834-4181-8 (e)

Because of the dynamic nature of the Internet, any web addresses or links contained in
this book may have changed since publication and may no longer be valid. The views
expressed in this work are solely those of the author and do not necessarily reflect the
views of the publisher, and the publisher hereby disclaims any responsibility for them.

Any people depicted in stock imagery provided by Thinkstock are models,
and such images are being used for illustrative purposes only.
Certain stock imagery © Thinkstock.

Lulu Publishing Services rev. date: 11/19/2015

WEATHER FORECAST

This is the second book of the series written in memoriam to those 'Wonders of Wythenshawe' that set out each day to either deliver weather or to use their unique skills to perform unbelievable tasks.

'Making rain and other things is our business' introduced readers to the crew of the Nimbus and provided a taste of what they got up to both romantically and work-wise. 'A Cloud's Life' elaborates on both.

Fire-fighting, delivering a spy and undergoing training set the scene, whilst saving a ship in distress provides further evidence of a cloud's life. Add to this, helping the Navy and delivering whisky-making water and the scope becomes enormous.

A Cloud's life is never far from tragedy in one form or another and whether it is on the Isle-of-Man or in the far north of Scotland the crew battles on to overcome adversity.

Romance in one form or another is never far away from the cloud machine scene and when jealousy strikes, the Chelsea Flower Show gets the sticky end.

If all this is not enough, you can always count on the skipper of the Nimbus letting you know what he thinks about the way the country is being run. If you think you can put up with all this weather stuff, read on, but be prepared for a stormy ride.

This book is dedicated to all cloud watchers. If you watch from below them, above them, or within them, it makes no difference to me; it's still dedicated to you!

If you are a star gazer, and have your hobby interrupted by a cloud, it could be one of mine. Unlike the stars and the rest of the Universe mine are not natural; they are just a man-made figment filling a need and the odd empty lake.

If in true British tradition you find the weather something to laugh about, this book is for you, but if you get wet, don't blame me.

CONTENTS

Maps

Preface

Background to the stories

From very small beginnings in 1985 the weather making-industry began and its clientele were very young. The industry has grown and its current clientele span a very wide age group from around the Globe.

My first book – **Making rain and other things is our business!** – takes the reader from those early beginnings into the modern day hurly-burly of making rain and other things. **A Cloud's Life** – continues the revelations.

There has always been a fascination with weather and the idea of being able to produce it on demand has long been an ambition of man. World War Two spurred rapid development in many areas, notwithstanding weather, but much of it has been kept secret.

The secrets of Wythenshawe Weather Centre and its weather-making as finally been revealed to an unsuspecting population. The many facets of weather-making, some surprising, some less so, are now available for anyone to read about. The whole business is now very well developed and encompasses both manufacture and training.

There is a great camaraderie between the crews of the cloud machines that operate from Wythenshawe and, as in all walks of life, they are a collection of people with different virtues, aspirations and codes of morality. They all have their own job preferences and romantic encounters as well as their own political viewpoints and they bring a special charisma to every weather making occasion.

These crews are innovative, creative, humorous and mad and along with these attributes, they bring romance, tragedy and patriotism to their daily work....honest!

There's a lot more to tell about weather-making. Let's face it; it goes on 24/7 but for the moment, read these accounts. You won't believe them but I bet you'll be taking a second look at clouds from now on.

July 17th 2013
Tony Smith

Acknowledgements

As with my first book, 'Making rain and other things is our business!' this latest contribution could not have been created without the help of three particular people. My neighbour Helen cast an eye over my work for spelling, punctuation and other mistakes. I suffered a comma syndrome at one point and they dropped on the pages like confetti. Without Helen I could never have cleared away those that were not necessary. Andy Cooper from Draw & Code Ltd produced the charismatic front cover that captures the spirit of the book and Eddie Challoner, now a Wing Commander in the RAFVR (T), updated the pilot's cockpit details for the Nimbus. I am indebted to each of them but if they intend visiting me I do hope they remember, I don't like grapes.

INTRODUCTION

Weather is both a natural phenomenon and man-made, but in the case of the latter, it has long been a Government secret that Manchester is the home of man-made weather manufacture.

Man-made weather is produced on demand by specially produced cloud machines, which, in cloud form of many alternative types, convey rain, of different levels to wherever it is required. Lightning, thunder, snow and a myriad of other weather forms are also available on demand.

Manchester is the only place in the World where cloud machines are manufactured, and Black, Black & Blakemore's in deeper Salford, are the specialist in this field.

Cloud machine owners are registered and certificated. Their machines have annual MOT tests to keep their 'certificates of airworthiness' current, and they are operated in strict accordance with the 'Cloud Machine Operators Rules of Operation Manual'.

Work available for cloud machine owners is always advertised in Wythenshawe Weather Centre, and agreements are made there. Cloud machines not in use are normally kept in a hangar at the Centre. There are many other weather centres around the World but they generally only deal with natural weather.

The stories told have as a central figure cloud machine owner Captain Cirrus Cumulus and his faithful engineer Percival White, generally known as Puffy, who crew the Nimbus.

The Nimbus and its crew performed a variety of jobs that most people would never associate with a cloud, but perform them they did. Fighting forest fires may seem appropriate enough but delivering spies, guiding a lost ship, helping families to keep their doting offspring apart, and posing for Calendar photos is stretching it a bit, but that's what they did, as well as help with funerals.

A cloud's life is fraught with problems and the crew of the Nimbus learned to cope with the many eventualities they faced by attending one of the courses organised by The Guild of Cloud Owners and conducted at Bishops Court Training Centre. The value of their training is regularly put to the test.

Mishaps in the cloud business are not infrequent. A crash, a freeze-up and a kickup the…. were all just an everyday part of life for a cloud, but we are simply not aware of these things.

Passion, jealousy and sabotage may seem strange bedfellows but where would a cloud be without their influence? Here is a chance to find out.

WHAT'S THE NEXT JOB?

Contemplating in Slaidburn

Captain Cirrus Cumulus CDM was sitting in the comfort of the lounge in his Slaidburn home. It was mid-morning, and his companion and faithful engineer, Percival White, known to everyone as Puffy, had already brought him his cup of coffee, and the daily paper, known as the Daily Gloom to the pair of them. Cirrus was busy scanning the paper to locate the five per cent that normally interested him. Usually, anything to do with the state of the country would attract him, but he also had a fixation about reading the 'stars'. He claimed that he didn't believe a word of them but he never failed to consult his own, Sagittarius or Saggy Arse, as Puffy called it. Today there was little gloom to whet his appetite, but there wasn't anything else either that he had an inclination to ponder on.

Several weeks had passed since the pair of them had taken a job on in their cloud machine, the Nimbus, which currently lay dormant in the large hangar at Wythenshawe Weather Centre. Cirrus felt no pressure to go hunting work. Financially, he was well off at present having already completed a number of lucrative jobs earlier in the year, but he was not anxious to spend a long period doing nothing. Having recently visited St. Kilda, on a rather special mission, he felt a fresh pulse of energy and couldn't wait to get started on something, but preferably something new.

There was always work available with Eddie Stormbart's convoy runs around the world, but that was pretty boring stuff in general. Each convoy simply consisted of a form-up somewhere over the Atlantic, followed by taking on board large quantities of water to be converted into cloud, and then a long journey to a dry place, to make rain, and then start all over again. The money was good, but Cirrus wanted more than this.

The Nimbus was in good condition; no maintenance or repairs were currently needed and its Certificate of Airworthiness had only recently been renewed. Both Cirrus and Puffy had current cloud machine pilot and engineer licences so there was nothing required in these directions that could have occupied them.

That's a thought, thought Cirrus, there might be a course we could take a look at doing!

"Puffy," yelled the Captain.

"Aye, aye skipper," replied Puffy.

"Bring me the latest copy of The Monthly Downpour will you?"

"Right away skipper."

The Monthly Downpour was the journal produced by The Guild of Cloud Owners, and had a section devoted to courses.

The Captain carefully scanned the page with all the relevant details. The list was not long: First Aid, General Maintenance, Air Law, Health and Safety Regulations, Meteorology, Navigation. There was nothing that really inspired him.

Scratching his head, the Captain was clearly at a loss as to what to do, and Puffy was not much help either. He wondered what some of his colleagues may be doing, at least those that were not working for Eddie Stormbart. What about Abigail Windrush, and her sister Lucy? Now there was a thought! Abigail and Lucy, both stunning looking young women, both intelligent and independent and both most pleasant to be in the company of.

An important call

"Captain there's a phone call for you."

That brought the Captain back from a potential day dream.

"Who's it from?"

"The Superintendant from Wythenshawe Weather Centre."

"I better take it then."

It's usually something special if the Superintendant calls, thought Cirrus, and he picked up the phone with a degree of trepidation.

"It's Spite here, is that you Cirrus?" enquired the Superintendant.

"Yes it is, what can I do for you?"

"Cirrus I need you at the Weather Centre pronto. Get here as fast as you can."

"It sounds like you have got something big on, Mr Spite."

"I can't talk about it on the phone; just get here as soon as you can."

"I'm on my way."

With that the Captain called his engineer Puffy to join him.

"Puffy there must be an emergency on of some kind. We are to make our way to Wythenshawe as fast as possible, so get our standby kit together, and sling it in the back of the car."

"I wonder what that can be?" remarked Puffy.

One and a half hours later, the crew of the Nimbus arrived at the Weather Centre and dashed inside to Mr Spite's office. Cirrus knocked on the door and it was opened by his secretary, a red haired young woman, that everyone called 'Goldilocks'.

"Mr Spite is in the Planning Centre," Captain Cumulus.

"Thanks."

They rushed to join the Superintendant and had quite a surprise when they entered the Planning Centre. Both Abigail and Lucy were present, along with Wally Lenticular, and Albertino Insomnia.

"Good to see you Cirrus," said Mr Spite.

"Now let's get straight to the point. There is a huge fire running out of control in the Kielder Forest, in Northumberland, and the Fire Service has requested our assistance. So, here we are! In a nut shell, I want you to check your machines over, and take aboard any supplies you need. When it's dark I want you to get airborne, and get over the Irish Sea and create a cloud. Then you can proceed to Kielder, and make contact with the Fire Chief."

"What supplies do you think we will need?" asked Abigail.

"Well apart from fuel for your fan duct motors, I think you should take enough food and drinking water for a few days. We can't be sure how long it's going to take to put this fire out."

"Who is the Fire Chief, and how do we contact him?" asked Wally.

"The Fire Chief is Mr O. V. Wrought, and on arrival at the location you can call him on the radio using a frequency of one, two, two, decimal two, two. Have you all got that?"

There was a unanimous reply of yes, and without any further ado, they all dispersed towards the huge hangar that made the Centre so identifiable.

Preparing the cloud machines

Inside Wythenshawe's huge hangar the presence of five cloud machines left the place looking decidedly empty. Nevertheless, each of the identical looking machines looked impressive. Bullet-shaped with two fan duct motors on each side, they looked futuristic. Each machine had two large saddle tanks on each side, one for fuel, and one for water. Other lumps and bumps hid various kinds of antennae for the various bits of kit on board.

Captain Cumulus approached the Nimbus, which stood ahead of him on its retractable undercarriage. He climbed the entry ladders and stepped inside to gain entry into the crew compartment where he sat in the forward-facing pilot's seat. He had a good view outside through the cockpit windows, but they were of limited value. Normally being surrounded by cloud, his view of the outside world would be provided by a pop up TV screen which received its image from an infra-red TV camera mounted above the machine in what looked like a periscope. The beauty of this device was that it could be rotated through 360° to give an all-round picture. For the moment it was time to focus on the fuel gauges.

Puffy dragged a fuel hose in the direction of the Nimbus and, as he did so, he couldn't help noticing Lucy making her way to her machine, the Softly Blows, with her engineer Peter Arnolds. He couldn't help thinking how lucky Peter was, but he didn't spend much time thinking about it. With a figure like she had, and a superb backside, his mind wandered to more embracing thoughts. That didn't last long either for, on reaching his destination, it was time to plug the fuel hose in and give his Captain the thumbs up before starting the fuel flow.

The same refuelling process occupied the crews of the Softly Blows, the Hurricane, the Discovery and the Astro. With that job out of the way the skipper of each machine checked out all the various systems whilst their respective engineers loaded the rest of the supplies they would need. Having stocked the galley, each engineer took up his or her position seated behind their pilot, facing rearwards at their instruments. It was the engineers that were responsible for atomising water down on the Earth's surface and either storing it as water in the machine's two saddle tanks or freezing it into ice and storing it in the onboard refrigerators. Some of the atomised water would be turned into cloud vapour and dispensed out into the atmosphere through grill-covered dispensers mounted along each side of the fuselage. This would enable the cloud vapour to immerse the machine in its midst, hiding its presence from the whole of humanity.

The engineer could control what type of cloud the machine produced, Westmorland Whites, Cumberland Greys and Manchester Blacks being the more usual. The clouds could be turned into rain, and here again there was a selection of options: intermittent, light, heavy, steady drizzle, torrential downpour and so on.

There were also other things that these versatile machines could do, but they can be referred to at a later date. In addition to this weather function each engineer looked after all the communications with mother Earth, or other machines, using either the radio equipment, or the on board telephone.

Fully loaded, and tested, the crews of the five machines got together to determine the plan of action. From the Nimbus came Captain Cirrus Cumulus, and his engineer Puffy White, from the Hurricane its skipper Abigail Windrush, and her engineer Josh Harrop, from the Softly Blows its skipper Lucy Windrush, and engineer Peter Arnolds, from the Discovery its skipper Wally Lenticular, and his engineer Bert Drummond and finally from the Astro, its skipper Albertino Insomnia, and his cracking-looking engineer, Carol Aspinall.

Captain Cumulus assumed command, but none of the other male crew members were really concerned, they were more interested in where Albertino had been hiding his engineer Carol. Wherever it was, they would like to be in hiding with her.

The Captain began, "As soon as it is dark I propose we head off over the Irish Sea and load up with cloud stuff. Then we can make our way to the Kielder Forest and make contact with the Fire Chief and take it from there."

"Who will navigate?" asked Wally.

"I will," replied the Captain. "And you all follow me. Once airborne check your radios using the appropriate call sign. Any Questions?"

When no-one responded it was time for a brew up, and a bit of a wait until it got dark. In spite of the urgency of the forest fire, cloud machines were not allowed to be seen by the general public; they were at all times to be hidden by their own cloud.

For the next hour or so the conversation revolved around Albertino's engineering beauty and how she had escaped everyone's notice, at least the men's notice!

Setting off

Captain Cumulus entered the Nimbus followed by Puffy, who then retracted the entry ladder into its stowage position below the side door which he then closed making a deep sounding thump as it did so. The entry portal led to a corridor which ran down the length of the machine. Turning left led to the aircrew cockpit whilst turning to the right led to the stern of the craft and the toilet and washroom. On each side of the corridor there were a total of nine compartments consisting of six refrigerators, a mixer, a sublimator and the all important galley. Dim strip lighting in the corridor ceiling gave a special atmosphere to the craft.

The crew of the Nimbus entered the cockpit, which was always an exciting place to be. The first thing that hit you on entry was the pilot's position, which had a large, comfortable, forward-facing, leather seat in front of a flight deck peppered with dials and buttons, and above it a series of windows which gave an excellent view out, which at the moment was the inside of Wythenshawe Weather Centre's huge hangar.

Sandwiched between the pilot's seat and the flight deck was a typical aircraft control column, and if you looked down, you could see what appeared to be a set of aircraft rudder pedals. They did the same job as those on a real aircraft, and would yaw the machine left and right, but they did it without a rudder, they swivelled the direction the fan duct motors faced instead. To the left of the pilot's seat was a Plan Position Indicator. It was a floor mounted device which held a display at seat height so that the pilot had an easy view of it. When operating, the PPI display was like a round TV picture, which displayed in green the lay of the land at ground level. A horizontal line extending from the centre of the screen to the outer edge rotated through 360°, and as it did so, any aircraft or cloud machine within 50 miles of the Nimbus would appear as a dot. Data at the side of any dot would give its height and identity, but the latter depended on the ID system being switched on in the other craft. The position of all these other sky travellers in relation to the Nimbus could be seen quite easily, since the very centre of the screen represented the Nimbus itself.

To the right of the pilot's seat was a box, out of which protruded four throttle controls, one for each of the fan duct motors. To the right of the throttles there was a position where a spectator could stand and watch, and a hand rail ran along the top of the flight deck.

Behind the pilot was the flight engineer's position. A rearwards-facing leather chair faced a small table top above which there was a myriad of dials and controls to do with clouds and rain, along with communication equipment. The table was used to place a chart on, if one was needed for navigation purposes. Most crews also found this table top useful when eating a meal.

Looking to the right of the cockpit there was another leather seat, but forward-facing. This was for any passenger or observer that may be aboard, and just in front of the seat, but set into the starboard fuselage side, was a drop down double bunk, which was very handy if you were on one of Eddie Stormbart's convoy runs.

Once in position, the crews started up the fan duct motors and taxied their machines out of Wythenshawe's hangar and into the outside darkness. Each made a vertical take off and rose steadily into the black abyss. As they ascended, the street lights of Wythenshawe presented a more attractive vision of the place than its daylight counterpart, but the detail was lost as each craft continued aloft until reaching 5000 feet, at which height they headed West, out to the Irish Sea on a heading of 270°.

On the journey to the sea each cloud machine checked its radio, and Puffy got to hear the different call signs;

"This is the Hurricane calling."

"This is the Softly Blows calling,"

"This is the Discovery calling."

And then the delicious voice of Carol Aspinall calling out, "This is the Astro calling."

The mere sound of Carol's voice had Puffy in a quandary, and he had to be prompted by his Captain to get on with it, and use his call sign.

"This is the Nimbus calling."

That was a pretty useless thing to be saying to that gorgeous thing in the Astro, thought Puffy, but he couldn't do anything about it right now, but given half a chance?

When the five machines reached a position over the Irish Sea halfway between Liverpool and the Isle of Man, Captain Cumulus called them to a hover, and issued the instruction to atomise 4,000,000 gallons of sea water each. He had been able to see them all up to this point on both his TV screen and his PPI but soon that would change.

After one hour, each of the five cloud machines was filled to the brim with 4,000,000 gallons of Irish Sea, some stored as ice and some in its natural state in the vessels saddle tanks, and now it was time to wrap each other up in cloud.

"Now listen in everybody, this is Captain Cumulus aboard the Nimbus speaking. I want you to create a Manchester Black around yourself and report back to me when you have done so."

With that the flight engineer on board each craft operated the various controls required to turn water and ice into the cloud vapour which, when dispensed out into the atmosphere, would surround them until they had become the very centre of a huge and menacing Manchester Black. These kinds of clouds are particularly frightening in daylight as they extended thousands of feet upwards and took on the shape of an anvil at the top. Most people knew that when these things were about, torrential rain was not far away and would set about taking shelter.

Not everyone had set their controls identically, and the Manchester Blacks were not all finished at the same time, but when they were, it was time to make the journey to the Kielder Forest.

Navigating in the dark

The five Manchester Blacks started on their way to the fire in a long line with the Nimbus leading. Captain Cumulus navigated using his PPI and he headed north over the Irish Sea. On the starboard side was the English coast line and Blackpool, and as they made progress with the help of a south-westerly wind, they passed between the Isle of Man and the Cumbria coast. Getting level with Workington, it was time to set course for Kielder.

"Puffy, give me the latitude and longitude for Kielder will you?"

"Aye, aye skipper."

Puffy spread the chart out on his table and worked out the details his Captain had asked for, and gave them to him.

Cirrus punched the information into his navaid, which looked like a large calculator with all its function buttons. In fact on the Nimbus, the navaid was an early version for cloud machines and was designed to enable them to navigate to various sources of water, and then atomise it for storage and cloud-making when they got there. The device had been called a Soakometer, the first four letters standing for Seek, Overland, Absorb and Karry. The absorb function had been disconnected. These days, the device simply had the job of navaid, but it was still called a Soakometer by the crews.

A radio call was made to the other cloud machines.

"This is the Nimbus, to the Hurricane, Softly Blows, Astro and Discovery. I am about to turn onto a heading for Kielder, so be sure to follow me on your PPIs. If you have difficulty doing that, contact me, and I will give you the lat and long to punch into your Soakometers."

The Captain could have given them the lat and long in the first place, but experience told him that, if he did that, he would probably end up with five Manchester Blacks going to five very different places. This way he might keep some control over things.

The Nimbus turned onto its new heading and the other four machines fortunately followed. At a height of 5000 feet above sea level they would have ample clearance of all the hills on the way to Kielder.

"Puffy swap places with me for a moment will you? I want to look at the chart."

Reluctantly Puffy sat in the pilot's seat. He was nervous looking at all the dials and buttons on the flight deck, but his Captain was reassuring.

"Just look at the compass and keep us on the heading we are on now. You can steer the Nimbus just like a car, but use the rudder pedals as well, if necessary."

With that the Captain moved to his engineer's table to study the chart and make some notes. Puffy on the other hand gripped the control column very tightly, and couldn't take his eyes off the compass. For him this was a genuine white knuckle ride.

Cirrus did not want to arrive at Kielder until daybreak, and he wanted to hold over a known location about an hour's flight time from his destination. Much of the country he would be flying over had few easily recognisable features that would show up on his PPI, and that was the problem. The TV camera on board was of little use in the middle of a Manchester Black, so he had to rely on his PPI to be sure of exactly where he was. After some time he decided that he would come to a hover over Carlisle airfield, at a place called Crosby. He could spot that easily on the PPI and it was on the same heading that he was flying on. When the Nimbus crossed the Cumbria coast at Maryport, it would be about an hour's flight time to Crosby.

Puffy was greatly relieved when his Captain took the helm again.

"Puffy, call the others up and tell them that in an hour's time we will come to a hover over the aerodrome at Crosby, and will remain there for about two hours, before setting off again, so there will be a chance for everyone to grab a bite and maybe a short kip."

"Right you are skipper."

The hour passed without incident and the airfield at Crosby was easily spotted on the Nimbus PPI. Captain Cumulus brought his machine into a hover and all four machines following also did the same. A Manchester Black occupies a considerable area and the Nimbus itself more than dwarfed the airfield below. The other four stretched back as far as Carlisle, and a little beyond, and that's where they would remain for the next couple of hours, much to the consternation of anyone down below that would be up at such an early hour. There's nothing as alarming as a Manchester Black immediately overhead. The sensible thing to do when faced with this situation is to take cover and fast.

Puffy took the opportunity to nip into the galley and soon the smell of bacon was circulating around the flight deck, much to the pleasure of Captain Cumulus, who couldn't resist the aroma. A cup of coffee, a bacon butty and a leisurely chat was something to be relished at times like this.

"What did you think of Albertino's engineer?" asked Puffy.

"Very nice indeed. It's always nice to have some good looking girls around. It makes the job that bit more pleasurable. But I must say I think Abigail is the more attractive, and her sister is a good looker too."

Bless me, thought Puffy. It's unusual for the Captain to talk like that.

"Who do you fancy Puffy?"

"Well it used to be Lucy, but now it's definitely that curvy Carol girl."

"When this job's done, we will have to invite all the crews to Slaidburn."

Brilliant, thought Puffy.

On board all the other machines it was a similar story of eating and drinking, together with chatting, and a short snooze. But whilst all this was going on, a layer of natural stratus cloud was flowing in a north easterly direction, directly below them at 4000 feet. For the moment their crews were oblivious to the outside world being nicely cocooned in the centre of a huge storm-bearing cloud, raring to downpour.

Time to move

With one hour to go to daybreak Captain Cumulus gave the order to move, and the five lumbering great Manchester Blacks set off, on the final part of their journey to dampen the flames raging in Kielder Forest. In one hour's time they could do what they had come to do- rain, and very heavy rain at that. As usual, nothing ever went completely to plan!

The Nimbus was first to pass between places called Roadhead and Bewcastle, although the crew were not aware of it. Since both places were so small, they didn't show up on the PPI. The Captain was flying on a heading, and timing the journey with a stop watch. What was below was a bit of a mystery. However, as the Astro, which was third in line, reached the same spot, it began an unscheduled torrential downpour which descended to Earth through the layer of stratus below it. There was only livestock to complain, and apart from the odd 'moo', 'baa' and 'neigh' there was little else happening on the now rain-soaked ground. There was, however, an important outcome to this, for the Astro rained its useful fire fighting load and, in its new shrunken fashion, was reincarnated as a Cumberland Grey.

"This is the Astro calling."

"Come in Albertino," replied the Captain.

"I'm terribly sorry, but I've lost my rain."

"What do you mean; you have lost your rain?"

"Well, you see it was like this. My engineer Carol, well she decided to sit on the chart table and do her nails. As a result, and without her realising it, she inadvertently altered the controls on the Astro to create a torrential downpour, and here we are now, a Cumberland bloody Grey."

"Damn it Albertino, you are a dozy sod. Anyway, when we get to Kielder you better move south east over the reservoir, and standby to top up in case you're needed," replied an annoyed Captain Cumulus.

With thirty minutes to go, it was time to call the Fire Chief Mr O. V. Wrought. Puffy dialled in the frequency to be used by his radio transmitter, one, two, two, decimal, two, two, or in normal language 122·22Mhz.

"This is the Nimbus calling Fire Chief Overought."

"Just call me bloody Fire Chief, and who the dickens are you?" came the reply.

"You better let me handle this Puffy."

"Aye, aye skipper."

"This is Captain Cumulus on board the cloud machine Nimbus and I am accompanied by four other machines that have come at your request, to help put the fire out."

"Ah, at last! You've taken your time anyway. Where the hell are you?"

"We will be over Kielder in approximately ten minutes, at least I will be, and the others are following in line astern. I will hover over Kielder when I arrive and call for your instructions."

"Very good Cumulus, and about time!"

Judging by the gruffy response of the Fire Chief, they must have had it rough down there, thought Cirrus, but at least we will give some help now.

Daybreak arrived and the Nimbus came to a hover over Kielder. Behind the Nimbus three other machines did the same and the order consisted of the Hurricane, the Softly Blows, and the Discovery, each with 4,000,000 gallons of fire-quenching water. The Astro took up a position on their starboard side over the huge Kielder reservoir, which would be their topping up source if needed.

"This is the Nimbus calling the Fire Chief."

"Where the bloody hell are you? All I can see is a layer of cloud covering the whole of the damn sky," shouted the Chief, over the radio.

"We are going to have to descend through the stratus layer, Chief. When we pop out of it let me know, because you will be able to see us, but we can't see you in our present form."

"Well get on with it then."

The Captain was a bit apprehensive because although his altimeter showed the Nimbus as being at 5000 feet, it was 5000 feet above sea level, and in this area the land was about 1800 feet above sea level, and that meant that they were only 3200 feet above the ground.

"This is the Nimbus to the Hurricane, Softly Blows and Discovery. I want you all to descend slowly, and stop as soon as the Fire Chief tells us to. There is a layer of stratus cloud below us that we must get below, so the Chief can guide us to where he wants us to rain. We must be careful because we are only 3200 feet above the ground as it is, so don't be fooled by your altimeters."

Four cloud machines descended slowly together, or at least they thought they were descending together; in reality they all descended at slightly different rates. They didn't know it but they reached the top of the stratus at 4500 feet on their altimeters, and popped below, and into the Chief's view at 4000 feet. It was not until they had reached 3000 feet that the Fire Chief gave the instruction to stop. They now had a height above ground of about 1200 feet.

The Fire Chief was amazed as he looked up at the Nimbus. The part of it that he could see was pretty menacing, large, widespread and very black. It extended up to, through and above the stratus, although the Chief was not aware of that.

"Ok Nimbus, follow my instructions. Come forward, stop. Left a bit, stop. Now rain!"

The Nimbus began a torrential downpour that landed on a number of acres that soon turned from a hot cauldron to a soggy quagmire, and after thirty minutes the Manchester Black was changed into a small Cumberland Grey, just like the Astro. The Nimbus was instructed to leave the scene and join the Astro, and standby for refuelling if necessary.

The Hurricane was called forward and it did its bit on another number of acres of burning forest land. The Fire Chief was most impressed with the effect of these monstrous Manchester Blacks, delivered by the Wythenshawe Weather Centre, and he made a mental note to thank the Superintendant, Mr Spite, at the earliest opportunity. Then it was the turn of Lucy Windrush in the Softly Blows, but once directed to her allocated location there wasn't as much as a spit, and panic set in. Her engineer, Peter Arnolds, dashed down the corridor to check a part of the machine's dispenser equipment that was notorious for developing problems. A sharp banging in a strategic place with a small hammer cured the equipment's reluctance to work, and the spit turned into the usual torrential downpour, that would turn the forest land below into a walker's nightmare, but done so legitimately.

What was left of the Softly Blows now moved sideways to join the Nimbus, Hurricane and Astro in the direction of Kielder reservoir.

The Fire Chief was now confident that one more dousing like the first three should completely extinguish the forest fire and he and his fellow fire-fighters could all go home or to the pub, whichever they preferred.

Wally Lenticular followed the Chief's instructions just like his colleagues had until he was in such a position that he could finish the job they had started. He generated the fourth deluge which was to prove to be the final straw for any flame that dared to show itself in the woods of these here parts. With the flames extinguished and the Discovery only a small shadow of itself, Wally could now see for the first time, on his pop up TV screen, the results of his handy downpour. A blackened landscape as far as the forest below extended was a new scar on the Earth's surface, but Mother Nature would heal all that at an unbelievable speed. Bert Drummond, the engineer on board the Discovery thought it was amazing how the craft's TV camera had begun to see as the cloud density diminished with the downpour. The picture quality was really good too.

With the job complete, there was no reason for anyone to hang around, and bidding Overought, the Fire Chief, farewell the happy five headed back to Wythenshawe.

A reason to party

Mr Spite was there to greet the five returning fire-fighting cloud machines as they descended in the dark. They had dispensed their Cumberland Greys over the Irish Sea on their return journey, fulfilling their obligation never to be seen naked in the public eye. Having landed, all five machines taxied straight into Wythenshawe's huge hangar and parked up in their allocated spot. When the hangar doors were closed, the crews disembarked and gathered around the Centre's Superintendant.

"Congratulations everybody! That was a job well done and Fire Chief Wrought says you are all to be commended. Now take a rest before you take on anything new."

With that Mr Spite left the group and Cirrus quickly jumped into his speech spot.

"I want to take the opportunity of inviting you all to my place for a party, and I think we should do it soon, what do you all think?"

Puffy certainly thought it was a great idea and it got better as he looked Carol up and down and then down and up again. He was beginning to feel dizzy with all this up and down business before Abigail popped the first question.

"What about next Saturday Cirrus?" asked Abigail, who went on, "All of us seem to be free then?"

"That's fine."

"But where can we all stay? If we are going to have a drink we must stop the night somewhere," said Wally.

"You leave that to me," replied Cirrus.

"We may need to do a bit of doubling up but we can sort that."

Doubling up, doubling up! What a brilliant idea thought Puffy. And I know who I want to double up with.

With that the five crews dispersed to make their way home.

On the journey to Slaidburn, Puffy was feeling a warm glow of contentment, which was probably mixed with a degree of optimistic lechery. But where would everyone sleep? True, the Cumulus abode in Slaidburn had four large bedrooms, each with a double bed, but that would only accommodate eight people if they doubled up and there were ten of them. And what about food? Was he going to have to cook for everybody? Should he approach his Captain now or hold his counsel till later? Looking at the smile on the face of Cirrus, he thought better of it, and decided to put it off until another day.

A couple of days after the Nimbus crew had returned home, Puffy took the 'Bull by the Horns' and approached Cirrus regarding the food and accommodation arrangements for the forthcoming party.

"I think we will book us all a meal in the Hark to Bounty, and then all we have to worry about at home will be the wine and spirits, and some nibbles. Oh, we better make sure we have something in for breakfasts as well. On the accommodation front I think we can cope if we put a camp bed in each of the spare rooms, and one in yours."

That last suggestion put a damper on Puffy's ardour.

16

Slaidburn's big day

They all seemed to arrive at once, but Puffy managed to escort them all into the lounge to meet his Captain, who announced that for this weekend, he was to be addressed as Cirrus. That might be a bit difficult for someone like Puffy, for all said and done, old habits die hard.

Looking at those shapely legs of Abigail, Lucy and Carol, who were all wearing skirts, it must be spring thought Puffy. They always come out in spring! Walking behind them down the hallway and into the lounge was another joyous experience. The way they moved! It was poetry in motion.

Once in the lounge it was greetings all round. Peter and Josh, the engineers that worked with Lucy and Abigail, Carol's skipper Albertino and the crew of the Discovery, Wally and Bert; they were all there, the fire-fighters. There was just time for a glass of wine before walking to the pub and time to take a good look at the ladies.

Cirrus had never seen the ladies wearing make up before and he was clearly taken by them. Abigail and Lucy wore a little lipstick and whatever it was on their faces in small quantities to highlight their best features. They didn't need much, they were both stunningly attractive and Cirrus could only despair a little that he wasn't younger. Whilst he was reserved by nature it didn't prevent him from enjoying something or someone that was beautiful, and he was perfectly capable of passing a compliment which he duly did. Carol was more gregarious and her make up gave her away, but it did something for both her and Puffy who for once, felt that his pseudonym was a disadvantage, but that didn't stop him from arresting her waist in his right arm, a gesture she clearly did not find unpleasant.

Conversation started to flow, but it was soon time to walk the short distance to the oldy World 'Hark to Bounty' pub, through the attractive village. The atmosphere in the pub was convivial and they all felt immediately at home and the conversation continued over an excellent meal. It all seemed over in a very short time but it had taken a couple of hours to consume the food, and digest the conversation, and they all made their way back to the warmth and comfort of the Cumulus establishment.

Some sat and some stood, but they all drank, nibbled and talked, and Wally, along with all the rest of the men, looked at and admired the ladies' legs, as they sat comfortably with their skirts riding above their knees.

Isn't it wonderful how ladies sit and show off their legs, without showing their knickers? thought Wally, and six other men.

But it was nice to look!

Around the room there were all kinds of Cumulus memorabilia, which attracted a fair amount of interest. In a glass case hanging on a wall was Cirrus's CDM.

"Are you ever going too wear this medal Cirrus?" asked Peter.

"Oh yes, I will put it on for the annual St. Swithin's Day parade at the Weather Centre."

"Oh what a good idea, I never thought of that," replied Peter

"And what do the letters CDM stand for?"

"It's the Cloud Defence Medal," replied Cirrus.

Josh was fascinated by a book called 'The Nimbus' that he found resting on the sideboard. Apart from the text, which described how it had been designed and manufactured by Black, Black and Blakemore's in deeper Salford, he found the pop- up pages particularly interesting. They started with a cloud, a Westmorland White, and when that page was lifted the Nimbus was revealed in the cloud's interior. Lift that page and the interior of Nimbus was revealed. Other pages illustrated the pilot's cockpit and the flight engineer's station. Whilst Josh was all too familiar with the internal details of a cloud machine, he had not seen a publication like this before, and he found it enthralling.

On the coffee table in the middle of the room was a splendid model of the Nimbus, rather like an Airfix model. It was very detailed and the top could be lifted off to reveal the interior layout. All the external lumps and bumps enclosing the craft's various antennae were there, along with the saddle tanks for fuel and water. The periscope was on top, and four fan duct motors fitted, two on each side. It looked very impressive, sitting there on its undercarriage.

"Who is this?" asked Abigail, pointing at a photo of a rather stern male in flying kit. It said Biggles underneath but she didn't believe it.

"That was my Dad, I called him Jim Biggles," replied Cirrus.

"Did he fly?"

"Yes he did. He loved flying light aircraft."

"Did you fly light aircraft, Cirrus."

"I did start to learn, but I had to stop. It was too expensive. I did learn to fly gliders though."

"What did Jim Biggles think of that?"

"He used to embarrass me in front of his friends about it. He would pat me on my shoulders and say that when I grew up I could fly one with a fan on the front."

Lucy picked up a Cd and started to read the label on it. It was a Cd made by Leyland Band and featured several pieces by the composer Lucy Pankhurst: 'Mr Sonnemons Unusual Solution', 'A Pondering Prince and a Captain's Calamity', 'The Great Cloud Parade' and 'St. Kilda's Fling'. She had heard of the first three numbers and she had listened to Leyland Band play the last when she had returned to St. Kilda for what had been called 'The Great Shin Dig'.

"I never knew Cirrus that Lucy had composed all these pieces for you. Are there going to be anymore?"

"I'm not really sure, but I have an idea for a piece which I may call 'The Wonders of Wythenshawe'.

"Wow, that's a great title!"

It was well past midnight when Cirrus decided that he was desperately in need of sleep and announced the arrangements for the others before departing. Bert and Peter would be in with Puffy. Wally, Albertino and Josh would share a room, leaving Abigail, Lucy and Carol in the one remaining bedroom. Abigail made a point of intercepting him before he left and gave him a most affectionate kiss that didn't go unnoticed. They all followed shortly afterwards, with Puffy thinking to himself how crafty his Captain was, saving a double bed for himself. But still, there had to be some privileges for him, especially since he had footed the bill for everything.

The group slept well that night, but Puffy thought he heard the door of the room Cirrus slept in being opened and closed several times during the night. It could have been a dream, and he wouldn't dare ask any risqué questions. What was not a dream was that it had been a great weekend, and everyone left after breakfast, profusely thanking both Cirrus and Puffy, and requesting that they be invited again.

A Case Of National Security

The Nation Needs You!

That's unusual, thought Cirrus, as he sat in his living room gazing at the tranquil scene through the window of his Slaidburn home. The noise of a motorbike coming up the drive had roused his interest. A sharp knock on the front door was answered by his engineer and compatriot, Puffy.

"Captain, you had better come and sign for this," shouted Puffy down the hallway.

Cirrus got up from his favourite chair and strolled to the door where he met an all- leather clad, motorcyclist, with an official looking clipboard and pen.

"Are you Captain Cirrus Cumulus?"

"Yes, I am."

"Can you provide any evidence of your identity, please?"

Cirrus thought for a moment and then remembered his passport. Excusing himself, he went off to find it, and whilst he did, Puffy tried in vain to engage the visitor in conversation. Then his Captain returned.

"There you are; my passport."

"Thank you sir."

The passport was scrutinised and after examining Cirrus, and his passport photo, he was satisfied that he had found the right man.

"Would you just sign here sir?"

Cirrus signed in the space shown to him on the motorcyclist's clipboard, and had an official brown envelope thrust in his direction. The first thing he noticed on the envelope were the words **Restricted,** and **In Strict Confidence.**

Having made his delivery, the man in leather made a hasty retreat, sending a pile of gravel into the air as he sped towards the entrance of the Cumulus drive way.

"What's it about?" enquired Puffy.

"Let me take a look and I will let you know," answered Cirrus.

He carefully opened the envelope and took out an official OHMS letter, which also had the word **Restricted** across both the top and bottom, and it was a very short instruction that was being served on Captain Cumulus.

> **To Captain C. Cumulus CDM**
> **Officer in Charge – Cloud Machine Nimbus**
> **From The National Security Council**
>
> **Captain C. Cumulus is instructed to attend Wythenshawe Weather Centre on the 4th inst. at 1000 hours prompt, where, he will receive a security briefing. Photo identity must be brought. You are not to speak about this communiqué, or your pending brief, to anyone. On receipt of this notice you will at all times be working in accordance with the Official Secrets Act. Non compliance will result in a prison sentence.**
>
> **I am sir, your obedient servant,**
> **Major K.Oss OBE**

"I'm afraid I can't tell you anything Puffy, except that in a couple of day's time, I must attend a meeting at Wythenshawe Weather Centre."

And with that the Captain placed the letter back in its brown envelope, and then folded it before placing it in his wallet.

The journey to Wythenshawe was distinctly free from conversation as the Captain contemplated what would transpire. Really he didn't have a clue as to what it would all be about.

On arrival Cirrus suggested that Puffy look the Nimbus over, and make sure that everything was ok, as he made for the Superintendant's office. The Superintendant's secretary, known to all as Goldilocks, welcomed Cirrus, and explained that he would have to wait a few moments for Mr Spite, who had been called out of the office. This only heightened the Captain's anxiety, but wait he had to. In due course Mr Spite returned, and after exchanging pleasantries, he invited Cirrus to follow him into a room that he had never been in before. He was quite surprised by the fact that there was an armed guard on duty at the entrance to the room, but duty called and in he went.

"Allow me to introduce you to Major K.Oss."

"How do you do Major."

"Ah, you must be Captain Cumulus?"

"That's correct sir."

"Please sit down and let me brief you."

At last, thought Cirrus, I'm going to find out why I am here.

Major Oss began, "You are probably aware that the world we currently live in is a precarious place at the best of times. You are also probably aware of the fact, that around the globe there are a number of countries which don't look too favourably on the West. Indeed there are a couple of countries that, according to our intelligence, are contemplating retaliating against the West for the sanctions they have imposed on them. Without putting too fine a point on it, I am of course referring to Iran and North Korea. The North Koreans have a nuclear capability, and a means of delivering it, and the Iranians are striving to have their own. If either of these countries should strike, it could encourage the Taliban to make a grab for Pakistan's nuclear arsenal, and then we have a conflagration of enormous proportions."

The Captain couldn't help thinking how crazy it seemed, under the circumstances, that the Government saw fit to continue the run down of the country's defences. The two scenarios simply did not match up in his mind, and the strength of that view was reinforced by the fact that the Americans were busy strengthening theirs.

Major Oss continued; "Our intelligence suggests that neither North Korea nor Iran could be making the military progress that they are, without outside help. We think that the Russians are helping them with 'know how', and some special resources but we don't know what."

"Why would the Russians do that?" enquired Cirrus.

"The Russians feel weak materially in relation to the West and anything they can do to alter that would strengthen them politically. Giving aid to those with a disliking of the West could get them to do what the Russians would benefit from."

Where is all this talk going? thought the Captain.

"Our intelligence people have been doing some good work and have found indications that things are being masterminded from a place called Perechyn, which is situated in the Carpathian Mountains, in the Ukraine."

What we intend to do

Major Oss paused for a moment at this point, and consulted the documents in front of him before continuing.

"Everything you hear at this meeting, Captain Cumulus, must not in anyway be divulged to anyone. Is that clear?"

"Yes it is, but if you are ultimately thinking of using the Nimbus, my engineer, Percival White, would have to know some details," replied the Captain.

"That may be so, but we can cross that bridge when we come to it. Now let me continue. It is of paramount importance that we find out what is going on in Perechyn. We have no-one on the ground in that part of the Ukraine that is capable of infiltrating the organisation that we think is masterminding aid to Iran and North Korea. We don't have any spies locally, but we do have a safe house in Perechyn that could accommodate one of our agents, and give some limited support."

The Captain began to feel uneasy at this point, thinking to himself that the Authorities may be thinking of sending him. But that would be crazy; he didn't speak Russian for a start.

Whilst the meeting was going on, Puffy was busy checking over the Nimbus, but it was going at a very slow pace. Alongside the Nimbus in Wythenshawe's huge hangar was the Astro. Its skipper Albertino Insomnia was nowhere in sight, but its engineer Carol Aspinall certainly was, and Puffy was giving her more attention than the Nimbus. Carol was giving the Astro a wash down to remove a year's grime. A ladder, a bucket, and a sponge provided the tools for the job, and once up the ladder they all provided a spectacle that Puffy couldn't resist watching.

"Haven't you seen a cloud machine washed down before?" she enquired, as Puffy gazed in awe.

"Not with equipment like that I've not."

"Well don't just stand there, come and give me a hand."

With that, the Nimbus was forgotten and the Astro had a new crew member, and Carol got a doting helper, but she was pretty good at doing that.

"I am not suggesting that you, Captain Cumulus, should be sent to Perechyn," remarked Major Oss.

Cirrus was greatly relieved to hear that.

"We need an agent who speaks not only Ukranian but also the local Russian, someone whose looks would fit in with the local population, and who is familiar with the customs of the area. We need someone with the scientific knowledge and political nous, that could get to the bottom of what is going on."

"Those are a lot of complicated requirements, Major Oss. Is it likely that such a person exists?"

"You may be surprised Captain, but yes he does. We have a man that must remain anonymous; his father came to England from the Ukraine during the Second World War, and stayed. He worked in the Yorkshire coal mines, and was a member of his local Ukranian Club. There they practised their old traditions, and spoke Ukranian and Russian. His father passed on these traditions to his son, who has been working for us for some years."

"That's most opportune," remarked Mr Spite, who had remained silent up to this point.

"We are more fortunate than that," went on the Major.

"The safe house in Perechyn is owned by a relation of our agent's father."

"Would you believe it!" remarked Mr Spite, who himself was beginning to wonder where this was all leading.

Puffy's great moment came when he was holding the ladders for Carol. As she descended, she neatly placed her shapely backside in his face. Apart from feeling ecstasy, he almost lost his grip, but of course he had to to let her get off the ladder. He made his first move as she turned round, once she had placed her feet on the ground. He placed a kiss on her pink cheek, which she thought was sweet, but she carefully extracted herself from a potential embrace, whilst reminding him that there was a job to be getting on with.

Puffy was invited inside the Astro for a coffee, and the two got into conversation.

"How come the Astro is not on a job?"

"I could ask you the same about the Nimbus," replied Carol.

"I suppose so!"

"As a matter of fact, Albertino did have a job. You know that in the south east of the country there's a bit of a drought on, and the Chelsea Flower Show were desperate for some rain. They hired the Astro to come down and rain in the night."

"Well how come you are here then?" asked Puffy.

"Albertino overslept, and they sacked him."

"What's it like working for him, they tell me that these Latinos are very amorous?"

"He's Italian not Latin American, and yes he can be amorous, although I would call it more randy than amorous, but that's only when he can stay awake."

"We intend to place this agent in Perechyn, and get him to find out what is going on there, and that's going to be tricky," said Major Oss.

Cirrus wanted to delay what he thought was coming next and asked,

"What will you do when you find out what's going on?"

"That depends on what we find out. Whatever we discover, we will have to discuss both at Government level, and with our allies, before deciding on a course of action."

We all know what that means thought Cirrus. How many times have I heard this before? By the time a decision is reached, the nature of the problem changes, and the course of action taken is irrelevant, and when carried out, it simply generates a new problem. They call this democracy at work!

Before Cirrus could think much more, the punch line finally came.

"Our problem is getting our man into Perechyn undetected, and that's where you come in Captain Cumulus."

Although he half expected this, Cirrus was still shocked when he finally heard it from the Major's mouth, and he coughed and spluttered for quite a time until he had digested what he had just been told.

Cumulus – Special Cloud Agent

"We want you to get our agent to Perechyn."

After a long pause the Captain asked, "Why can't you get your agent there by any other means?"

"If we tried to get him in by road, or rail, the Russian authorities would know that he was in the country, and although they may not know that he is working for us, they would probably put a tail on him to check him out. The same would apply if we flew him in, or sent him by sea. The other thing is that we want to get him straight to Perechyn, and avoid any journeying through the country."

"Why not drop him by parachute, or smuggle him in by truck?"

"We couldn't fly an aircraft over Russian airspace to parachute him in without being picked up on Russian radar, and that would provoke an International outrage. And the risk of being detected trying to smuggle him in by truck, is simply too risky. No, we must get him in to Perechyn without the Russians having the slightest idea that he is there. That way, they will not be expecting him, and no special security arrangements may be in place."

Cirrus had a lot to think about; he wasn't trained for this kind of work, and what if something went wrong. Major Oss could see that Captain Cumulus was chewing things over in his mind.

"Look, there is a huge financial reward involved in doing this job for us."

"Maybe there is, but how do you think I could get your agent to Perechyn undetected? I might only be a cloud, but the Russians would get a radar return off the Nimbus, and that would be the end of it."

"That's not the case. You could enter the Ukraine as a ground mist, and travel in that form all the way through the Carpathian Mountains to your destination, and then drop the agent off to walk out through the mist. At ground level you wouldn't be picked up by radar, and in that part of the world ground mists are quite common, so you wouldn't arouse any suspicion."

"You seem to have it all worked out. What will happen to the agent when he gets there?"

"That's not really your concern, but as he emerges from the mist, he will rendezvous with his distant family relation and be taken to the safe house from where he can plan his next step."

"And what will happen when your agent as done his job?"

"You will go back to Perechyn and collect him."

"Two journeys; that's a bit risky isn't it?" asked the Captain.

"Well, that's the job. Take it or you may be ordered to do it," said Major Oss.

"I need time to think about it, and I do need to discuss it with my engineer."

"Very well Captain. You have until 1030 hours tomorrow to decide, and you will advise your engineer that he is compelled to act in accordance with the Official Secrets Act."

When the meeting was concluded Cirrus left the room and walked passed Goldilocks, who was busy filing her finger nails.

"You do look in a grumpy mood Captain," she said as Cirrus hurried through her office, but he ignored her, and pressed on to the huge hangar.

There was no activity around either the Nimbus, or the Astro and so Cirrus entered the Nimbus to find Puffy. A quick search of the interior did not yield any results, and he decided to check if anyone was aboard the Astro, since its entry ladder was extended to the ground, and its door open. As he stepped inside Albertino's machine, he was greeted by the sighing sounds of two individuals clearly enjoying each other. Stealthily, Cirrus moved towards the machine's cockpit, and the sounds got louder and of a more ecstatic nature. He peered into the cockpit and discovered that the drop- down bunk bed in the starboard fuselage was in full use, accommodating an attractive Carol wearing little in the way of clothing, and an equally undressed engineer, who went by the nickname of Puffy.

Cirrus did not hurry in announcing his presence, and had his education widened in terms of sexual relationships, but before it exhausted him, he decided that all things sexual must come to an end some time. He leapt into the confined space of the Astro's cockpit, and announced it was time to be going home. The shock of his arrival brought about the break up of a wonderful embrace, which was followed by a scramble for clothes, but Cirrus made a discreet retreat with a nice pink bra shovelled into his pocket. He had no idea what he would do with it, but waited outside the machine for a reaction.

"What have you done with my bra?" shouted a frustrated Carol.

"I haven't seen it," said Puffy.

"You've seen more than my bra, Percival White."

At this point a bedraggled Puffy clambered down the steps of the Astro, and was escorted by his Captain to their parked car. Before getting in, Cirrus handed the bra to Puffy saying, "This might have something to do with you!"

On the journey back to Slaidburn, Cirrus broke the news about his meeting with Major Oss. Puffy found it all hard to believe, but was in no doubt that they should do the job, and especially if a rich reward would be coming their way on completion. Neither of them cared to think too much about the consequences of being caught in the act.

On arrival in Slaidburn, it was time to reflect further on the pending operation, and to assist them, they turned to their charts of the area. They found Perechyn in the Ukraine and thought what a long distance it was from Wythenshawe.

"Will we start at Wythenshawe?" asked Puffy.

"I have no idea. No details of how the operation is to be performed were discussed, but let's take a look at the chart and see where this place is."

The chart was spread out, and they found Slovakia, and the border with the Ukraine. Just beyond the border, the Carpathian Mountains ran from North to South, and in one of the valleys, not far from the border, was Perechyn.

"How far is it from Wythenshawe?" asked Puffy.

Cirrus got his navigator's ruler out, and measured.

"It's one thousand, four hundred and eighty two nautical miles."

"That's a long way. How long would it take us to get there?"

Well if I assume no wind is blowing, and we flew at thirty knots, the maximum we are allowed to do, then it would take approximately fifty hours."

"Just over two days then," said Puffy.

"That's right, and that means just over four for the journey there and back."

"It's going to be pretty tiring, and I wouldn't want to be tired when I have crossed the Russian border," remarked the Nimbus engineer.

"Let's not get too far ahead. I will let the Major know tomorrow that we will perform the operation, and then we can find out what the plan is."

How 'Lucky' fits in

The journey to Wythenshawe was turning out to be tedious. The traffic was heavy, and in places there were delays due to road works. Cirrus and his engineer passed the time by chewing things over before the forthcoming meeting with Major Oss. Puffy would be present this time. The conversation was not confined to the work of secret agents.

"Are you going to see Carol again?" asked Cirrus.

"I'm going to see as much of her as I can," replied Puffy.

I wonder what exactly that means, thought Cirrus. He's already seen most of her.

"Don't you think you are a bit old for her?"

"I'm as old as she'll let me feel," replied Puffy, feeling a bit aggravated at being asked this.

On arrival at the Weather Centre it was the same procedure as before. Goldilocks beckoned them in to her office, where they remained whilst she checked to see that the Major and Mr Spite were ready for them. Then she escorted them past the armed guard, and into the room where the meeting would be held. It was still off-putting to be in a room that required an armed guard at the door, and it certainly reinforced the fact that this really was classified official business.

"Good morning gentlemen, and allow me to thank you both for volunteering to carry out this Government mission," began Major Oss.

Mr Spite spoke next; "I will tell you how much you will get later."

"Now before I talk about the plan, have you got any questions?"

"Yes," said Cirrus; "Is the operation to be mounted from Wythenshawe?"

"A good question and the answer is no. The operation will be mounted from a village in Slovakia, called Lucky."

"Well we should be so lucky," commented Puffy.

Major Oss continued, "Lucky is handy for a number of reasons. Firstly, it is only twenty six nautical miles from Perechyn, in the Ukraine. That means that you could reach your destination in an hour or so, depending on the wind, drop our agent, and be back again in another hour or so. The whole mission could be accomplished in a night, under the cover of darkness."

"How sure are you that the Russians will be unaware of what is happening?" asked Cirrus.

"You are going to make the journey hugging the ground, just like a ground mist. Russian radar will not detect you, in fact they will not have the slightest suspicion that something is going on, as there is nothing unusual about ground mists in the Carpathian Mountains."

The Major was making it all sound so easy, perhaps too easy, thought the Captain.

"On the South side of Lucky is an isolated barn, which is big enough to hide the Nimbus in before the operation begins."

"What about a water source?"

"Just North of Lucky is a man-made lake of substantial size, and it's called Zemplinska Sirova. That's your source of water. You can atomise it to create a cloud, and you can rain on it to get rid of one. What could be simpler?"

"It looks as if you have sorted everything," remarked Cirrus.

At this point the Major produced two maps, one of which showed the whole of Western Europe and the Western part of Russia. The border with Russia was clearly shown, stretching in the North from Poland to Romania in the South, with Slovakia and Hungary in the middle. The second map showed in much more detail the border between Slovakia and Russia, or The Ukraine to be more precise.

The second map was spread out on a large table and the Major indicated the location of Lucky and Perechyn, together with Zempliska Sirova.

"You can see from the map what a short distance it is between Lucky and Perechyn."

"The Carpathian Mountains stand in the way though," remarked Cirrus.

Yes, they have to be crossed, but it's not a mammoth challenge. They only rise to about nine hundred metres, that's approximately three thousand feet, and the gradients on the route are not fantastic."

The discussion then moved to the subject of the agent.

"Where do we pick the agent up from?"

"He will be waiting for you in Lucky, and we have a safe haven in the village that will look after you all. A kind lady, who will be known as Jitka, will be there to greet you and look after all your needs."

Puffy's ears picked up at this point, and his imagination started to work on the name Jitka, but he didn't get far as the conversation was about to move on.

The Major did not want to get involved in the detailed plan at this stage, but gave a brief outline of the operation.

"Your job will be to make your way from Wythenshawe to Lucky in the Nimbus, arriving under cover of darkness. On arrival you can rain on Zempliska Sirova before landing at the isolated barn. Jitka will meet you and you will be accommodated in the safe house, until the operation is mounted."

The Major continued, "The operation will take place at night, and the agent will board the Nimbus just before take off. You will proceed to Zempliska Sirova and atomise water to create a cloud, and then descend to ground level before making your way along a route that we will provide you with details of, to Perechyn. There you will drop off our agent at a selected spot before returning."

"You do realise Major, that on board the Nimbus, we only have a crude navaid in the form of our Soakometer." said the Captain interrupting him in full flow.

"I know that, and we are going to fit a sophisticated satellite tracking system for you, that will keep you on course," replied the Major.

"Will we return to Lucky and wait to collect the agent?"

"No. We have no idea how much time will be required to find out what the Russians are up to, so you may as well plan to go straight back to Wythenshawe."

After that brief outline, the Major handed to Cirrus the two maps along with the latitude and longitude of the landing sites at both Lucky and Perechyn, and the flight path between their Slovakian start point and Ukranian destination.

"Now I want you to go away and make your plans for getting to Slovakia and back home again, and when you have done that, study the route over the Carpathian Mountains."

Strategic planning

The crew of the Nimbus decided that it would be better to do their planning in the privacy of their Slaidburn home, away from the prying eyes they would be subjected to at Wythenshawe. They knew that they needed to arrive over the man-made lake known as Zempliska Sirova around 0100 hours. If they allowed a full hour to rain and hence get rid of their cloud, they could be at the isolated barn on the outskirts of Lucky village at 0200 hours and their arrival should go unnoticed. If they worked on a ground speed of thirty nautical miles per hour, then they would need to depart forty eight hours before their intended arrival at Zempliska Sirova, and that meant departing Wythenshawe at 0100 hours two days before. They would have to adjust the throttle settings as the wind dictated to achieve the required ground speed.

"Captain, I think we need an extra crew member for the journey to Lucky," said Puffy.

"I've been thinking the same thing," answered Cirrus.

"We need to be able to rotate crew on an operation like this, and have two on duty at all times."

"Who would you ask, and who could you get clearance for?"

"I think Abigail would be ideal, and I will just have to make a case out with the Major."

"Would you take her to Perechyn?"

"No, I wouldn't put her at such risk. We could drop her off at Lucky and call back for her after completing the operation."

With that settled, contact was made with the Major, and he agreed, providing Abigail travelled no further than Lucky.

The route was carefully planned using the chart that the crew had obtained at Wythenshawe, but in reality they only needed the lat and long of their starting position and their destination over the lake North of Lucky. Punch these co-ordinates into the satnav currently being fitted into the Nimbus, and the machine would find its own way there. The crew would simply control the height and speed at which they flew.

Once over the lake they could punch in the co-ordinates for their landing spot in Lucky, whilst the Nimbus was busy raining, and then let it take them there. Nothing could be simpler.

With the plans for getting to Slovakia sorted, Cirrus contacted Abigail Windrush.

"Abigail its Cirrus here, have you got anything on?"

"What a personal question but yes I have: knickers, bra, a blouse and a skirt."

"No, no, I don't mean are you wearing any clothes, I mean, have you got a job to do?"

"As a matter of fact I have two: I have some clothes to wash, and a pile of ironing to do."

"I don't mean that kind of job, I mean, do you have a job to perform with the Hurricane?"

Abigail knew exactly what Cirrus had meant, but she also knew how to get him agitated, and she was taking advantage of that. She was attracted to Cirrus when he felt awkward. There was something very likeable about him at these times.

"No I don't have any work to do in the Hurricane. Why, do you want to hire it?"

"No, but I want to hire you for a few days."

"Doing what exactly?"

"I can't tell you over the phone. Can you get down to my place?"

"When do you want me?"

Even Cirrus thought that that was a leading question but he declined from giving a flippant or for that matter too true an answer!

"I need you to get here asap, and bring enough gear to keep you going for a week or more, and not a word to anyone about this."

Abigail was intrigued by the conversation, and seriously wondered if Cirrus was about to proposition her. She lost no time in throwing some clothes and toiletries into a large canvas bag that she had for just this kind of purpose. Not that she was regularly propositioned!

In no time at all, the Windrush home drive experienced the rapid acceleration of Abigail's car. It was not a sports car, or very powerful in engine terms, but Abigail was adept at getting out of it all it could deliver, and not necessarily within the law. Only emergency vehicles could reach Slaidburn with the same sense of purpose that Abigail did, and her arrival in the drive of the Cumulus home coincided with a shower of gravel onto the well-kept lawns. It would certainly be unwise to use a lawn mower after this deluge.

"Come in Abigail, come in, nice to see you," said Puffy as he greeted the windswept pilot of the Hurricane.

"Let me escort you through to the Captain."

Now don't overdo it, thought Abigail.

Cirrus was seated in his favourite chair in the lounge and didn't get up as Puffy escorted Abigail in.

"Hello Abigail, come and sit down. We have something important to talk about."

Miss Windrush was a little disappointed with her greeting, but was still intrigued, and was anxious to find out why her presence was required.

"What I am about to tell you is strictly confidential. I am compelled by the Official Secrets Act to say that if you divulge anything I say to you about your reason for being here, you may go to prison."

This is either really serious, or a big send up, thought Abigail.

"I need you to come to Slovakia, as a member of the crew of the Nimbus."

Cirrus then went on to explain about the journey to Lucky, but gave nothing away as to what would be going on when they left her behind and proceeded to Perechyn.

She could understand the reason for the Nimbus needing an extra crew member to get to Slovakia, but was mystified about the purpose of going there in the first place, but accepted that Cirrus must have a good reason for not telling her. She was impressed with the fee she would get, and had no qualms about agreeing to help. She did not see any danger with the job, or at least, with what she had been told about it.

"Now I'm afraid you will have to leave Puffy and me to do so more planning. We have sorted a room upstairs for you, so if you would like to get settled in, please do. We only need an hour."

"When do you think we will leave for Slovakia?" asked Abigail.

"I don't know, but it could be anytime; I'm just waiting for a call from Major Oss."

That was a mistake, he hadn't intended giving that away.

He'd better be more careful, he thought.

Major Oss, that sounds interesting, thought Abigail. This could be a military operation, but so what, the money's good and as far as Cirrus was concerned, well, you never know!

In the next hour Cirrus, with the aid of Puffy, put the details together for the operation itself from Lucky to Perechyn, and then rang Major Oss to tell him they were ready.

Off to Slovakia

It was a couple of days before the Major rang the Slaidburn crew, but they were a pleasant couple of days. Puffy watched in earnest for any relationship developing between his Captain and Abigail, but Cirrus was too reserved to make a direct move, in spite of the signals being given. Still it was nice to have a good looking woman about the place; it was like a ray of sunshine on a winter's day!

When the call finally came in, the three of them had to make an early morning drive to Wythenshawe to get organised, although that would not take long. On arrival Cirrus went off to the Superintendant's office whilst Puffy refuelled the Nimbus, and Abigail made sure they had all the provisions they would need. She assumed a week's supply would be adequate.

Major Oss greeted Cirrus and began by checking over the route he was taking to get to Slovakia. Satisfied with that, he went over the route for 'Operation Inquisitive'. Satisfied with all that he had seen, he introduced Cirrus to a facsimile of the satnav he had had installed in the Nimbus, and demonstrated how to use it. It was quite simple and Cirrus had no problems understanding it.

"Now Captain, let's go over the plan. I want you to depart at 2300 hours and get over the Irish Sea and atomise some water and make cloud, then get back here for a 0100 hours departure for Slovakia. When you arrive over Zempliska Sirova forty-eight hours later at 0100 hours, make rain, and land at Lucky at 0200 hours. It will then be Saturday morning and Jitka will rendezvous with you on your arrival. Any Questions?"

"No, that's straightforward enough."

The Major then went over the details of the Operation itself which would take place in the early hours of Sunday morning. The logic behind this was that it was considered to be the best time, since most of the population of Perechyn would still be in a stupor from a night of celebration on the vodka. They would meet the agent that they were to take to Perechyn on arrival in Lucky.

"Once the Operation is over, get back here as soon as possible," said the Major.

"Do you want me to contact you when the Operation is accomplished?"

"No. Keep radio silence. Jitka will let us know."

"Now let's take a look at the weather forecast."

Conditions were not bad, with broken cloud covering the whole of Europe, and a moderate south westerly wind at ten knots. Satisfied with all he had heard, Cirrus was ready to get to the Nimbus and both he and the Major got up at the same time to depart.

"Good luck to you and your crew, Captain Cumulus," said the Major, who shook his hand at the same time.

As he was departing the room, Mr Spite intercepted Cirrus, and expressed his best wishes, and hoped he would be back soon. To add to all this good wishes stuff, Goldilocks collared him, embraced him, and crash-landed a pair of lipstick covered lips on his left cheek, leaving a whopping tattoo where the impact had occurred. Cirrus was both surprised and flattered, and departed with a mild blush to add to his new tattoo.

The arrival of Cirrus in Wythenshawe's hangar was greeted by one or two wolf whistles which foxed him, but he smiled in a nonchalant fashion and proceeded to the Nimbus to meet his fellow crew members.

"So, what's the score Captain?" asked Puffy, with an ear to ear smile.

"I have been over the plans with the Major."

"And what exactly have you been planning," asked Abigail with a rather serious look on her face.

Cirrus couldn't make out why he was getting the kind of response he was, but decided he'd better put them in the picture anyhow.

"We depart for Slovakia tonight at 2300 hours and should arrive at our destination at 0200 hours on Saturday. Operation Inquisitive takes place in the early hours of Sunday morning."

Neither Puffy nor Abigail had heard this title before, and in fact Abigail should not have been told.

"Operation Inquisitive! I didn't know I would be involved in any secret Operation," remarked a perplexed Abigail.

"Sorry Abigail. I shouldn't have told you that. You're not involved; you stay behind at Lucky whilst Puffy and I do the Op."

"We leave Lucky at 0100 hours on Monday morning and head for home."

"So, we should get back to Wythenshawe on Wednesday next week," remarked Puffy.

"That's correct. Now let's get aboard and make sure everything is ok."

With that the crew boarded the Nimbus, but Cirrus sensed that Abigail was not very happy with him, and he wondered why.

Once on board, the process of checking everything began, and at a convenient moment when Abigail had gone to the back of the Nimbus, Cirrus turned to Puffy and asked what he may have done to offend her.

"Perhaps it's that tattoo on your left cheek."

"What tattoo?"

Puffy took a tissue from the box on his working table top and wiped away the evidence of contact with the female world, and then presented it to his Captain.

"So that was it," remarked a relieved Cirrus.

At 2300 hours the fan duct motors on the Nimbus were started up, and the sleek machine taxied out of the huge hangar and into the darkness of the outside world. A vertical take off took them into the blackness of the night sky, and reaching a certain height, it headed West towards the Irish Sea where the crew atomised a quantity of water to generate a cloud around them, before proceeding back again to Wythenshawe.

The Nimbus hovered for awhile over the Weather Centre until its departure time, and meanwhile Cirrus punched the lat and long of both his departure and arrival places into the satnav. At 0100 hours precisely, the Nimbus set off for Slovakia. The heading appeared to be about 110° and soon the throttles were being adjusted, so that the propulsion they provided, together with the tail wind, gave it a ground speed of 30 knots. Now it was a case of continuing like this for forty eight hours.

The drop-down double bunk was lowered, and Abigail used the lower, as she took the first rest. Cirrus and Puffy would share the top bunk, but for the next four hours they constituted the duty crew. They swapped over every four hours, but there were always two on duty. At 0500 hours Abigail and Puffy swapped over, and she joined Cirrus on the flight deck. She glanced at Cirrus and he blushed as he returned her glance.

"We are on course and everything is going ok," he said as they started their shared shift.

For the next forty eight hours the Nimbus ploughed a steady course across Europe. The Netherlands, Germany, The Czech Republic all passed below on an uneventful passage to Slovakia. Not even much conversation took place amongst the crew, but the ice appeared to be melting between the Captain and Abigail, who was beginning to wonder if her suspicions had any foundations.

Zempliska Sirova could be seen, even in the dark, from a considerable distance and they arrived over it to come to a hover at exactly 0100 hours on Saturday morning.

Whilst raining to get rid of their cloud, the Captain punched his next destination into his satnav and duly, the Nimbus, freed from its surrounding vapour, headed for the isolated barn on the outskirts of Lucky. Cirrus had no problems picking out the barn on his pop-up TV screen and a vertical descent saw them land right outside the place.

With the motors shut down, the crew made their way to the exit door which, when opened, allowed them to see quite a large group of people waiting for them, and it took them by surprise. The exit ladders were extended to allow them to meet the waiting party, and a young woman stepped forward to greet them.

"Welcome to Lucky! I am Jitka, and my friends are here to give you help pushing your machine into the barn."

That was a relief, and in double-quick time the Nimbus was pushed into the barn, the doors shut, and the party of locals all disappeared, except Jitka. It was difficult to make her out in the dark, but she escorted them to a nearby house, and showed them to a room with three single beds in it, and wished them all a good sleep before departing. When Jitka had gone, the three crew members couldn't wait to get their heads down after the last forty eight hours of duty.

"Puffy we better make sure we are up and about by 1600 hours."

"Aye, aye Captain!"

Operation Inquisitive

Puffy was up at about noon and left both Cirrus and Abigail asleep as he went to find Jitka.

"Good morning Jitka. Any chance of something to eat?" asked Puffy whilst he took a good look at his Slovakian host. Now that he could see her in the daylight he could appreciate both her good looks and slim figure.

"Where are the others?" asked Jitka.

"Still asleep, and I didn't want to disturb them."

With that, Jitka set about cooking Puffy a good breakfast, even though it was noon. Not much later Cirrus and Abigail made an entrance, and Jitka, most obligingly, cooked them something as well.

"What are your plans Captain Cumulus?" asked Jitka.

Cirrus thought he'd better be a little cautious about what he said to her. When all was said and done, he really didn't know her.

"I don't know just at the moment. I'm going to work things out, but you could help by getting a weather report for the next twenty-four hours."

"Very good Captain. Leave that with me."

When Jitka had left the Nimbus crew, Cirrus decided that he and Puffy ought to get organised for Operation Inquisitive.

"Abigail, would you check over the Nimbus for me?"

"I suppose you want me out of the way?"

"There's no point in anyone knowing about our plans that need not know," replied the Captain, at which point Abigail left, feeling a little disgruntled.

The two intrepid cloud fliers got down to business and studied the map showing this part of Slovakia and the adjacent Ukraine, extending to Perechyn. They pin-pointed their landing site on the north side of a river, at a point where it divides for a short distance before merging again. This position was an area of open land, just south of the town.

They both agreed that the Nimbus should put down at their destination at about 0230 hours to drop off the agent they would be taking.

"Where is the agent?" asked Puffy.

"We better ask Jitka and we better get a message to our contacts in Perechyn to let them know about our arrival time."

The pair of them then turned their attention to the route from Lucky to Perechyn, and finally the time for take off. If they lifted off at 0030 hours they could hover over Zempliska Sirova, make a cloud, and be ready to depart at 0130 hours to fly the short distance of twenty-six nautical miles to Perechyn.

Jitka burst into the room with the weather forecast, and she was asked to stay whilst they took a quick look at it. The wind wasn't going to be a problem, a westerly, at ten knots. Cloud base four thousand feet, which meant that the tops of the Carpathian Mountains would be clear. Four tenths cloud. Visibility with a half moon should be good.

"Jitka, we are going in the early hours of tomorrow. Conditions couldn't be more favourable. Can you have your ground team at the barn for midnight?"

"That is not a problem."

"What about the agent we are taking with us, is he here?"

"Yes Captain, he his here but my orders are that you will not meet him until take off time. I will arrange for him to be at the barn for midnight."

"Excellent. Now one more thing. Can you get a message to Wythenshawe for us to tell them that our arrival time at our destination will be 0230 hours? I cannot do that myself since a radio silence as been imposed on me."

"I can do that Captain. What time will you require a working party back here for your return?" asked Jitka.

"I am not going to hang around when the job is done. I will land at approximately 0330 hours, but I will be in cloud form. I want Abigail to come aboard. I will give her a mobile phone and speak to her as she enters the cloud to find the Nimbus. I don't think we should need a working party."

"Fine. I will go now and do as you instructed. I will make you a good meal for 1900 hours."

With that Jitka left, displaying a Slovakian wiggle as she did so, and it didn't escape the notice of the Nimbus crew.

"They even have nice girls in Slovakia, isn't that Lucky," remarked Puffy but Cirrus resisted from agreeing, even though he did.

"Abigail, Puffy and I will be departing at 0030 hours tomorrow, but we should be back for 0330 hours, and I want you to come aboard at that time so that we can depart immediately for Wythenshawe. We will be in cloud form when we land, so here is a mobile phone which

41

we will use to guide you through the cloud to the Nimbus. For security purposes I think we need to agree a password."

"Knickers," shouted Puffy, and it was immediately agreed.

"If we don't return, Abigail, I want you to promise me that you will post this letter for me."

Cirrus handed the letter to her and waited for a response.

Abigail had given no thoughts to the risk being taken by the Nimbus crew and was suddenly embraced with a degree of admiration, tinged with a feeling of compassion.

She looked at the name and address on the envelope, but the details meant nothing to her.

"Who is it to?" she asked.

"It's my Uncle George. I have no immediate family," replied Cirrus.

He has no Uncle George either, thought Puffy. What's he up to?

Abigail embraced Cirrus and kissed him passionately, only stopping when Jitka re-entered the room.

So that's his game, thought Puffy!

At midnight, the Nimbus crew joined the working party at the barn, and Jitka was there to give orders. The agent joined them without exchanging a word. He was a big hunk of a chap, but in the darkness they couldn't make out what he looked like. The barn doors were opened and the Nimbus was pushed out into the darkness. The three crew went aboard, raising the entry ladder and closing the door behind them. The motors were started and at 0030 hours, a vertical take off lifted the machine into the night sky. The craft was steered over Zempliska Sirova and came to a hover whilst a cloud was manufactured, casting a shadow of ever growing proportions as it did so, necessitating the use of the pop-up TV screen and TV camera to give the Captain visual awareness of the outside world. During the cloud-making, the agent sat in the spare cockpit seat, in silence.

The lat and long of the present position of the Nimbus and its destination were punched into the satnav, and at 0130 hours the journey to Perechyn began on a heading of 095°. As soon as they got underway they took the cloud down to ground level, and Cirrus was forced to focus intently on his TV screen to prevent hitting any obstacles that he came across, but at this height there was certainly no shadow. Visibility was quite good and Gajdos could be seen on the starboard side before they passed Nizna Rybnica, and then, further out on their starboard side, Sobrance, and after forty minutes they reached the Carpathian Mountains. Up to this point the journey had been fairly easy, the few obstacles being barns or other buildings which the Nimbus had simply been steered around. What those on the ground made of this fast moving ground mist was anybody's guess. It was a bit different in the mountains, it was all up and down like a roller coaster, and to maintain a steady ground speed meant constant adjustments of the throttles. Navigation, being under the control of the satnav, presented no difficulties at all. At 0220 hours, the border fence between Slovakia and the Ukraine came into view and Cirrus steered the Nimbus between two guard towers, although it was not possible to see if they were manned or not.

Crossing into the Ukraine was a bit of an anti-climax, but no matter, the sheer concentration involved told its tale. Both crew members were saturated in sweat with the effort required, and throughout all this, the agent still uttered not one word. The river that flows past Perechyn came into view at 0230 hours and Cirrus had no difficulty following it to the landing Spot just south of the town. Touch down was easy from a height of just thirty feet and Puffy went aft to open the exit door and lower the access ladder. On the TV screen, Cirrus could see the figure of a man just on the edge of his cloud and turned to point this out to his passenger who rose from his seat to take a look. He tapped Cirrus on the shoulder and said thanks before exiting the craft. Cirrus watched him for a moment on his tv and then, when Puffy had returned, and confirmed that they were ready for off, he punched the co-ordinates of his current position and that of the barn in Lucky into his satnav, and they departed Perechyn.

The Nimbus, now on a heading of 275°, was moving into a headwind, and although it was only ten knots, the throttles needed advancing somewhat to maintain the same groundspeed as before. The first twenty minutes of low-level flying through the mountains was again energy sapping, and both men continued to sweat profusely with the concentration involved. It must have been a confusing experience for anyone they passed over, or any other observer, to see a ground mist moving in a direction opposite that of the prevailing wind, but nevertheless the border fence was passed without incident, and both of the crew were only too glad about that. The rest of the flight to the barn at Lucky passed without incident, and at 0340 hours the Nimbus touched down. Cirrus could see both Jitka and Abigail waiting for him on his tv screen, and Puffy passed him the mobile phone to speak to her, before he went aft to open the door and lower the access ladder again. It was good to be in Lucky!

Back to Wythenshawe

The two ladies came aboard the Nimbus and made their way to the flightdeck. Jitka embraced Cirrus, kissed him passionately, congratulated him for being a brave man, and then did the same to Puffy before speedily departing. No sooner were the two of them recovering from this enjoyable experience, than they got a second helping from Abigail, who was determined not to be outdone. Regaining their composure became the new mission in order that they could concentrate on getting back to Wythenshawe, but it had felt great, especially when the ladies had embraced them and they felt their female bodies pressed up against them.

With the door closed and the access ladder retracted, Cirrus fed the appropriate start and finish co-ordinates into the satnav and began to ascend, and this time to a less demanding altitude of about three thousand feet. It was now 0400 hours and if they maintained a ground speed of thirty knots, they should arrive back at Wythenshawe at 0400 hours on Tuesday morning, a journey of forty eight hours. This was not what had originally been planned, but so what! Once underway, Puffy went aft to change out of his sweat ridden clothing, and Abigail went into the galley to make some breakfast. Cirrus was left in control, and soon the smell of bacon permeated the cockpit to replace his body odour induced by the exertion getting back from the Ukraine. The three of them chatted whilst eating, but then it was down to business and a crew rota was imposed for the duration of the return flight, allowing each one of them to get short bursts of sleep, and Cirrus took the opportunity to change into odour free attire.

The Nimbus cruised steadily for the next forty eight hours, and the Czech Republic, Germany and The Netherlands all passed under them on their way to the North Sea. Since the prevailing wind was still a westerly, it must have looked strange to those on the ground. A single cloud moving in the opposite direction to all the others is not what anyone would expect to witness, and under normal circumstances, this would not be allowed. The journey should be done in the dark, in stages, but that would take several more days. When the sky is covered with a layer of stratus cloud, then the Nimbus could operate above the clouds and out of sight. These conditions did not apply on this operation; they had been given special dispensation.

Duly, the English coast came into view and the Nimbus crossed it near Grimsby. Cirrus was in no mood to hang around as he got nearer to Wythenshawe; his only interest now, was getting back to Slaidburn, getting a good sleep in his own bed, and then putting his feet up by the lounge fire. He was duty-bound to get rid of his cloud before landing, and without any due consideration for those down below, he got Puffy to start the rain one hour out from their destination. It was still dark, it was the early hours of Tuesday, and he really didn't care about anything now except getting back. He felt weary. Without Puffy asking, he gave the instruction for a torrential downpour and the remaining part of the Nimbus flight was marked by a travelling, drenching, downpour, served on all places going west, starting with Chapel-en-le-Frith, Whaley Bridge, Poynton, Bramhall, and Cheadle Hulme. Fortunately, at such an early hour, few people were about, but those that were, were not expecting what they got, and what they got was a good soaking.

A naked Nimbus arrived over the Weather Centre at 0400 hours and Cirrus commenced the descent which placed it at the entrance to the huge hangar. Wythenshawe's duty crew had opened the doors and the Nimbus taxied straight in. With the motors shut down, the crew disembarked and Puffy pressed the external button that automatically retracted the entry ladders and closed the door. They were rather surprised that there was no-one to greet them. They had at least expected the Major to be there, and it was all a bit of an anti-climax.

"Well Puffy, we might as well get the car and get going to Slaidburn."

"Will there not be a debrief?" asked Puffy.

"There's nobody here, so who's going to do it? Forget it, we are going. What are you doing Abigail?"

"My car's at your place Cirrus, and anyway, I wouldn't mind a few days with you two after this trip. Would you mind too much?"

"We would be delighted Abigail. Come on, let's get going."

A few days later in the lounge of the Cumulus home, the three intrepid fliers were having coffee and swapping thoughts about their recent experience when the postman delivered a letter which had to be signed for. In it there was a cheque for a substantial sum of money to be split between them for their part in Operation Inquisitive. Accompanying the cheque was a short letter to thank them and congratulate them on a job well done. There was no mention of recovering the agent they had dropped in Perechyn, or the removal of the satnav fitted to the Nimbus.

"How strange," remarked Cirrus!

"How could they determine that everything went ok without debriefing us?"

That's where the matter had to end for the moment and sadly it was time for Abigail to leave; she had a job to do with the Hurricane.

Cirrus would miss her, thought Puffy. They had both been sharing the settee of late and moving steadily closer. The speed at which Cirrus moved in an amorous fashion should result in a passionate embrace roundabout Christmas. I hope she can wait that long? he thought.

It was some four weeks after the Nimbus crew had returned from Slovakia that Cirrus spotted an article in the Daily Gloom that related to Operation Inquisitive. It didn't refer to the Operation by name, but there was no doubt that that was the topic of the article.

"Puffy, Puffy, get in here sharpish," shouted the Captain.

"What is it Captain?"

"I have just read this article in the paper, and I'm sure it's about the agent we dropped in Perechyn."

"What does it say?"

"It says that British Intelligence have discovered how the Russians are breaking sanctions imposed on Iran, and North Korea. They have discovered a plant in the Ukraine that is manufacturing essential materials, and setting up places to use them in both countries."

"Go on Captain."

"You will never believe this. They are setting up Burger Bars, and exporting Rostov Burgers using amongst other things Minsk Meat to put in them. Evidently, they are selling like hot cakes."

"Don't you mean Hot Burgers?"

"You may think its funny, but I don't. We took a considerable risk carrying that Operation out, and just for a bloody burger bar."

Once the indignation that Cirrus was feeling had subsided, he rang Mr Spite at Wythenshawe.

"I know how you must feel Cirrus, but that's the way it goes sometimes, and anyway, isn't it better to discover that the Russians are exporting Rostov Burgers and not Molotov Cocktails, or nuclear weapons?"

Cirrus could only agree with this.

"What about the agent we dropped off, when are we going to recover him?"

"Oh don't worry about him, he could be there for some time yet."

"How come? You know what the Russians are up to now."

"That might be so, but he has another mission now. He's got a job in the Burger factory in Perechyn, and his job is to put horse meat into the Burgers!"

CCMO/8/13

Something to learn

Cutting the grass and washing the car was tedious at the best of times, but when you have been doing it almost exclusively for a few weeks, it becomes extremely boring, thought Cirrus. He never tired of looking at the local scenery, but he was in need of a fresh challenge, and until he got one, he was going to get progressively more aggravated, and his faithful engineer, Puffy White, was the one that would bear the brunt of his frustration.

Although he would admit it to no-one, Cirrus was actually missing Abigail whom he had not had the pleasure of seeing for some time, since she was on a job captaining her cloud machine the Hurricane. He had no idea where she was, or what she was doing, but he did miss her. Carol Aspinall on the other hand, had been to the Cumulus home several times recently, and had shown no sign of embarrassment when meeting Cirrus under a new set of circumstances, and the subject of her pink bra was never brought up. The relationship between Puffy and Carol seemed to be growing on a weekly basis at least that was the conclusion one would get, witnessing the passionate embraces they exchanged around the house.

Cirrus was not a man who could cope without a mission of some description, and unless that happened soon, there was going to be no way of coping with him. Morning coffee and the Daily Gloom only heightened his desire to groan about something. His pet hate was the political class, and he despaired of the career politicians who tried to convince everybody that they knew best about what should be done to keep the country going, but couldn't agree amongst themselves. He had long reached the conclusion that they served their own interests, rather than the country's. If Puffy gave him half a chance he would go on all day about what he thought of politicians, and it was a bit repetitive to say the least.

It was fortunate that Cirrus spotted an advert in the paper one morning that took his interest. An appeal was being made to attract self-employed persons to attend courses that would enhance their ability to cope with emergency situations. The Government was urging small companies to consult the associations that worked on their behalf, and look at the courses they were providing on this important subject.

What kind of emergency situations are they talking about? thought Cirrus.

"Puffy can you bring me the latest copy of The Monthly Downpour?"

"Aye aye, Captain."

The Monthly Downpour was the journal produced by The Guild of Cloud Owners, and had a section devoted to courses. They rarely interested the crew of the Nimbus, but nevertheless, Cirrus flipped through the pages until he reached the section he was looking for. The Guild had a training centre in Northern Ireland at an old airfield called Bishops Court in County Down. It was quite handy for the Nimbus crew because of its proximity to their second home in Ballyhalbert. Both of the crew had attended courses there, and learned a lot, but it was some time since they were last there. The list of courses looked quite interesting for a change, but Cirrus was looking for something in particular.

The Guild of Cloud Machine Owners
Courses for Cloud Machine Crew
Bishops Court Training Centre
2013

Feb 11th – 15th	Cooking in a Confined Galley	CCMO/1/13
Mar 11th – 15th	What to Wear on Board	CCMO/2/13
April 15th – 19th	Know your Clouds	CCMO/3/13
May 13th – 17th	Navigating Planet Earth	CCMO/4/13

June 10th – 14th	Creating Special Effects	CCMO/5/13
July 15th – 19th	The Law and Making Weather	CCMO/6/13
Aug 12th – 16th	Preparing for your Pilot's Examination	CCMO/7/13
Sep 9th – 13th	Coping with Emergency Situations	CCMO/8/13
Oct 14th – 18th	MOT Regulations for Cloud Machines	CCMO/9/13
Nov 11th – 15th	Drinking and Flying	CCMO/10/13

CCMO/8/13 was the one Cirrus was looking for, and he turned to the page that gave details, and he was struck by the opening paragraph.

Have you given any thought to how you would fight a fire on board your machine whilst on a mission, or how you would treat an injured colleague?

Have you practised using your machine's emergency parachutes?

Do you know the drill?

Would you be able to vacate your craft in flight?

Can you complete an incident report?

All these important factors are covered in Course CCMO/8/13.

This really caught the eye of Cirrus and he had to admit that he was not really competent in any of the things that this course covered. It could be an interesting challenge for both Puffy and himself, and they could combine it with spending a bit of time in Ballyhalbert.

"Puffy, have you got a minute?"

I wonder what he wants to moan about now. thought Puffy.

"Just take a look at this course at Bishops Court, and tell me what you think."

Puffy scanned the information and was equally as interested as his captain.

"Looks good to me, Captain. I'm up for it."

That was the response Cirrus was looking for.

"We could spend a bit of time in Ballyhalbert at the same time."

"That sounds good," said Puffy.

The cost of the course was not prohibitive, and now it was only a question of completing the course application form.

Meeting fellow course members

Ten cloud machine crew members gathered at Bishops Court on a Sunday evening in readiness for the start of the course the following day. It was something of a pleasant reunion, for they all knew each other. Apart from the crew of the Nimbus, there was Abigail Windrush and Josh Harrop from the Hurricane, Lucy Windrush and Peter Arnolds from the Softly Blows, Albertino Insomnia and Carol Aspinall from the Astro, and finally Bill and Ben Jones from the Skylark. They had been expecting Wally Lenticular and Bert Drummond from the Discovery, but at the last moment they discovered they had another commitment.

It was no accident that Abigail was on the course. Cirrus had pulled a few strings, and Puffy had been placated by arranging, in a devious way, that Carol would also be present. It was to be hoped that romance would not hinder learning, but the morrow would soon reveal if that was to be the case.

The atmosphere in the training centre bar was congenial, and the ten new students caught up on each other's news, although that proved to be a challenge for Albertino. They had collectively rained on many parts of the globe in both nice and not so nice ways. The rising cost of raining, along with new EU laws that may be introduced in the near future, were also a focal point of discussion before an argument broke out about the best quality water to use when making Westmorland White clouds. It seemed like a close run thing between Lake Coniston, and Loch Ness, but no definite consensus was reached. It was interesting to see Bill and Ben, known affectionately as the rain men, taking a keen interest in Lucy, who appeared to reciprocate the advances of both of them. Maybe coping with emergency situations was not a bad title for the course, but would it cover what Cirrus was thinking?

Fire Fighting

The following morning, after a hearty-breakfast, which most course members thought would be the best part of the course, they gathered in the centre's lecture theatre.

"My name is George Brown, and I will be your tutor throughout the course, so allow me to welcome you all to Bishops Court, the Guild of Cloud Owners Training Centre."

A number of formalities then took place, and Mr Brown became acquainted with his students, before moving on.

"This morning you will be dealing with fire-fighting, and this afternoon will be devoted to first aid."

"Crikey, that's a good start!" remarked Albertino, in one of his rare outbursts.

Mr Brown led the course members out of the lecture theatre and into what looked like a large garage from the outside, but inside it was quite impressive. A single cloud machine was parked in the centre of what was quite a sizeable hall which had a lot of extractors in its ceiling. Placed in the floor around the machine, were what looked like the end of hose pipes that could spray something onto the machine. There was an abundance of fire extinguishers, and several fire hoses on reels.

Mr Brown introduced Albert Melrose, who would be their fire-fighting instructor.

"Morning all, hope you all had a good breakfast. Now I will be taking you through the first half of today's course which will deal with fire-fighting."

It turned out to be far more informative and interesting than most of them expected. They began by going aboard the centre's cloud machine and Mr Melrose highlighting what they needed on board their own machines as a precaution against fire. Red and black extinguishers had been placed in strategic positions on board, and signs indicated clearly where they where, and what they were for. A fire blanket was placed in the galley, and there was even breathing apparatus stowed away. Cirrus made a note of these things, for he could see already some of the deficiencies of the Nimbus.

Next came a demonstration of using the different extinguishers and the fire blanket, but this took place initially outside the machine, before they were introduced to fire- fighting inside it. In the confined space of a cloud machine, there was an emphasis on team work, and Mr Melrose was joined by an assistant. Before going aboard, they went to a corner of the hall which had been set up like a small cinema, and here they saw a film about fire-fighting in a confined space. The need for breathing apparatus became obvious and, reluctantly, they were led back to the centre's demonstration machine to don the equipment. They went aboard two at a time with Mr Melrose and his assistant, and the door was shut behind them. The machine filled with smoke, and the business of fighting fire in this unpleasant environment began. It was all very realistic.

The course stopped for a break around mid-morning, and they exchanged thoughts.

"I never expected things to be this real," said Carol.

"Neither did I, but it's pretty good to go through all these things," replied Peter.

"I will certainly be updating my fire-fighting procedures on the Skylark."

There was general agreement that things had got off to a good start.

"Now we are going to take a look a look at fire-fighting externally," began their instructor.

"Obviously, this is confined to the time your machines are on the ground. The greatest risk of an external fire is when you are refuelling on the ground at your respective Weather Centres, although I think that in your case, that will be Wythenshawe. You can't use just any extinguisher to fight a fire involving the fuel used by your fan duct motors. It must be a foam extinguisher like this one."

A large cream-coloured extinguisher was wheeled into place before Mr Melrose took them back again to the corner of the hall to view another film, which acquainted them with its operation. Then came the scariest bit of the morning. The extractor fans were switched on, and then the little hose jets in the ground sprayed fuel over the cloud machine, which was then ignited to create sheets of flame that seemed to embrace it, and create lots of thick black smoke that kept the extractor fans busy. Mr Melrose and his assistant sprang into action with their portable foam extinguisher, and went to work fire-fighting, with great gusto. Their performance was worth an academy award. They soon had the fire out, and then it was the turn of the course students. No-one was spared from this experience, and no-one was particularly confident. The anxiety each pair of fire-fighters felt had been taken into account by their instructor, who with the aid of his assistant, carefully supervised and advised them, so that on five occasions, the fire was successfully extinguished. There was great relief when this aspect of the course was completed but everybody thought it was extremely worthwhile.

"What happens if we get an external fire when we are airborne?"

"Your machines should have built in extinguishers in each of your fan duct motors, and buttons on your flightdeck should activate them, and by the way, there are also danger lights that come on to warn you that you have a fire."

"Suppose it's not the motors?"

"In that case you need to land asap, and disembark fast, but that's covered later in the course."

First Aid

After a light lunch, it was back to work in the lecture theatre.

"I'm Geraldine McWhirter, but you can call me Gerry. I'm your first aid instructor."

Gerry was a lady of substantial proportions, but a true lady in every sense of the word. She had a lovely smile and a motherly aura that made everyone comfortable in her presence.

"There will be two sessions on first aid, the first this afternoon, and the second on Thursday afternoon. You may find that there is a lot to take in on the subject, and that's why it has been decided to split the subject into two sessions, with a break in-between."

"It must be obvious to all of you, that if anything happens to a crew member when you are flying, then you only have yourself to do the necessary for your colleague. To help you do that, you must have on board a first aid kit with the appropriate items in it, and the location should be clearly identifiable."

At this point several of the students looked at each other in rather telling ways. The course was already paying dividends.

Gerry provided a demonstration first aid kit for each crew, and went over the various contents before embarking on the rest of the curriculum.

"I'm going to start with some of the possible scenarios that you may have to deal with."

First came drowning, which surprised everyone, but when they considered how much time they spent over water, they agreed it was important. A practical session involving artificial ventilation followed, using a dummy, which was a great disappointment since there were three female students that would have been delightful to practise on, and it would have been even better if they had been wearing swimwear. Gerry then moved on to smoke inhalation, and after the last session on fire-fighting, this seemed most appropriate. Choking and treatment of bruises came next, and a little practical work before a break, and a little respite. There was lot to take in, and it was all relevant.

After the break, Gerry began again by introducing everyone to the ABC system, which in this case meant Airways, Breathing, and Circulation. Checking for a heartbeat proved not to be so easy, and a number of the living were pronounced dead, but they all got revitalised by the prospect of mouth to mouth ventilation, only to be disappointed again when a dummy was provided for practice. There are occasions when mouth to mouth ventilation is not possible, and an alternative method was demonstrated and practised, and it went by the name of the Holger Nielson method. The afternoon's session was rounded off by learning how to put someone into the recovery position.

After evening meal, the cloud machine crews retired to study the handouts they had received during the day's sessions, and no-one frequented the bar until 10-00pm, and even then only for an hour. Conversation was almost exclusively course related, and the only highlight was the refusal of Abigail, Lucy and Carol to act as dummies for their male counterparts to practise on, but morale was unaffected.

"What have we got on tomorrow?" asked someone.

"Using a cloud machine's emergency kit, it says on the programme."

"Oh that should be interesting."

Internal parachutes

Tuesday morning was going to be very different from Monday. The ten students gathered in the lecture theatre to meet their instructor for the next two days. Alec Pain had a great deal of experience in relation to dealing with life-threatening emergencies, and was an expert in crisis management.

Once Alec had got acquainted with everyone, he went on to describe what they would be doing during the morning.

"I want you all to imagine that you have created a cloud, and are in the process of delivering it overland. You have a catastrophic failure of all four fan duct motors, which results in a loss of your electrical power, and hence your various systems. What do you do?"

"Pray."

"Well, you could do that, but you could also deploy the machine's parachutes, which will allow you to descend safely to earth."

"But we wouldn't be able to see where we are landing without the TV camera providing us with a picture, and suppose the place we were going to land was a bad one?" said Ben.

"Those are very good points, so let me deal with both of them. But first, let me take you all to the cloud machine simulator."

It was only a short walk to the building that housed the simulator, which took the form of the cockpit area that accommodated both crew members, and it was mounted on three hydraulic legs which provided it with three axes of movement. A removable bridge allowed the crew access, and TV cameras in the cockpit roof provided an image of what the crew was doing, on TV screens mounted outside the simulator. The whole scenario was high-tech, and stunning in its brilliance. Alec had an assistant who was already sitting in the pilot's seat.

"I'm going to ask my assistant to indicate to you the position of the lever which deploys the craft's parachute." Watching the TV screens, the students noted what they were shown.

"Now let me answer the point about seeing where you are going to land. Without electrical power, the craft's TV camera will not function, but there is a back up battery, but you must activate it by using the switch, which my assistant John will now point to."

John complied and they all watched again.

"Finally, let me respond to the problem of finding yourselves about to land in a bad location. There is not a fantastic amount you can do about this, but you have some limited control by using a steering control that pulls on the strings of the parachute."

As Alec was talking about this control, John pointed to its position.

"Has anyone got any questions?"

"What about the undercarriage? Can it be lowered for the landing?"

"Yes it can. I forgot that. John, point to the lever please."

John did so and Alec continued, "You have to crank the lever up and down to lower the undercarriage, and when you have succeeded a green light will flash."

"Have any of you ever used the emergency parachutes on your machines?"

There were no responses to this question.

"Well you are going to get the opportunity now. Each crew will go aboard the simulator in turn, and join my assistant. John will demonstrate the procedure, and then it will be your chance to handle the experience."

Cirrus and Puffy went aboard first and observed John start up the motors. They could see the TV screen come to life, and an image appeared of the interior of Wythenshawe's huge hangar. The machine was taxied out, and the sound and feel of the undercarriage was experienced. Then came take off and the machine was flown overhead a lake, and atomising commenced to create a cloud. The craft then began its overland journey, and it was all so convincing. Suddenly all four fan duct motors stopped, and power was lost, but all this had been induced by Alec, sitting in front of a console somewhere else. John operated the parachute deployment lever, and switched on the emergency power battery which brought the TV screen back to life and provided some dim cockpit lighting.

"Now, I'm going to steer the craft whilst it descends, with careful reference to the picture and, whilst I do this, I want one of you to lower the undercarriage with this lever."

The bump could be felt as they came into contact with 'terra firma'.

The demonstration must have lasted no more than about twenty minutes, but it seemed a lot longer, and then it was the turn of Cirrus and Puffy to have a go. The whole experience provided an adrenalin rush that was felt by all the other crews as they took their turns. By the time the five crews had finished, it was time for lunch and an excited group conversed about the experience, which all had found most valuable.

In the afternoon, the course students assembled again in the simulator building, and Alec Pain was waiting for them.

"Now I want to carry on from where we left off this morning. I want you to imagine that you are delivering rain in a cloud form once more, but this time you are cruising in a maritime setting, in other words you are over water not land. You have a failure of all the motors and a corresponding loss of power. Now you know some procedures already, would anyone care to say what they are?"

"Deploy the emergency parachutes."

"Good."

"Switch the emergency power on."

"Excellent, but this is where things get a little different. There would be no point in lowering the undercarriage, but a great deal of point in operating the control that will deploy and inflate the machine's buoyancy bags that will keep you afloat on landing. Now, John will identify for you the position of this control."

They all moved to the cinema area at this point, to see a film that showed the buoyancy bags inflating, and a cloud machine being kept afloat.

"Now I want to show you how to put your life jackets on correctly, and how to inflate them before my assistant shows you where they are stowed aboard your machines."

The life jackets were not difficult to put on or to inflate and only a short time was taken making sure everybody could do it before Alec began again.

"Now just like we did this morning, we are going to take one crew on board the simulator at a time, and John will demonstrate the procedure before you are given the opportunity to practise it."

The rest of the afternoon was taken dealing with an emergency landing at sea, but things were not quite over.

"Right folks, one last thing before you finish for the day. Each life jacket has a SARBE fitted to it and if you don't know what that means, it is a Search and Rescue Beacon, which, when activated, emits a signal telling the emergency people that you are in need of assistance and where you are."

Alec then showed the beacon to everyone, and how to activate it.

"If you land on land, it is a good idea to take a life jacket out of its stowage and use this device. It's also worth bearing in mind that the battery which powers it needs to be periodically checked."

"Before you all go, I just want to mention that it would not be a good idea to have too much to drink tonight."

A slightly bemused group headed back to their accommodation, wondering what could be in store for them tomorrow.

Most of the course students retired early, especially with all the handouts they seemed to have accumulated, but also in view of the comments made by Mr Pain as they left. Anyone with any desire on the amorous front was declined an opportunity, but they remained optimistic that their luck would change in the near future.

Dangling from a real chute

Mr Pain met the course students in the lecture theatre as usual.

"Today, we are going to deal with the worst case scenario. Imagine you are carrying cloud over water and a catastrophic fire breaks out on board your machine. Your only course of action in the event of not being able to put the fire out is to exit the craft and parachute to safety.

Several course members started to murmur and a certain amount of apprehension could be felt.

"Now I'm going to take you over to the evacuation hall and we can become acquainted with the procedures."

As they walked across to this special facility, an unhealthy conversation kicked off.

"He's not going to get me jumping out of a cloud machine," shouted Peter.

"Me neither," said Ben.

"Don't be a set of wimps," retorted Carol, and a sudden silence descended.

Entering the evacuation hall, a mock-up of a cloud machine suspended high up in the ceiling could be observed, and access was via a metal stairway and walkway, which went around the sides of the building.

"What I want you all to do to begin with, is to put these life jackets on."

A few moments elapsed whilst everyone did this.

"Now do try and remember how you inflate them, and how you activate the SARBE. Next I want you all to put a parachute on like this."

Alec gave a quick demo, and then everybody donned theirs.

"This is the 'D' ring that you pull to deploy the chute, and you pull it like this."

Alec's chute did not deploy, since his was a dummy.

"Ok, you are all kitted out now to escape your burning machine, but before we do the drills, you must learn three things, first you need to learn how to land without breaking any bones, and you do it like this."

A demonstration followed and then it was time to practise. When Alec was satisfied with what he had seen, he called for a harness to be lowered, and he fastened himself into it and was hoisted high up. He called on everyone below to watch carefully. A whistle was blown by his assistant and the hoist was released to allow the instructor to descend at the rate he would, if using a parachute for real. He dropped into a circle painted on the floor and keeled over in the manner previously demonstrated.

"Right, now it's your turn to do it."

The ten course members were duly hoisted up to try the experience and they clearly enjoyed it the second time round.

"Okey dokey, let's move over now to the mock-up in the corner there."

This was another cloud machine but without a cockpit. Its main feature was the exit door which had a safety mat placed on its outside. Inside the mock-up, there was only a platform behind the closed door and it was big enough to accommodate them all.

"Look carefully at where my right hand is pointing. This is the button that you press to jettison the exit door." And that's exactly what he did.

"The second thing you need to learn is how to jump out of the machine without colliding with its motors and you do it like this!"

He took a good run, and jumped as far out of the open door space as he could, to land at a point on the mat beyond an orange coloured line.

"Now, that's not too bad so you can have a go."

Each of them coped ok but it did take a bit of getting used to when they did it with a life jacket and parachute on.

After completing this second task, Alec took them back again into the centre of the hall where a lowered harness was awaiting them.

"When you are descending by parachute you have a chance to pick out where you want to land, but the wind may prevent it if you don't steer your descent using the parachute lines."

Alec fastened himself in the harness again and after a whistle was blown, he was hoisted aloft before descending, and as he did so, he tugged on the harness lines to demonstrate how they could be used to get him to the landing spot he had chosen. A large fan was then activated to simulate a wind and the instructor demonstrated the process again, landing inside the circle on the ground. There was considerable enthusiasm to have a crack at this and the experience proved to be a lot of fun.

The final exercise involved walking up the stairs to get to the mock-up they had observed when they came into the hall. When they got to it, they could see it had no roof. This allowed a student to attach himself or herself to a harness that was activated by pulling the 'D' ring on their chute after taking a jump out of the empty door space; clearly this was a much bigger challenge. Fists could be seen gripped, jaws tensed, and serious facial expressions adopted. Their nervousness was not relieved as Alec leapt out of the doorway, pulled the 'D' ring, and descended at a less rapid rate, whilst pulling on his lines to land in the circle.

"Bloody hell, this is scary!"

"Yeah, but better than doin'it for real!"

This last comment placated no-one.

In spite of their apprehension, all ten cloud machine crew members jumped, and apart from the fact that several of them dropped outside the circle, the exercise was a huge success.

"Ok folks, that was a good morning's work so go and get some lunch, but no alcohol."

With that, a high spirited group of ten, feeling rather pleased with themselves, headed off for a light lunch.

Immediately lunch was over, the students were taken by minibus to a location on the airfield where a twin-engined aircraft was parked. Tension mounted, especially since they had not been made aware that a real parachute jump was part of the course. Some members were excited by the idea, others were less so, and one in particular was petrified. They were greeted by Alec Pain as they disembarked, and he guided them to a small building in which they put on a flying suit and parachute before getting into the aircraft which was devoid of seats.

"I know that some of you may be nervous at the prospect of jumping out of an aircraft whilst it's flying, but you know the drills and it will prepare you for a real emergency. You are not compelled to do this and it will not be held against you if you decide to withdraw, and now would be the best time to do it."

"I'm not jumping out of a bloody good aeroplane! You must be mad," commented Peter, Lucy's flight engineer.

"Don't worry, Peter. If this is something you do not wish to do, that's fine. Just wait for us in the minibus until we return."

The rest boarded the aircraft along with Alec and the pilot, who had been waiting for them, and the aircraft's engines were started.

"Wait, wait!" shouted Peter as he ran toward the aircraft to join the others.

A great cheer rang out as he boarded the aircraft and Alec gave him a big pat on the back.

Alec gave them all a quick brief before the aircraft started to move.

"When we get airborne, the aircraft will do a circuit of the airfield so that you can become acquainted with the aerial view. You will notice a big yellow circle in the middle of the runway, and that is your aiming point. As you approach the aircraft door I will attach your 'D' ring to this harness, and when you jump, your parachute will deploy. That's just in case you forget. Now enjoy the jump, and don't forget to use your parachute lines to get you inside the circle."

With that, the aircraft began to taxi out to the end of the runway and, turning into the wind, the aircraft's throttles were opened and the surge of power accelerated them down the runway. In no time at all the aircraft was airborne and climbed to 1000 feet before completing a circuit that took them over a small part of the Irish Sea and Gun Island before coming back over the airfield.

Bill and Ben, the rain men, jumped on the first two circuits and everyone watched their descent with great interest. It was Peter's turn next, and he was clearly petrified at the prospect. When the time came to jump he didn't hesitate, but he did close his eyes and narrowly missed colliding with the door surround as he exited the aircraft. When he found himself dangling from his chute, his fear suddenly disappeared, and he had no problem controlling the direction of descent. He got a cheer from both Bill and Ben and Alec's assistant, John, who was there to collect everyone as they landed. The three ladies went next and they were followed by Josh and then Puffy. When it came to Albertino, he had to be woken up first. He had slept through all the jumps made so far and amazed both Alec and Cirrus as he gave a great yawn before leaping into space. Cirrus was the last to jump, and it had seemed like an eternity waiting for his turn. He had to admit to himself that he was nervous, but he wanted to do it and jumped right on call.

Suddenly falling towards earth and then feeling the reassuring tug of his parachute as it deployed was amazing, and in no time at all, Cirrus had raised his arms above his head to grab the lines of his chute to use them to guide himself down, so that he landed bang in the centre of the big yellow circle painted on the runway. His audience clapped to congratulate him before John gathered in his parachute and hurriedly got everyone into the minibus to clear the runway. Soon after they had departed, the twin- engined aircraft landed.

There was great revelry in the bar that night as everyone recounted their experience. There was no doubt that it had been an action-packed day, and one they could feel proud of. Judging by the chatter and enthusiasm, course CCMO/8/13 was considered by all as a great success, but it wasn't over yet, and they'd better watch how much they drank. Tomorrow had a lot more in store for them.

Abigail, Cirrus, Carol and Puffy may not have had much opportunity to advance their romantic fortunes, nor Lucy for that matter, but any disappointment in that direction was more than made up for by the euphoria of the day's activities.

By chute to water

Over breakfast, each of the course students was told to bring their swimming costumes with them. The male members were rather heart-warmed by the prospect of seeing their shapely female colleagues' figures in swimwear, and proceeded to the lecture theatre in high spirits to be greeted by their instructor, who turned out to be Alec once more.

"Good morning all. I trust you all slept well after such an active day yesterday. It's not going to be much different today, and we are going over to the Training Centre pool where I want you all to put on your swimwear and a wet suit, which John will provide you with."

The next time they all saw each other it was on the side of the pool in wet suits, so, so much for seeing the ladies in their natural glory.

"Yesterday, you made a parachute jump and landed on dear old mother earth, but you could just as easily have to jump over water."

Before Alec got any further it became obvious that there was an inclination to decline any invitation to do that if they were asked.

"No, I am not telling you that you will go and parachute into Neptune's Lake. You are going to practise here in the pool."

There was a great sigh of relief upon hearing Alec's words.

"Please put your life jackets on. Now I am going to demonstrate to you, what you do when you land in the water on the end of a parachute."

A hoist dropped down from the ceiling and Alec clipped himself into it, saying that this was his parachute harness. He waved an arm to his assistant who blew a whistle, following which he was hoisted up and over the centre of the pool. The whistle was blown again and Alec descended into the water at the speed he would do so if it was for real. On entering the pool, the hoist was released, and then the life jacket was inflated. Finally, the SARBE was activated.

"There you are, that's all there is to it. Want a go?"

"Nothing to it," remarked Albertino, who was turning out to be the star student.

The rest of the morning was spent practising this drill, and by lunchtime, they were all famished.

"Its Thursday lunch already. Hasn't the time flown by?" remarked Josh, to which there was unanimous agreement.

"What's next on the agenda?"

"First Aid."

Geraldine, or Gerry as she preferred to be called, was waiting for them all as they entered the lecture theatre.

"I hear you have all had a very busy day and a half since I last saw you. Well you won't be as physically involved this afternoon, but you will be mentally. I think you will all agree after what you have been through, that your ability to administer first aid is of the upmost importance."

Everybody naturally agreed, and Gerry plunged into talking about, and demonstrating, how to deal with, 'wounds and bleeding', 'shock', 'heart attacks' and 'unconsciousness', after which they took a break.

"Blimey, there's so much to remember on this course," which of course, there was.

"Right everybody, we still have a few more potential medical problems to deal with, so let's get on with it."

Gerry was certainly professional.

Fractures came next and the practical resulted in some miraculous looking dressings, but they got better on the whole. Sprains, burns, and scalds came next, and the afternoon session ended by covering the sequence of actions that are required in any emergency situation, which when summarised, cover assessment, diagnosis, treatment, and disposal which in the case of the latter, means onward movement to the next stage of medical help.

On arrival back at the accommodation block, it was clear that an evening of swotting was in store before the end of course examination on the following afternoon. One more training session in the morning and they would have covered the entire syllabus.

In spite of a great desire to have a farewell celebration, it was conceded that the course exam had precedence, and although they did get together for an hour at the end of the evening, it was a somewhat quiet affair.

The last day

Course tutor, George Brown greeted everyone in the lecture theatre on this their final day on course CCMO/8/13.

"Good morning everybody! I trust you all had a good breakfast. This morning we will conclude the course by covering 'Incident Reporting'. This will be a rather dry subject after all the exciting activities you have been involved in, but it is essential. I have placed on your desks a copy of an incident report form, and this is the tool that researchers use to make decisions regarding cloud machine design, and particularly safety features."

Albertino was not totally satisfied with this statement and piped up to say so.

"They also use these reports to check up on you when something goes wrong. They are used as evidence to make judgement on you, so they can fine you, or ban you, or put endorsements on your licence."

Mr Brown knew that he had to treat this with a degree of diplomacy.

"It is true that reports are considered when something goes wrong, but it would be unwise not to, since the whole object of them is to learn from every incident that occurs, and to try and militate against them in the future. It is also true that cloud machine crews have been found guilty in some respect on the basis of these reports, but these have been in a very small minority of cases. I think it is obvious from what is being said here that it is of crucial importance that you fill these forms in correctly."

The group went over the incident report form in great detail before being given a copy of a story that described something happening on board a cloud machine delivering rain. After reading the story, they had to complete a form, which Mr Brown would analyse and comment on. The form had four sections which covered, 'what happened', 'action taken', 'injuries sustained' and 'safety equipment used'. Then it went on to ask what safety equipment was on board, and when was it last checked, and when was training last carried out using the equipment. It was all very thorough, and somewhat daunting. The form ended with a requirement for the date to be included, and a signature.

"It's never been the same since we joined the EU, all this flippin' paperwork and regulations," remarked Josh.

"You're right Josh, there's always an EU spy looking over your bloomin shoulder these days," replied Ben.

"Well that's it ladies and gentlemen. We have reached the end of the curriculum. All that remains is the examination this afternoon and then you can be on your way, and I do hope that you have enjoyed the course, and learned something useful."

There was complete agreement that the course had been excellent, and Mr Brown was thanked for hosting them.

"When will we get the results of the exam?"

"Probably in a couple of weeks."

Lunch was a slightly sombre affair as everyone was in deep thought regarding the pending examination, but once they had all returned to the lecture theatre and got started, their apprehension evaporated as they got to work.

Exam over, it was time to say goodbye and depart for home. The group had got on remarkably well and so there was a degree of sadness at the parting of the waves.

Cirrus, in a manner most unusual for him, approached Abigail whom he had hoped to get closer to whilst attending the course. There hadn't been much opportunity for that.

"Abigail, Puffy and I are going back to our place in Ballyhalbert which is not far from here, and I wondered if..." He faltered at this point, but then regained his composure, "if you might join us for a few days?"

That was the best he could manage.

Puffy had his arm around Carol, and put it straight to her, "Look here my beauty, you're coming back to my place for a few days before you head back to the mainland."

Abigail couldn't come to Ballyhalbert without her sister Lucy, and Lucy wouldn't come without Bill and Ben being invited.

Carol had to return back to England since her skipper, Albertino, had a job to do.

In the end no-one accepted the invitation, and Cirrus and Puffy were both disappointed. But it didn't stop them from making the best of a well-earned rest, and they were flattered by the way the residents of Ballyhalbert made them welcome.

THE NIMBUS PRANGS

Checking safety features

"When we get back to Wythenshawe, Puffy, I think we better take a look around the Nimbus, and locate those things that we were told about at Bishops Court."

"I agree, I think we should, and there are some bits of kit that we should acquire as well."

The course they had recently attended was something of a salutary lesson for them, and they both realised how neglectful they had been in relation to safety matters.

After this short conversation, Cirrus turned his attention to his copy of the Daily Gloom. Robberies, violence, crazy judgements passed by the judiciary, murders and of course, the irrelevant meanderings of an increasingly irrelevant Government, filled the pages to guarantee a daily diet of staple tripe.

Why does he read that stuff thought Puffy? It only gets him aggravated.

To prove a point, Cirrus got up from his chair, threw the paper onto his settee and turned to face Puffy, who was now braced to receive a barrage of suggestions as to what needed doing, particularly to politicians. He had heard it all many times before, but it didn't make it any easier.

"Puffy get the car out, we are going to Wythenshawe. If we can't put the Country in order, we can still put our own things in order, and when we have done that, we will invite Abigail and Carol over."

That was a welcome surprise and Puffy wasted no time in getting sorted out.

"Good morning Cirrus, how did the course go at Bishops Court?"

"Good morning, Mr Spite. It went very well indeed; in fact it is as result of that course that brings me here. I'm going to check the various emergency facilities on board the Nimbus, and bring everything up to scratch."

"A very sensible move! I'm glad you thought it was worthwhile."

In Wythenshawe's huge hangar there were a number of cloud machines parked up, which was a little unusual, and enquiries revealed that several of them were updating their emergency equipment. Word had already got back about the course at Bishops Court, which was not surprising, considering that all the attendees were from Wythenshawe Weather Centre, or at least their machines were kept in the hangar there.

Walking up to the Nimbus, Puffy pressed on two outside buttons near the entry/exit door. First the door automatically opened, and then the access ladder telescoped out from under it before angling down to meet the ground. As both he and his Captain ascended the ladders, the first thing they made a point of looking for, was the emergency exit door ejection button. It was just where Alec had said it would be. They had no idea why they had taken no notice of it before. They then proceeded to the Flightdeck to locate a number of other safety features that they had been told about. The most obvious was a vertical row of three buttons and a lamp to the left of the fuel gauges and tachometers. From top to bottom, there was a button to lower the undercarriage and under it a lamp, which would illuminate when it was down and locked. Below that came the emergency power button, below which was the button that would initiate the inflation of the craft's flotation bags. The crew were amazed that they had forgotten about the last two items, but they had never had to use them.

The emergency undercarriage lowering lever was on the left hand side of the pilot's seat, sandwiched between the control column and the Plan Position Indicator. The last items to pick out were the motor extinguisher fire alarm lamps, and their respective extinguisher buttons.

These they found positioned on the box that the throttle levers were mounted on, on the right hand side of the pilot's seat.

The Nimbus crew were satisfied that they had reacquainted themselves with all these safety features, and made a plan to periodically practise using them, and to keep a record of their drill periods. That would keep the Health and Safety people off their backs!

Inspecting the rest of the Nimbus scared the daylights out of the pair of them. They discovered they had no smoke detectors, fire extinguishers, or fire blanket, and no oxygen masks. To make things even worse, they discovered that they had no first aid kit, no parachutes, and no life jackets. Cirrus looked at Puffy with his mouth wide open. Both crew members were staggered by their own negligence, and even more staggered that they still possessed an MOT certificate for the machine.

"Puffy, we better get this lot sorted out before we take on another job," and with that, they set off to find suppliers for all that they needed.

It took about a week to purchase all that was required to meet modern safety requirements, and engineers from Black, Black and Blackemore's in deeper Salford did the necessary work to accommodate everything, but it did make a dent in the Captain's bank balance. When everything was done, Cirrus asked Puffy to contact their two lady friends to invite them to their Slaidburn home. It would be nice to have some female company thought Cirrus, but evidently his method of approach did not go down well. Abigail was not impressed. He should have asked her himself. Puffy faired no better, but the response he got was more straight forward.

"You can bugger off with your invitations. You only want me when you have nothing better to do." And that was that.

"Well so much for that idea," said Cirrus, and Puffy just agreed with him. Both men had to be satisfied with their own company, and Cirrus went back to the Daily Gloom.

Manx Whisky

Looking around the job's board at Wythenshawe Weather Centre, Captain Cumulus spotted one for the Isle-of-Man, and he studied it more closely. A resident of Peel intended to make whisky that was different. He intended to make it with a blend of Manx and Scottish water. What he needed was a method of shipping water from Scotland to the island.

"This looks interesting, Puffy."

Casting his eyes over the advertisement prompted Puffy to ask, "How can we deliver water to the island, other than in rain form?"

"You have something there. There's a phone number on the card, perhaps I ought to give them a ring."

The Captain popped over to the Centre's main office where Goldilocks was sitting doing her nails.

"Any chance I could use your phone, Goldilocks?"

"You're lucky! Mr Spite is not in today. He generally doesn't allow anyone to use the office phone, but whilst it's you Cirrus I will be kind and say yes, but don't tell anyone, mind you."

Cirrus kissed her cheek, and thanked her, and this shocked her no end and she began to blush.

Cirrus dialled the telephone number shown on the job card and, after a few moments, a female voice answered.

"Hello, this is the Peel Wine and Spirits Company, how can I help?"

"My name is Captain Cumulus, and I'm ringing from Wythenshawe Weather Centre."

Oh! Well we don't have any of that here."

"You don't understand. I believe you need some water?"

"We already have plenty of that; we just turn the tap on."

Cirrus started to get a bit frustrated. This conversation was going nowhere.

"Look, can you put me through to your chief engineer?"

"We don't have any chiefs, but we do have a manager."

"Well please put me through to him then."

"Righty-ho then, just two ticks."

"Mr Vannin here, how can I help you Admiral?"

"Hello Mr Vannin, this is Captain Cumulus. I am not an Admiral. I own a cloud machine called the Nimbus, and I have just picked up a job card of yours at Wythenshawe Weather Centre."

"Ah, that's good, I wondered if I would find any takers. What can I do for you?"

"My engineer and I are interested to know how you think a cloud machine can deliver water to you. We can bring a cloud and rain on you, but that wouldn't be as efficient as using a large tanker vehicle. If we rained on you, you would only get a small proportion of what we carry."

"That may be so, but I have developed a special piece of kit which I call a cloud condenser. If you take the job on, I will pay for the kit to be fitted to your machine."

"How does it work?"

"Well, you land here at my place as a huge cloud, and I walk into it to find you and connect a hose up to you. I switch the cloud condenser on, and your cloud gets sucked back aboard, via the dispensers. Once it's aboard, the condenser converts it to water which is then pumped out of your machine and into my own private reservoir."

"That's clever, but isn't it a bit expensive doing it this way?"

"Not at all! To carry the same amount of water as you can, would take at least ten tankers, and they would have to come across on the ferry. No, doing it this way is much cheaper, and that includes removing the cloud condenser when the job's done, so how about it, are you up for the job?"

Cirrus mused for a moment or two. It all seemed straightforward enough, but there were still one or two points that he needed to clarify.

"Where would you fit the equipment to the Nimbus?"

"I could arrange for that to be done at Wythenshawe, at your convenience."

"Where will the water be taken from?"

"Ah, now that's a bit tricky. I want water from the river Spey, but from a section in particular, a section that flows past Grantown-on-Spey. Now, that's very popular with a number of distilleries in that area, so it would have to be done at night."

"How many deliveries do you need?"

"With the amount of water you can deliver in one go I should have enough in my reservoir for a whole year. Does that answer your questions, Admiral?"

Cirrus had no difficulty confirming that he would take the job on. It would be different, and it would be intriguing to see how well Mr Vannin's cloud condenser worked. The Nimbus would be unique as the only machine capable of doing this work.

In due course, arrangements were made for an engineer to come over from the Isle-of-Man to Wythenshawe to modify the Nimbus, but Cirrus took the precaution of consulting the manufacturers Black, Black and Blackemore's, who would ensure that they had a representative present to see that all the other functions were in no way compromised.

Once all the engineering arrangements had been made, it was time to look at the charts and establish the latitude and longitude of both the source of the water, and its destination, since these co-ordinates would have to be punched into the soakometer/navaid to get them from A to B. Finally, they had to look at the highest points on the route from Wythenshawe to Grantown-on-Spey and from there to Peel on the Isle-of-Man, since that would determine how high they would need to fly to prevent hitting anything.

Grantown-on-Spey

The Nimbus was stocked with all the supplies that were required for the job in hand which would take several days. Cirrus pored over his charts to ensure that his flight plan was correct. He made the decision that twenty knots would be a better ground speed to work on. It would make fewer demands on his machine and was more achievable if the wind was to play a bigger part, but according to the forecast it should not be much of a problem. For the next few days it would be a north westerly at ten knots.

"We'll get airborne at 2110 hours Puffy. It should be dark by then."

"I suppose we will do the usual, and head out to the Irish Sea and make a cloud?"

"Not this time. I intend to head north as she is," commented the Captain.

That's unusual, thought Puffy, but he didn't feel inclined to probe any further at this point, working on the notion that all would eventually be revealed.

The crew amused themselves for a few hours before boarding their cloud machine. Once the entrance door was shut, and the access ladders retracted, they entered the cockpit to start the pre-take off checks. With all the preliminaries completed, Cirrus started the four fan duct motors, one after the other. Looking out from the cockpit window, he could see that the doors of Wythenshawe's huge hangar had been opened, and so he taxied the Nimbus out into the night sky. The Nimbus stopped for a few moments and then took off vertically as the fan motors were swivelled to the correct position.

Up and into the darkness the machine went, and it continued in this fashion until it reached five thousand feet, at which height it was brought to a hover. Cirrus punched the lat and long of Wythenshawe Weather Centre into his soakometer/navaid, and then he did the same for his destination. The Nimbus automatically turned onto a heading that would take it to Grantown-on-Spey and Cirrus noted on his compass that the heading was about 350°. He checked his watch. It was just coming up to 2115 hours and as it did so, he advanced the throttles until the Nimbus settled at a speed of twenty knots.

The crew settled down to the long flight ahead. The pop-up TV screen was now in action, but there was not a lot to see in the darkness. The Plan Position Indicator, on the other hand, gave an interesting display of the land they were flying over, and Puffy used the chart that his Captain had given him to follow their flight path. The machines Identification Beacon was activated, which was most important. The Nimbus would give a return on both ground radar and that on any aircraft in proximity, and it was essential that everyone knew who they were. If they were not identified in British airspace, there was every likelihood that the Royal Air Force would investigate by scrambling one of its new Typhoon fighter aircraft, and that could be embarrassing or at its worst, fatal.

The time passed awfully slowly, and at 2326 hours, the crew could make out Lancaster on their port side on the PPI.

"Puffy, make a brew will you?"

"I never thought you would ask skipper."

Having the galley so close at hand was very convenient, and the drawback of cooking smells was more than offset by its convenience factor.

"There you are skipper, a nice cuppa, and a buttered scone to go with it."

"Cheers Puffy, you're a good man."

"Shall I get my head down now?" asked Puffy.

"No. I want us both to stay awake through the night. We will both get the chance to sleep through the day tomorrow."

"Righty-ho skipper," and Puffy went back to his work table to drop crumbs on his chart, and log them on his flight log record, as it helped pass the time. He recorded, 'crumb spotted' on the starboard side as we passed to the east of Kendall. It wasn't official, but it did absorb a little time.

At 0137 hours, the PPI showed that the Nimbus was still east of the M6 motorway, and had reached a point north of Appleby. The journey was taxing both of the crew who were finding it a bit boring, with little for them to do, except maintain their height and speed, and monitor their position.

"Looks like Abigail and Carol have lost interest in us Puffy?"

"Ah, that's women skipper. Here today gone tomorrow."

Puffy seems to take it all in his stride, thought Cirrus.

"They'll be back. You mark my words skipper."

"I hope you're right."

Another couple of hours passed and by 0338 hours they had crossed the Scottish border and were somewhere over the Southern Uplands, although it was difficult to say exactly where, but the PPI showed Jedburgh off to their starboard side. As the Nimbus flew on, Edinburgh, and the Firth of Forth came into view both on the PPI and on the tv screen, as dawn began to show itself. At exactly 0600 hours, Cirrus brought the Nimbus to the hover over the Firth of Forth, and immediately got Puffy to start atomising the North Sea below them, to surround themselves with cloud, for they were sailing pretty close to the wind right now in terms of preserving their anonymity to the naked eye.

By 0700 hours, an attractive Westmorland White cloud was comfortably sitting above the Firth of Forth watching all the other clouds go by, and the two crew got their heads down for a well-earned sleep.

Cirrus woke to the smell of something good. His flight engineer was already busy cooking a very late breakfast for the two of them. Once out of his bunk the Captain neatly rearranged and folded all the blankets, and lifted the double bunk arrangement back into its stowage space in the starboard side of the flightdeck compartment. He had just enough time for a quick wash and shave before Puffy served up an enticing looking plate of egg, bacon, beans, sausage and fried bread. Washed down with a good cup of tea, it was a most enjoyable meal and now he was ready to face the rest of the day, or what was left of it.

"Thanks, Puffy. That was a most enjoyable breakfast."

"You're welcome skipper."

It was only 1600 hours, and with some seven hours left before they departed their present location, over the Firth of Forth, there was plenty time to kill. Cirrus looked over all the various systems to check everything was ok. The fan duct motors were running and set to keep them in the hover, fuel was fine, and the identification beacon was working. Next he looked at the Plan Position Indicator to see that they had not moved from the spot they had stopped over the previous night, and they hadn't. He looked at the tv screen and Rosyth was visible ahead. He rotated the periscope that had the tv camera mounted in it. As he looked east, the two Forth Bridges could be seen along with the town of Queensferry, and Edinburgh a little further on. To the south he could see Edinburgh airport, and Broxburn, whilst to the west he could see Grangemouth. The view was quite spectacular, and the panorama was enhanced by several ships coming and going along the Forth. The last thing he checked was the height at which the Nimbus was hovering. At 5,000 feet, nothing had changed, and everything could be left as it was before they moved off.

The crew of the Nimbus had a game of draughts, and a couple of cups of coffee before darkness came, which was at about 2100 hours.

Two more hours to wait and then they would be off. Cirrus paced up an down the corridor which linked the flightdeck with the toilet and washroom at the stern of the craft, and Puffy ticked off the number of times his Captain did this on a piece of paper. He should be doing this for charity thought Puffy.

Finally, 2300 hours arrived, and it was time to take leave of the Firth of Forth, and all the twinkling lights of the many homes on either side of it. They could make out moving vehicles by their lights, and a train crossing one of the bridges. Cirrus altered the angle of the fan duct motors by moving his control column, and the thrust that had kept them in the hover now provided the Nimbus with forward propulsion. The co-ordinates of their destination were already in the soakometer/navaid, so the Nimbus would automatically take them there. At a height of 5,000 feet they would clear all the mountains that lay ahead in the Grampians, so there was nothing to be overly concerned about.

For three hours the Nimbus flew north at a ground speed of twenty knots, and Puffy kept a careful watch on their position by viewing the PPI, and marking waypoints on his chart. The pop up tv screen had little to display after the first hour. Once Perth had been left behind they were over sparsely populated country, and in the early hours of the morning there were practically no house lights to observe.

Once the Nimbus arrived over the Grampian Mountains, the infra red facility on the tv camera came into its own. The view below was very good, and lochs and glens were easily spotted, and that was important. Cirrus had picked out a loch south of the highest mountain, Ben Macdhui, upon which to rain, and he peered with great concentration at the PPI to pick it out. At exactly 0200 hours, the Nimbus was brought into the hover. Down below them was a small loch that was rapidly going to get bigger. Satisfied that he was in the right place, Puffy was given the instruction to make it rain, and for the cloud the Nimbus had brought from the Forth to have fully precipitated in one hour. Puffy carried out his instruction, and steady rain was all that was required to get rid of a Westmorland White, which they had brought to this dark and isolated spot. Down below there was no-one to witness this event that would reveal, if it was light, the presence of a cloud machine.

The rain was over, and the Nimbus was nude in the night sky by 0300 hours, and Cirrus, once again, altered the angle of the motors to provide forward propulsion, to continue on to its destination, Grantown-on-Spey. It passed over Ben Macdhui with a thousand feet to spare, and the Grampians were left behind as it flew on to meet the River Spey, its source of water for whisky making in the Isle of Man. After forty-five minutes, the Captain was alternating between the PPI and the tv screen to pick out a bend in the Spey, just south of Grantown. He intended to hover over a straight section of the river that was to the left of the bend.

"There it is Puffy, that's the bend I was looking for, and I can see the spot that we are going to hover over."

The throttles were partly closed to slow the Nimbus down, to give Cirrus a better chance of hovering exactly where he wanted to atomise water. The craft was brought to the hover, and Puffy began the process of atomising that lovely Scottish whisky- making water that was about to find its way to the Isle of Man. By 0500 hours, the job was completed, and the Nimbus was a cloud again, and it was still dark.

Now for Manxland

Punching in the co-ordinates for both Grantown, and Peel in the Isle of Man, the soakometer/navaid would ultimately take the Nimbus on its important delivery flight. Cirrus would maintain a height of 5,000 feet and a ground speed of twenty knots. The distance to travel was one hundred and ninety nautical miles, and that would take nine and a half hours.

At just after 0500 hours, the Nimbus left its source of Spey whisky water in the Cairngorms, and headed off on the final stage of its journey. Glimpsing at the compass, the heading was about 190°. There was nothing left to do now except monitor the flight path, and occasionally check on the speed and altitude. In another hour it would be daylight.

It was daybreak by 0600 hours and, in a sky of broken cloud, the Nimbus made its way almost at right angles to the westerly wind. At ten knots, the wind was not very strong and should have caused them to drift to port, but the soakometer/navaid automatically swivelled the fan duct motors to compensate, and keep them on course. It must have been a little strange for those individuals down below to see ninety-nine per cent of the clouds heading east, and just one heading south west. None of this was really unusual in the cloud machine line of business.

By 0722 hours, the Nimbus was just south of the Grampian Mountains and Puffy had spotted Aberfeldy as they passed over it. Everything was going fine and it was time for a coffee. In fact, there were several coffees on this long journey, and the odd bacon sandwich. Cirrus was grateful for having such a congenial and helpful flight engineer and gratefully received all of his offerings.

The halfway point was reached at 0945 hours and directly below the Nimbus was the city of Glasgow. On course and on time, Cirrus was well satisfied, and the view on the tv screen was helping to make the journey both interesting and enjoyable.

Newton Stewart was just ahead at the three-quarters point, 1208 hours, and the Irish Sea was in view. The crew were taking a bit of lunch before the real work began. Just another two hours and twenty minutes and they would reach their destination at Peel.

In just less than an hour the Nimbus crossed the Scottish coastline at a point west of Whithorn, with Luce Bay and the Mull of Galloway on their starboard side. Further to the west, and clearly visible, was Northern Ireland and the Ards peninsula that was home to Ballyhalbert. Ahead lay the Isle of Man and its most northerly point, the Point-of-Ayr, was easy to pick out. It was on a day like this that the Captain could be thankful that a day in the office for him, was the splendour unfolding around the Nimbus.

Onwards the Nimbus flew across the Irish Sea and ever nearer to the Isle-of-Man. The flight path would take it down the west side of the Island to reach its destination. By 1319 hours, it was almost level with Jurby, and the airfield at which Cirrus had prepared for the Great Cloud Parade in 2012 was clearly in view. Suddenly, the Captain shouted out with an air of anxiety.

"Puffy, we have just lost five hundred feet."

"That's not all skipper, we have also drifted towards the Island."

What the dickens is happening? thought Cirrus. We shouldn't be doing either. But by the time he had got himself acquainted with the motion of the Nimbus, they had lost another five hundred feet, and it was time to take action.

"I'm going to open the throttles and give a bit more power to stop this descent," and he did, but it didn't stop the Nimbus going down, and it was doing so fairly rapidly.

"Bloody hell! I better try and alter the elevation of the motors."

Puffy was worrying by now, even though he had full confidence in his skipper, but they were down now to three thousand feet, and were almost at the Manx coastline as they continued to drift eastwards.

The Captain pulled back on the control column to check the craft's descent and noticed as he did so, that it was already slightly forward of the position it should have been in, and that would explain why it was descending. The pull back on the column didn't check the descent. With sweat beginning to trickle down the side of his face, Cirrus quickly closed the throttles, and thankfully the rate of descent was slowed, but not stopped, and now the Nimbus was down to two thousand five hundred feet.

It became obvious that the descent could not be stopped, and even if the throttles were fully closed, it would only slow it down. The more immediate problem now was the continuous drift to port. The Nimbus was just about to cross the Manx coast on a south easterly heading, and the heights of Snaefell looked perilously close.

There was only one thing for it; the fan duct motors would have to be swivelled to check the drift, and that meant that the throttles would have to be kept open to aid the process. Applying pressure to his rudder pedals that controlled the angle of swivel of the motors, Cirrus noticed that they were not centralised, they were in a position that would explain the drift that they were experiencing. Try as he might, the Captain could not get any response to the foot pressure he was applying.

Well below two thousand feet, and with Snaefell looming on their port side, there was nothing left to do other than close the throttles and wait to see if they cleared the mountain top. It was too late to don parachutes and bail out, but if they did clear the top they could try deploying the craft's parachute. Suddenly there was a loud bang and a crunching sound, and it all went very black.

Snaefell's new victim

Jimmy Ellan was riding his motorbike to work, and was making his way over the mountain road toward Ramsey. It was not far to his turning at that famous place on the Islands TT course called the Bungalow. Here he would turn left to ascend to the summit of Snaefell where he worked in the transmitting station for the 'National Air Traffic Services'. Jimmy could clearly see a very large grey cloud on his left, and it appeared to be moving closer fairly fast, and he could also see the cloud base lowering. Any minute now he fully expected to be riding through a thick mist, but that was not unusual on Snaefell.

As Jimmy expected, he was soon embraced by a thick, grey mist, and the temperature quickly dropped. Having adjusted his speed to cope with the drop in visibility, there was a loud crunching sound on Jimmy's left hand side, and immediately he suspected that an aircraft had just collided with the mountain, but of course he couldn't see anything. He stopped and listened out carefully, but there was no other indication that anything had happened. Nevertheless, he was convinced that something had impacted with the mountain, and felt compelled to do something. He got his mobile phone out of his pocket and called his colleagues in the transmitting station.

"Hello, it's Jimmy here. I'm on the mountain road, not far from you, and I suspect something has flown into the side of Snaefell, but I can't see anything. The summit is covered with cloud."

"Hi Jimmy! We didn't hear anything, and we are not aware of any aircraft in the area, but stay where you are and we will get the emergency services to you as soon as possible. Let us know when they reach you."

"Will do, thanks."

In due course the siren of an approaching fire engine could be heard, and it got a lot louder as it got nearer to Jimmy.

"Where is it?" enquired the Fire Chief.

"I don't know. I heard what I think was a collision. but it was over there in the cloud. That's all I can tell you."

An ambulance and police car arrived on the scene to assist, and everybody got into a huddle to determine what the appropriate action should be. If it was a crash, there could be somebody out there in the mist, desperately in need of help. It was decided that the local Mountain Rescue Team should be called out, since only they could provide the manpower to carry out a full search of the area. Meanwhile, a small scale search would be embarked on, with everyone fanning out into a long line, but all connected to each other by rope. Satisfied that this was the best course of action before the Rescue Team arrived, the Fire Chief ordered everyone to step forward into the mist, but to be extra diligent, and go slowly. Jimmy was to stay behind until the Rescue Team arrived.

It was rather strange to see a line of people, or at least a part of a line of people, walking into the mist and then disappearing in it. Jimmy checked the time; it was 2.00pm. It was thirty minutes or so since he had heard what he thought might be a crash. A full sixty minutes passed before the Rescue Team arrived, and for Jimmy that felt like an eternity. Considering the Rescue Team was made up of part time volunteers, it was something of a miracle that they had all left their places of employment to mobilise at their headquarters, and get here so fast, but it still felt like an eternity to Jimmy. The narrow road to the mountain summit was now clogged with emergency vehicles.

"Where is everyone?" asked the team leader.

"They have gone off into the mist in that direction to try and locate any crash site," replied Jimmy.

"Ok guys, it's the usual drill and make sure we have blankets and stretchers."

Jimmy was given hold of the end of a rope and told not to drop it, and at the other end, the Rescuers disappeared into the mist. The rope was their way of finding their way back.

"It's here, it's here," shouted one of the Fire Chief's crew, and a tug on the line brought the first team to the Nimbus.

"What the devil is it?" asked one of them.

"Never mind what it is, there may be someone inside, so let's get on with it."

It didn't take long to surround the machine, and the entrance door was soon found. But it was still closed, which meant that any occupants would still be on board.

"There's an 'open' button here."

"Press it."

Nothing happened, and a further search did not reveal any emergency exit, but through the cockpit window the shapes of two people could be made out, sprawled across the floor.

"We are going to have to break a window to get them out."

A burly member of the crew stepped forward, and a window rapidly vanished as a shower of Perspex. The rescuers soon gained access into the cockpit, and Cirrus and Puffy were only too glad to see them. A quick examination soon revealed a combination of severe bruising, a few lacerations, and possible leg fractures. The only way to get them out of the Nimbus would be on a stretcher, through the cockpit window, but a stretcher was not what they had. The Fire Chief called Jimmy on his mobile.

"Don't worry Chief, the Rescue Team are on their way to you, and they have stretchers and blankets."

The Fire Chief informed the crew of the Nimbus, and set about getting the paramedics from the ambulance to treat them as best they could, until they could evacuate them.

In due course, the Mountain Rescue Team arrived and passed the blankets and stretchers through the cockpit window. The Nimbus crew were soon brought out into the cold mist of its own cloud, but they said nothing about it. The Fire Chief was about to lead everyone back to the narrow mountain road as was his wont, but when asked which way it was, he had no idea. He had not taken the precaution of attaching a rope to Jimmy, as had the Mountain Rescue Team, who now rescued firemen, paramedics, and policemen, alongside the crew of the Nimbus. This was a rescue that the team would not forget, whilst the Fire Chief wished they would.

Jimmy was greatly relieved to see everyone emerging from the mist, for he was damned cold by this time, but he felt vindicated when he saw the two casualties. It didn't take long to get the two stretcher-borne casualties into the ambulance which, with siren blaring, travelled down the road towards Douglas. Once it emerged from the mist, which was not moving, it accelerated, to deliver the two crew members to Noble's Hospital for the experts in the 'A' and 'E' department to get to work on.

Hospitalisation

On arrival at Noble's Hospital, the two injured crewmen were wheeled straight into the Accident and Emergency Department, and in no time at all, both Cirrus and Puffy were surrounded by groups of medics all looking at different aspects of their injuries, whilst conferring. Those lacerations which could be dealt with fast, and without endangering any suspected fractures, were dealt with, and then it was off to 'X'-ray. Both of the Nimbus crew had hairline fractures of a leg, and the appropriate action was taken. With the fractures taken care of, the examination continued. It was generally agreed that both of them had got off relatively lightly, but they would be bed-bound for a few days for both of them were exhibiting symptoms of shock.

With one leg in plaster, and multiple dressings, each crew member was wheeled into a ward to join several other patients that had been involved in accidents. The ward sister made her presence known to them, and ran over their particulars to ensure that the paperwork was all in order.

"If you need anything, just ring this bell."

The sister left both of them to the mercy of the rest of the patients who wasted no time in asking them who they were, and what had happened to them. The Nimbus crew were obliged not to divulge too much and the vagueness of their answers did not endear them to their new bedfellows. After a relatively short time, interest in the new arrivals dropped to a low, and most went back to reading or listening to the radio, using the headphones supplied for that purpose.

After a good night's sleep, and a breakfast, which whilst good, did not match those cooked by Puffy, the two new patients had two new visitors. Two burly policemen had arrived to make some enquiries and their arrival roused considerable interest. A curtain was drawn around the beds of both crew members, but the privacy provided would not extend to any conversation, and the silence in the ward would, with luck, prove to be informative, at least that's what the other patients thought.

The first formality was to establish who Cirrus and Puffy were and where they both came from and then came the bit that the rest of the ward was dying to find out.

"Can you tell me what happened sir?"

Cirrus thought carefully before answering but knew he would have to give it away, since he may need their help in contacting various agencies, and more to the point, he couldn't run the risk of saying something different than Puffy.

"I was delivering a cloud of Scottish whisky water to Peel when a fault developed, and I couldn't stop colliding with Snaefell."

The police constable looked up from his note pad, pencil in hand, and looked at Cirrus in a puzzled looking way.

"Would you care to repeat that sir?"

Cirrus repeated his story, and the police constable noted everything meticulously without a smile or a smirk, which wasn't helped by the sniggers he could hear from around the ward. When he had done, he joined his colleague to swap notes, and couldn't believe it when he discovered that he had got the same story from Puffy.

"I don't know what my Sergeant is going to say when he hears this," and with that the two police officers left.

A buzz went around the ward.

"You need a psychiatrist mate!"

The Nimbus crew declined to respond, but made a request that they be moved into a side room, but the request fell on the deaf ears of the ward sister.

"Nurse, can you help me?" asked Cirrus.

"What's the problem?"

"I need to make a few phone calls in private. Can you help me to do that please?"

Nurse Eleanor, Ellie to her friends, was quite taken with the nice way she had been asked to help. Her day so far, had been an unpleasant experience, being the butt of bad tempers.

"Of course I can. Just let me check where the telephone pay trolley is, and if we have a spare side room."

A couple of minutes later, Ellie was back with a wheelchair, and Cirrus found himself alone with a phone and made his first call. Black, Black and Blackemore's would need to get a recovery team over to recover the Nimbus, and carry out any repair work back at Wythenshawe. The next call was going to be a bit more difficult.

"Hello, this is the Peel Wine and Spirits Company, can I help you?"

"This is Captain Cumulus. Can you put me through to Mr Vannin please?"

"Oh he's been expecting you for several days, just a mo."

"Is that you Admiral? Where the devil have you been? You should have made a delivery a couple of days ago."

Cirrus tried to explain as best he could, but detected a lack of sympathy.

"Well you're off the job, and make no mistake about it; I want my cloud condenser back."

The phone went dead and Cirrus was a bit flustered after this less than amicable exchange, but was glad he had got it over with. He called out for Ellie, and thanked her for her kind help, noting at the same time that he had an ally on the ward now.

Before the day was out, the skipper of the Nimbus had another visitor in the form of a police inspector, whom the ward sister introduced as Inspector Ramsey.

"I understand that you are Captain Cumulus."

"Yes, that's correct."

"I'm Inspector Ramsey, from the Island Constabulary, and I am in charge of the enquiry regarding your crash on Snaefell. I need to establish one or two things with you."

"That's ok Inspector, go ahead."

"I have spoken to the Fire Chief, and my officers who came to see you, and I understand that the cloud currently in residence on the mountain, is yours. Can you confirm that for me?"

"Technically speaking, the cloud belongs to the Peel Wine and Spirits Company in Peel. I was only delivering it to them."

"That maybe so sir, but having checked with Mr Vannin, he says that until he was in receipt of the cloud it was still yours."

"Well in that case, I suppose it is mine."

"Can I ask you if you have planning permission for it?"

"Planning permission! What do you mean, have I got planning permission for it?"

"If you don't have planning permission for it, you can't leave it where it is. We are getting a lot of complaints about it. People can't see the sun!

Every day is a grey day, and it's dangerous driving over the mountain road, and so on. Who put it there, and did they have permission? I'm sure you get my drift."

Cirrus could see the serious look on the Inspectors' face and was about to inform him about the arrangements he had made when his thoughts were interrupted.

"I'm afraid sir, that you must shift your cloud, and that if you do not do so in the next forty-eight hours, you will face a heavy fine or even imprisonment. Do you understand that, Captain?"

"Yes I do, but I do have a question to ask you Inspector. I'm worried about looters. Could you put a guard on it to make sure no-one gets on board? I would be most grateful if you could help."

"I'll see what I can do, but its most unusual putting a guard on a cloud."

Cirrus sincerely hoped that Black, Black and Blackemore's engineers would get to the crash sight fast.

Abigail was looking at the news board in Wythenshawe Weather Centre when she spotted the details of a crash in the Isle of Man. She read on, and to her horror, discovered that it was the Nimbus. The names of the crew were not listed; it simply said that the injured were recovered to the Noble's Hospital, Douglas. Good God, thought Abigail, I wonder how Cirrus is, and she discovered that he did mean something to her.

"I wonder if Carol knows?" she said to herself. Within a few hours, the two of them had booked a flight to the Island.

Cirrus was having a light nap when he felt a slight prodding on his shoulder.

"Hello. I'm Jimmy Ellan. I'm the bloke that heard you crash and reported it. I just thought I'd pop in and ask how you are?"

"Jimmy, I'm very pleased to meet you. I'm Cirrus, and over there is my Flight Engineer, Puffy White. I'm really pleased to meet you Jimmy. This is a chance to say thank you for saving my bacon."

"An' he does like his bacon," shouted Puffy, from across the ward.

A conversation then ensued, and Jimmy got the full story, which would make a great talking point with his colleagues in the transmitting station.

"Thanks for calling, Jimmy, and thanks for getting help to us."

With that Jimmy shook hands with Cirrus and Puffy, and left, taking with him the grapes he had brought, but forgotten to give them.

"You can't go in that cloud sir, not without authority," said the police constable, standing on the edge of the new resident on Snaefell.

"But I'm the bloody recovery engineer from Black, Black and Blackemore's."

"You can be from the Black Hole of Calcutta for all I care, but you can't go in there without authority."

"Look constable, what about all this traffic, it's going through the cloud isn't it?"

The constable was stumped by this observation and decided that a little discretion may be in order.

"Well since you are the recovery people, I suppose it will be ok."

The recovery team drove past the constable with their vehicles and into the cloud, whilst carefully following the narrow road that led to the summit and the transmitting station. After a short distance, the vehicles halted, and their crews disembarked. A rope was attached to one of the vehicles and, holding on to it, the recovery chief led his team further into the mist, off the road, and down the side of the mountain, fanning out at the same time. It was not too long before they discovered the Nimbus, and they gained entry through the broken cockpit window.

Inside the Nimbus, stuff had been thrown around by the impact, but on the whole it didn't look as if it was damaged internally. The emergency power button was pressed and this activated the dim strip lighting which improved their visibility.

"I think we need to get rid of the cloud first and then we can see what we have on our hands from a recovery point of view," said the leader, who was busy assessing the situation.

One of the team made his way to the flight engineer's station and looked carefully at the rain selector panel. He made the decision to create light rain to get rid of the cloud. Heavy rain would get rid of it faster, but that might make it boggy underfoot, and that would make it more difficult to recover the Nimbus. Light rain it was, and it took a good couple of hours to get rid of the cloud.

It was a strange phenomenon to observe, from the summit, a shrinking cloud that ran down the mountainside until it was simply no more, but the poor policeman on guard duty got a good soaking in the process.

"Get some tarpaulins over the thing quick. We don't want to give too much away," barked the recovery leader, who then took a look around to assess the damage. On the whole the Nimbus had survived quite well; the majority of the impact had been suffered by the two port fan duct motors which would have to be replaced. Other than that, there were a few dents here and there, but nothing too serious. There would have to be an investigation to establish what had happened, but that would be done back at Wythenshawe.

Once the Nimbus had been covered by tarpaulins, it was winched off the mountainside and lifted onto one of the trucks to be taken to the ferry terminal in Douglas. Within another twenty-four hours it was back in Wythenshawe's huge hangar and being carefully inspected. What was more, Cirrus was saved from paying any exorbitant fine, which was not such a bad thing under the circumstances.

Armed with the standard patient's recovery present, grapes, Abigail and Carol entered Noble's Hospital and made their way to the ward shared by Cirrus and Puffy. Their entry was observed with considerable interest, but no wolf whistles. They were not appreciated by the ward sister who controlled everyone with a rod of iron. The majority were disappointed when the two charming looking lovelies headed for the crew of the Nimbus, who seemed to be getting most of the attention around here.

"Cirrus, how are you my dear?" asked Abigail.

"I have been so worried about you."

"Now that was a turn up for the book," thought Cirrus, "but I'll take it!"

She leaned over the bed revealing something of her delightful assets in the process, and then proceeded to kiss him passionately. Whilst this was something to relish, Cirrus couldn't cope with it being so public, and broke into a severe blush, which he didn't recover from for some time. Puffy on the other hand, seemed to be very satisfied wrestling with

Carol, public or not, but the ward sister was less impressed, although she did refrain from refereeing.

It was great to see the two women in their lives, and to discover that a passion existed between them, but it was also a relief when the ward sister called 'time', and all the visitors had to leave, but it was not done without making a promise to get together in Slaidburn when they got back.

Just before departing, Abigail gave Cirrus a letter, saying it had arrived at Wythenshawe for him, and then finally left, complete with a bag of grapes. He opened the letter which was from Bishops Court informing him that he had passed the examination on the course CCMO/8/13, 'Coping with Emergency Situations', which was a little ironic, given their present circumstances.

"Hey skipper," shouted Puffy. "I passed the exam, how did you get on?"

After a week in hospital, Cirrus and Puffy were both discharged. They both still had a leg in plaster, at least up to the knee, but that was not debilitating. In spite of being very well looked after, they were glad to be heading home and the ward sister was glad they were going. Since their arrival there had been a constant stream of visitors, and especially policemen, and she had had a frustrating time keeping the media out. At least that pressure would disappear. She had, however, developed a bit of a soft spot for the two of them, and shed a tear as they left the hospital in a taxi for Ronaldsway Airport. But she rapidly changed her mood when two reporters approached her asking what she could tell them about the two injured cloudmen. She declined, but told them in no uncertain terms what they could do to themselves. The medical terms she used went straight over their heads, which was perhaps just as well.

The investigation

A close investigation of the Nimbus by the engineers from Black, Black and Blackemore's back in Wythenshawe, led to the conclusion that the problem had been caused by the machine's fan duct motor becoming jammed in a position pointing slightly downwards and to the left, and this they had concluded, had been caused by some damage done to the motor movement mechanism when Mr Vannin's cloud condenser had been fitted. The investigation went on to make two recommendations. The first was to fit all cloud machines with an emergency exit door above the cockpit, and the second was to fit seat belts on all three of the cockpit seats.

An insurance claim was made against the Peel Wine and Spirits Company for the damages incurred by the Nimbus, due to the negligence of their engineer when fitting the cloud condenser, which had subsequently been removed and returned. Mr Vannin, when faced with big increases in his premiums, dropped his whisky-making project, and concentrated on drinking it from then on.

A Ship In Distress

The Glasson Voyager

Joe Solomly came from Glasson Dock, a small port just south of Lancaster. He came from a seafaring family and he was the Captain of the Glasson Voyager, a cargo ship of no great size. Joe brought timber to Barrow in Furness from Halifax, Nova Scotia, and did so on a monthly basis. He just about broke even doing it, but money never figured high on Joe's priority list; he was something of a carefree character and enjoyed his independence immensely. There had never been any special woman in Joe's life. He considered the opposite sex as too 'bossy' and interfering.

If appearances are anything to go by, Joe would be considered scruffy, which he was, but that would mislead anyone who would make a judgement about him on that basis. Joe was intelligent, and kept himself informed about what was happening on the World stage. He was however, carefree, and had little time to keep up appearances. His clothes were well worn, and often he didn't bother shaving. He was of the opinion that crossing the Atlantic he was not likely to get visitors dropping in. Dentistry was not one of his strong points either, and he would go for days without putting his dentures in.

The Glasson Voyager had an appearance in keeping with that of its skipper, namely, neglected. The ship's paintwork was a patchwork quilt of combined rust of varying ages, and the odd bit of colour. Even the compulsory Plimsol line was faded to a point that made a determined search a pre-requisite to finding it. Loaded with Canadian timber, it sailed low in the water, and rough seas cascaded in waves over its focsle confining its small crew to below deck.

Joe's navigator was Bert Drew, who had spent most of his seafaring life aboard the deep-sea trawlers that used to fish out of Fleetwood. Bert was well acclimatised to the vagaries of the ocean, and could cope with almost any sea conditions. Like Joe, Bert was carefree and easy going, and had developed a professional dedication to neglect. He could navigate using charts and radio direction-finding. He could use a sextant to navigate by the stars, but since he left the world of deep sea fishing, he didn't see the point of bothering with these skills any more. He still carried charts and spread them out on his chart table, but these days he used a satellite navigation piece of kit to plot his journeys. The radio direction-finding equipment had fallen into disrepair, and he left his sextant at home. More than likely, his charts would not be current, but the world didn't change that much each year, thought Bert. He did have an aldis lamp for signalling purposes which he was quite proficient with, but he could never work out why.

Boat drills and fire drills were not the strong point of the Glasson Voyager, but no-one could tell that from the paperwork. Captain Joe Solomly was of the firm opinion that when a ship was loaded, its sole purpose was to make for its destination, and as long as the ship's engines worked, and the galley brought forth good food, then the crew should take advantage by putting its feet up whilst enduring the passage. Anyone entering the Ship's Bridge would find Joe in his skipper's seat, next to the helmsman, and with feet up, watching the horizon, and the waves breaking over the bow of his ship. Bert had is navigator's cabin just behind the skipper and often Joe would call out,

"Where are we, Bert?"

Bert would reply by giving a lat and long, and that seemed to satisfy his skipper.

Down in the ship's engine room, two rather old Parsons diesel engines provided the vessel with propulsion. These engines had served the Glasson Voyager with great loyalty over the years, and they were treated to a tender servicing every couple of years or so in Barrow shipyard. On a more regular basis, their needs and wants were taken care of by the ship's engineer, Taffy Davies, who always dressed splendidly in oil-stained brown overalls. Newspapers laid out on a chair in the galley marked his regular eating place, which he shared with no-one. Taffy and contamination were bosom partners, but the rest of the crew loved him. He had never been to Wales and consequently, his fellow crew members often wondered about the total appropriateness of calling him Taffy, but it didn't get them down.

The two Parsons engines supplied power to the ship's electrical generator, which in turn kept a number of other things working, such as the ship's lights, radio, and heating system, not to mention the cookers in the galley. Taffy had the responsibility for looking after the generator, but was less proficient with electrical things. The Glasson Voyager did have an electrician aboard normally, but he had been left behind in Nova Scotia, suffering from a severe shock sustained when he was repairing a washing machine for a local lady. It was rumoured that the washing machine was still full of water when he was working on it, but it was only a rumour. 'Sparks', as the electrician was known as, was currently recovering in hospital, but the washing machine was less fortunate after the local fire brigade had had a set to with it.

The journey across the Atlantic from Halifax to Barrow generally took about fifteen days. The Glasson Voyager made about ten knots, and with a distance of some three thousand six hundred nautical miles to cover, it was a slow and laborious time. Joe and his crew had made the journey many times before and had learned to cope with the sheer boredom of such a long and uninteresting voyage over a featureless ocean. They had also learned how to cope with its changing moods. Once they were at sea they had no option but to cope with it, and the Atlantic Ocean had a foul temper that would spend itself on any vessel taking advantage of its surface. The temperamental fluid separating two continents made many a sailor pay the price.

About seven days out of Halifax on a calm sea, the Glasson Voyager was just about at the halfway point of its voyage when, suddenly, the ships lights went out.

"Taffy, what's going on?" barked the skipper down the telephone, but there was no response, the line was dead.

"Bert, go below will you, and find out from Taffy what's going on."

Bert returned ten minutes later. "The ship's generator has just packed in."

"Can Taffy not repair it?"

"He's trying now, but he's not sure he can do it."

"This is where we miss 'Sparks'. What about the standby batteries? Can we not switch to them?"

"They're not charged up."

"That's a bugger. Anyway, we'll have to wait and see how Taffy gets on."

An hour later, the ship's engineer appeared on the bridge.

"Joe, I'm afraid we have lost all electrical power. The generator is well and truly clapped out."

"I see, so we have no lights above or below decks, no heating, no cookers, no radio, no washing machines."

Before he got any further Taffy butted in, "and no refrigerators."

"Ok Taffy. Now you go and organise some storm lamps for below decks, and keep the ship's engines running."

Joe then called out for a couple of deck hands to come up to the bridge.

"Now I want you to organise a rota for the 'crows nest'. We are going to have to man it twenty-four hours and keep an eye out for other shipping. Without our lights, and no radar, we will need to keep a sharp lookout to avoid a possible collision, so away you go, and take care of that."

The second deck hand was sent to get the chef.

"Bert, are we ok on the navigation side of things?"

"Not really Joe, my satnav won't work without power."

"I thought it was battery powered?"

"I operate it off the mains supply. I don't have any batteries."

Before the skipper could respond the chef appeared on the bridge.

"Look 'Cooky', we have lost power, so we have no cooker or refrigerator. What can you do to keep us all fed?"

"Don't worry Joe, I have an old oil burning stove. It's not been used for some time, but I'm sure I can get it going. The fridge is a bit of a problem, but the stuff that's in it is eatable for about forty-eight hours.

After that we'll have to make do with tinned and packet stuff, but we can cope."

"Thanks' Cooky', at least that's some good news."

Joe then turned his attention back to Bert.

"So Bert, we don't know exactly where we are, or exactly where we are headed?"

"It's not so bad. We know where we were when the power failure happened and we know what our heading was when it happened. We still have our compass, so all is not lost."

"That may be so, but you know as well as I do, that several changes in heading are required to get us to where we are going, or we will end up somewhere else. What about the sextant?"

"I left it home Joe."

"Well how about getting a signal off to another ship for help? Can't you use the aldis lamp?"

"I'll do that right away."

What Bert didn't tell his skipper, was that the ship's compass wasn't working properly. The ship's hull was in need of degaussing, and until that was done the compass simply couldn't be relied on.

On the port side of the Glasson Voyager, the Celtic Ranger was heading west, and its bridge lookout spotted the winking light of Bert's aldis lamp. At first it was considered a novelty, but when the same sequence was repeated several times, it was taken more seriously. Someone conversant with Morse code was found, and the message was taken down on paper and translated.

'Ship's electrical power system lost. Navigation systems lost. Need assistance to find our way. This is the Glasson Voyager, bound for Barrow'.

The message continued to be repeated but the Celtic Ranger could not reply, it did not have an aldis lamp.

A message passed on

Flight Lieutenant Matt Johnson was on duty in the Air Rescue Co-ordination Centre at RAF Kinloss when the message came in from the Celtic Ranger.

"You'd better take a look at this boss."

He read the message that had been handed to him. 'From Celtic Ranger, stop. Vessel known as Glasson Voyager with cargo of timber en route Halifax, Nova Scotia to Barrow in Furness, stop. Vessel has lost electrical power, stop. Navigation systems down, stop. Aid requested, stop'. The message then went on to give the lat and long of the vessel in distress.

The Flight Lieutenant crossed over the room to look at the large electronic chart to locate the position of the Glasson Voyager. It looked as if it was mid-Atlantic, which meant about one thousand eight hundred nautical miles away. That was a considerable distance. He called together a few of the Centre's watch team to discuss what should be done.

"If the vessel used an aldis lamp, we can assume it has no working radio."

"Good point."

"Yeah, and if it's saying its navigation systems are down, perhaps we should also assume that it has no radio direction-finding equipment functioning, or satnav."

"And you can add to that, that it doesn't have a sextant, or anyone that can use one."

"They must have a compass though. They should be able to cope with a compass and chart, and navigate by dead reckoning."

Flight Lieutenant Johnson welcomed the thoughts of his colleagues. In this line of business, several heads were always better than one.

"Gentlemen, I think we should assume that they have no means of navigation and our job is to work out how we can assist."

"Has the Navy got a ship in the area that could guide them back?"

A check was made on one of the Rescue Centre's computers, but it drew a blank.

The modern Navy, with around fifty ships, would be hard pressed to fully protect the Manchester Ship Canal, let alone scour the Atlantic, thought the Flight Lieutenant, who was not impressed with what his Government was doing to the Armed Services.

"Can we get an aircraft out to the vessel?" enquired one of the team.

"We don't have any. This is when we miss the Nimrods."

RAF Kinloss had been home to several squadrons of this maritime patrol aircraft and one was always on permanent standby for just this kind of emergency.

"What we need is a guiding star."

That last comment was the catalyst of the solution.

"What about using a cloud machine?"

The phone rang in Wythenshawe Weather Centre and Goldilocks picked it up.

"Wythenshawe Weather Centre speaking, how can I help you?"

The caller was put through to Mr Spite.

A full five minutes passed without Mr Spite speaking a word, but he made notes on a pad at a furious rate.

"You leave that with me, Flight Lieutenant. I will get on to it right away."

This place is getting famous, thought Mr Spite, and the idea of providing 'A Guiding Cloud', well that was a novel idea, in fact, a first in his experience.

"Miss Black, get me Captain Cumulus on the phone will you?"

Mr Spite always spoke to his secretary in a formal way.

It was a bit ironic that Miss Black had red hair, which was the reason for her pet name 'Goldilocks'. Everyone else used 'Goldilocks', but her boss liked to keep her in her place which, he thought, was behind the office desk. Others tended to think it should be on their laps.

"Cirrus, I have a special task that I think you are just the man for, so get yourself and your flight engineer over here asap, and be prepared to get airborne almost immediately."

Ninety minutes later, Cirrus was going over the details of the task with Mr Spite whilst Puffy checked out the Nimbus, and got provisions on board.

By the time the Nimbus was likely to take off, a full twenty-four hours would have passed since the Celtic Ranger had picked up the message from the Glasson Voyager, which meant that its position would have changed. The Celtic Ranger had estimated the speed and heading of the Glasson Voyager, and armed with that information, they were able to estimate its current position. The lat and long of its estimated position could be used initially to provide a heading for the Nimbus, but it would need to be reviewed every few hours or so.

Cirrus calculated that with the current wind speed and direction, he could make a ground speed of 20 knots, and if the Glasson Voyager was making 10 knots then they were converging at 30 knots. The distance to reach them would be about one thousand five hundred and sixty miles, and Cirrus estimated that would take them about fifty-three hours, allowing time to create a cloud.

The next bit was a bit trickier. How can the Nimbus identify itself to the vessel in distress, and how can it act as its 'Guiding Cloud'?

The solution came to Cirrus in an inspirational flash, and Mr Spite was in awe at the idea.

"I'll arrange to get the dye loaded immediately," said Mr Spite.

"How's things aboard the Nimbus?" enquired Cirrus.

"Everything is fine, skipper. Black, Black, and Blackemore's did a good job repairing the damage after the prang in Manxland, and we have seat belts now."

"Did they install an emergency exit?"

"Yup, we have one of them too. It's right over the top of the cockpit."

"What about our supplies, are they all aboard?"

"They are indeed skipper. We are ready to go."

With that they both boarded the Nimbus to begin their new role as a 'Guiding Cloud'.

An Atlantic search

Captain Cumulus was just about to start the motors when Puffy spotted Abigail through the cockpit window. She had a shopping bag in one hand and a small suitcase in the other and was hurriedly walking towards the Nimbus.

"There's Abigail, and she's walking towards us."

"You better let her come aboard Puffy."

"Aye aye, skipper."

The door of the Nimbus was opened and the access ladder lowered, and Abigail came on board and made her way to the flightdeck.

"I didn't expect you, Abigail," remarked Cirrus.

"This job will take you several days, and you know from your experience of convoy work that it is much easier with a third crew member aboard, so here I am, and I have brought my own rations with me."

"That's brilliant, but tell me, how did you find out about what I am doing?"

"I have my friends, so let's leave it at that."

Puffy was delighted that he would be sharing the cockpit with such a cracking looking lady, but wished it was Carol. Never mind, he thought; one nice bum to look at is just the same as any other nice bum!

As usual it was dark as the Nimbus taxied out through Wythenshawe's open hangar doors, and on exiting it, it stopped for a few moments to allow the Captain to perform a quick instrument check. The vertical ascent into the blackness was fast, and the large hangar rapidly diminished in size until it became obliterated in the shadow made by street lights. It was always a relief reaching five thousand feet in the vicinity of Wythenshawe for it was located next door to Manchester Airport, and it would be catastrophic if they were to collide with an aircraft landing or taking off. Cirrus often questioned the wisdom of locating the Weather Centre so close to a busy International Airport. The comings and goings of cloud machines were not however, left to chance. There was a link up between the Weather Centre and the Airport Control Tower and cloud machines were given the all the clear to take off or land by Wythenshawe's own control set up.

Once in the night sky, the Nimbus headed west for the Irish Sea, and the identification beacon was activated to warn aircraft and ground radars as to who it was. Liverpool and Birkenhead were easily observed by their many twinkling lights and the River Mersey which was sandwiched between them. Ahead lay nothing but darkness over the Irish Sea, and once the Nimbus had left Liverpool behind, it was brought to the hover whilst Puffy operated the atomiser, to create the cloud that they would be for this latest operation. A Westmorland White would do for this job, and it had the advantage that it wouldn't merge too comfortably, with all the Cumberland Greys that had been forecasted for the next few days over the Atlantic.

What is the name for this operation thought? Puffy and he asked his Captain.

"ARCC at Kinloss have called it Operation Glasson."

Original, thought Puffy.

With a cloud around them to protect their anonymity, the crew prepared to get on their way to find the vessel in distress. Cirrus looked at his PPI and, from it, got the lat and long of his current position which he punched into his soakometer/navaid. He then punched in the lat and long of the last known position of the Glasson Voyager, and with that the Nimbus got under way. The westerly heading would be into wind for the next few days and the throttles had to be advanced a fair way to achieve a ground speed of twenty knots. With this throttle setting, fuel consumption would have to be monitored carefully.

Abigail took the opportunity to acquaint herself with the operation.

"How long will it take us to reach the ship?" she asked.

"From our present position, fifty-two hours."

"Is the ship underway?"

"Yes, she's making ten knots."

"So she won't be in the position you just punched into the navaid?"

"No, that's right Abigail, but on our present heading we should spot her if she stays on her present heading. I have calculated our intercept position and Puffy has marked it on his chart if you want to take a look."

Puffy began to breathe heavily with the proximity of Abigail's shapely figure. His temperature began to rise as she pressed against him to get a good view of the chart on his table. He was both pleased and disappointed when all physical contact was broken off and he went back to the business of keeping an eye on their position, but he left one keeping an eye on hers.

The crew of the Nimbus settled down to a workable sleeping rota with Abigail taking the first break. It was 2200 hours when the craft had got underway and at 0400 hours the following morning, it was crossing the coast of Ireland, just north of Dublin. For the next eleven hours the Nimbus made passage across Ireland towards Galway. Its flight into the wind and in the opposite direction to nature's creations caused no stir with those below, for the Irish are made of stern stuff, and the unusual was very much a part of their cultural usual anyway. At 1500 hours the Nimbus departed Galway Bay and began the crossing of the Atlantic Ocean. It would be another thirty-seven hours before it would reach the Glasson Voyager.

Skipper Joe Solomly sat in his usual seat on the bridge with his feet up. He stared into the distance, watching a grey monotonous ocean reach out to the horizon until it met a grey sky. Up above was and endless convoy of Cumberland Grey clouds, journeying in the same direction as the Glasson Voyager, but they were not carrying the same load of timber as the Voyager was.

"Joe, do you think our heading is ok?" asked Bert who really didn't know what their heading was.

"Don't you worry your head about that. The helm has not been moved an inch, and if we just keep going we will bump into land eventually."

It was the bump that Bert had on his mind, and he went on, "Do you think that ship we saw got our message?"

"I don't know, but just you watch, before long something will turn up."

As long as the thing that turned up was not a great rocky cliff, Bert didn't mind. He left his skipper to his wave-spotting and went off to find 'Cooky'. He needed a strong brew.

By 2200 hours it was blackness in every direction. A layer of stratus cloud at seven thousand feet blotted out the stars, making it a bit eerie. The only indication of where the Nimbus was had to be worked out from the PPI and Puffy's chart. The PPI displayed nothing below them, but at least the present lat and long could be read off, and plotting that on the chart enabled its current position over the ocean to be established.

Cirrus reckoned they still had some thirty hours to go, and there was a long night ahead of them.

Thirty long hours later, the Nimbus had arrived at the position over the Atlantic where they had estimated the Glasson Voyager would be. It was 0400 hours and still dark, which was not helpful. They PPI indicated a ship below them but Cirrus didn't know if it was the one they were looking for.

"Puffy, have you put the dye in the mixer?"

"It's all set, Captain."

Abigail had joined Cirrus and Puffy on the flightdeck to watch the mysterious master plan put into operation.

"Right Puffy, illuminate the Nimbus."

"Bloody hell, look at that!" cried Jim Crow, the helmsman on board the Glasson Voyager.

"Call Joe, he needs to see this."

"What's the problem, Jim? It better be good, disturbing my sleep is not something I enjoy."

"You ever seen a green cloud, Joe?"

"Have you been on the bottle again?"

"See for yourself," he replied, pointing up into the night sky, and there it was, a beautiful green Westmorland White cloud heading west.

"Puffy, connect your Morse key and signal to the ship. Tell them who we are, and that we have come to guide them home."

The Nimbus blinked in green Morse and the Glasson Voyager stood witness to the miracle.

"In all my time at sea I have never seen anything like it," exclaimed Joe.

"It's a Guiding Cloud," said Bert, who was spellbound.

"Signal back with the aldis lamp. Acknowledge who we are, and thank them for their help."

The green Nimbus stopped winking, and having seen on its TV screen the ship's signal, Cirrus announced that he was going to turn around. Abigail was enthralled to be a witness to this momentous event. The Nimbus was brought about to face east, and Puffy was ordered to pass the message, 'Follow me'.

Down below on the ocean's surface, the Glasson Voyager's full crew had gathered on the bridge which was now full to bursting. The Nimbus turning in the night sky was a sight to see.

"It's signalling again," shouted 'Cooky'.

"What's it say?" said Joe.

"Follow me," and a great roar of applause was heard above the song of the waves and the chorus of the wind, mixed with the accompanying thump, thump, thump of the ship's engines, but it all blended in well with a green, winking cloud.

Going home to Barrow

The Nimbus descended to three thousand feet and remained green to ease recognition on the journey back to Barrow in Furness. Puffy noted their present position and gave the details to his Captain. Cirrus punched the lat and long into the soakometer/navaid. He then punched in the details of the position of their destination and everything was set for the flight to the port where the Glasson Voyager was headed. Puffy noted the time, 0430 hours.

No more than fifteen minutes had passed when Cirrus, looking at the PPI, realised that the Glasson Voyager was trailing behind the Nimbus. He rotated the craft's periscope, which housed the TV camera, to get confirmation of what his PPI was telling him. After a full one hundred and eighty degrees of rotation, the Glasson Voyager appeared on his TV screen, and it was winking at the Nimbus.

"Puffy, take a look at this will you?"

Joe was flabbergasted as he saw the Nimbus steadily leaving his ship behind. At this rate it would completely disappear in a few hours. The Glasson Voyager simply couldn't keep up with it. What's the bloody point in finding us if you're going to leave us again, he thought.

"Bert, get that aldis lamp of yours and signal to that damn green cloud that we can't keep up with it."

Bert started frantically signalling.

"It says we are going too fast for them, and we are leaving them behind."

"Ask them what speed they are doing?"

"They say ten knots skipper, and we are doing thirty. We have a tail wind now."

Cirrus brought the Nimbus to the hover so that the Glasson Voyager could catch up, and then resumed their journey at ten knots. Joe was relieved that a potential problem had been averted and put his feet back up and enjoyed a good cup of 'Cooky's' tea.

Breakfast was cooked on board the Nimbus at 0800 hours and Abigail joined her male companions, having had a couple of hours sleep after the excitement of locating the Glasson Voyager.

"Where are we, Puffy?" she asked.

Puffy indicated their position on his chart.

"And where are we going?"

Again, Puffy indicated their destination on his chart, Barrow in Furness.

Abigail looked at the compass and noted its heading.

"On this heading, we will eventually reach the Irish coast around the Galway area. If you stay on this heading, the ship will run aground. It can't fly over Ireland like the Nimbus."

Overhearing this conversation Cirrus started to feel a bit embarrassed. He had not taken this into account, although he did think that it would have raised its head sooner or later.

"We need to guide the ship around the north of Ireland and into the North Channel. Just make a note of the lat and long of this position here," said Abigail as she pointed to a place on the chart north of Mallin Head on the Donegal coast. Puffy noted the figures and gave them to her, and she turned around, and in a most charming manner suggested to Cirrus that he might consider adjusting his heading for these new co-ordinates. He could hardly refuse such a request, and punched all the relevant figures into his navaid.

"Puffy, how long will it be before we reach Mallin Head?"

"Four days and twenty hours," came back the answer.

"That's an awful long time, but I suppose that's because we are only doing ten knots."

"I'm sure we can amuse ourselves," said Abigail, in a voice that had both men quivering with anticipation.

Down below, the Glasson Voyager faithfully followed the new course of the Nimbus, and Ireland was saved from being bumped by this old and neglected rust bucket from Nova Scotia.

The next forty-eight hours were pretty routine, ploughing along at ten knots at three thousand feet. Eating, sleeping, working, and chatting with the delightful Abigail, and down below it wasn't much different, except that on board the Glasson Voyager the crew had a little more space to pass the time in. But all this was about to change.

"Captain, I have just had a weather warning on the radio. There is a storm catching us up and should be with us in the next hour."

"Ok Puffy, let the ship know, and Abigail, can you make some sandwiches and flasks of tea? When we are in the storm we won't be able to use the galley."

The Nimbus winked its message to the ship below and Abigail busied herself in the galley, and then the crew braced themselves for the storm.

One hour passed before the first effects were felt. The approaching black cumulonimbus clouds were preceded by strong winds which buffeted the Nimbus about, and the crew fastened their seat belts. Cirrus took his machine down to five hundred feet as the base of the approaching clouds from behind was lowering. It was important to allow the Glasson Voyager to keep them in sight. The buffeting seemed to last forever and was joined by heavy rain as the storm clouds eventually arrived overhead. Buffeting and heavy rain is not enjoyable when you are flying in it and when it is joined by thunder and lightning and you are right underneath it all, it is quite frightening, and the crew of the Nimbus were hanging on to each other for support. The electrics were temporarily out of action and both the TV screen and the PPI were blank. All that they had to keep on course was the compass, but that didn't appear to be too useful either at the moment, and they had no idea what was happening on the tempestuous ocean below.

There was nothing new about a storm, as far as Joe was concerned aboard his ship; they were just a nuisance to be periodically put up with. The Glasson Voyager simply continued following the green Nimbus on its present course and 'Cooky' popped onto the bridge occasionally with bacon butties, and a half-filled mug of tea, which was full when he had left the galley.

"I bet they're having it rough up there," commented Joe, who by this time was finding it a little difficult to keep an eye on it, due to the poor visibility.

It was almost three hours before there was any let-up for the Nimbus, but eventually the horrible cumulonimbus storm clouds were ahead of them, and the air was much clearer, but the buffeting continued. This was a very tiring experience, especially for Cirrus, who had to keep on track as well as the right way up by using his control column and rudder pedals. Abigail had been a great asset in this respect, and had taken the controls periodically to give him a rest. As the storm clouds moved ahead it became lighter, and the PPI and TV came back into operation. The buffeting got less, and life aboard was getting more bearable. It was good to see that the Glasson Voyager was still faithfully following them. When the buffeting finally stopped, the Nimbus ascended back to three thousand feet and the crew viewed the storm on the horizon ahead of them, as it progressed on a westerly wind.

"Puffy, just check the state of our cloud will you?"

"Aye aye, skipper."

Fortunately, the green cloud surrounding the Nimbus was as good as new, and Joe and his crew were having no problem following it.

The boredom of routine that everyone experienced for the next two and a half days was relished by the storm-ridden crew, and the sighting of the Irish coast, reinvigorated everyone. Abigail gave her companions a hug and a kiss, which they both enjoyed tremendously. A few calculations determined that the Nimbus and her following ship would reach their current destination north of Mallin Head at 0630 hours the next day, and then they would need a new heading as they entered the North Channel.

At three thousand feet, Mallin Head to starboard and Islay ahead and to port were clearly visible to the Nimbus, but less so from the bridge of the Barrow bound Glasson Voyager. Cirrus punched a new set of lat and longs into his soakometer/navaid for his next waypoint, which would be a position in the North Channel between Larne and the northern end of the Mull of Galloway, a distance of one hundred and twenty nautical miles.

The next twelve hours allowed the crew of both the Nimbus and the Glasson Voyager an opportunity to enjoy a passage through an interesting Channel. On the port side Islay came first followed by the Mull of Kintyre, and the dome-shaped island of Ailsa Craig which is so distinctive, and finally the Mull of Galloway and the entrance to Loch Ryan. On the starboard side was a changing vista of Irish coastline with Rathlin Island thrown in for good measure. It was 1830 hours when both vessels reached the position Cirrus had intended and another set of figures were now used to get them both to a point between the southern end of the Mull of Galloway and the Ards coastline. This was a short distance of twenty nautical miles which would only take a couple of hours, but it was also an area in which a number of other ships would be encountered making their way between Belfast, Larne, Liverpool and Stranraer.

A large number of passengers on a ferry from Stranraer to Larne were most surprised to see a green cloud moving sedately along in the sky, although no-one linked it with the rust bucket of a cargo ship directly under it. Mobile phones sent messages around the country and in some cases even further, and the odd photo was taken as well. News of this phenomenon reached the offices of the Belfast papers and the following morning's editions would carry some interesting headlines.

At 2030 hours, at the southern end of the Mull of Galloway, it was time for yet another set of figures to be used, and the vessels would now head south east to reach the Point-of-Ayr on the Isle-of-Man, some fifty nautical miles away. They should reach this point at 0130 hours the following morning.

News had reached the Isle-of-Man regarding a green cloud heading their way and the pundits had already calculated its probable time of arrival at the Point-of-Ayr if it continued on its present course, and the information was given out on the ten o'clock news. What was making this all the more incredible was the fact that this green cloud should be going in the direction of the prevailing westerly wind, but instead it was moving south east and at an angle to all the other clouds, which made it stand out all the more.

By midnight a large crowd had gathered at the Point-of-Ayr, and more were arriving every minute. Word was spreading that the Martians were on their way. Whilst many folks were happy to go out and greet them, the feeling was not shared by everyone and some locals started to barricade themselves into their own homes. The crew of the Nimbus were oblivious to all that was transpiring in Manxland, whilst Joe and his crew were busy sharing a dram as they followed their guiding green cloud.

"There it is, there it is," shouted the first individual to spot the Nimbus in the distant night sky.

"Wow, it's beautiful!"

Many other compliments were paid by the many spectators that witnessed this great event, and it was a great pity that the crew in the sky were unaware of it at the time.

Soon another set of co-ordinates would be punched into the soakometer/navaid to get both vessels to the mouth of Morecambe Bay, and Cirrus looked at his PPI to check when he should alter course. Abigail kept her eye on the TV screen and she turned the camera to get a view of the Isle-of-Man. There were many twinkling lights around the area of the Point-of-Ayr and she zoomed in.

"You won't believe this Cirrus, there are thousands of people down there watching us."

Cirrus and Puffy turned to look at the screen and were amazed at what they saw.

"Send them a greeting, Puffy."

The Nimbus winked at those below, as Puffy used his Morse key.

A great awe descended on those gathered at the Point-of-Ayr, for no-one had ever seen a winking green cloud in their lives before, and most thought it was definitely Martians signalling to them.

On board the Glasson Voyager, the crew were a little mystified by the message being winked at them by the Nimbus.

'Good morning Manx people', seemed a bit pointless and the skipper, Joe, told his crew to ignore it and carry on drinking. In fact, that's what he thought they must be doing up there on cloud 99.

The two vessels left the Manx people and proceeded for the next six hours on a course that would get them to the mouth of Morecambe

Bay. In the darkness there was little to see of the Cumbria coastline on their port side and the Isle of Man fell astern as they continued their journey. At daybreak, the many windfarms in this area could be clearly seen, and Barrow was also in view. The entrance to Morecambe Bay, which is clearly marked with a buoy, is south of Barrow, and on arrival at 0730 hours they turned east to enter a shipping lane to Heysham. Cirrus didn't need any co-ordinates for this last part of the journey; he could see where to go, and it would only take them another hour. The Glasson Voyager headed into the shipping lane and after a short distance turned to port into another that headed north into Barrow in Furness.

News had already reached Barrow that the Martians were heading their way, and those that had risen were busy preparing for work or school. Joe Solomly was glad to reach his final destination and was most grateful to his Guiding Cloud, the Nimbus, and he got his navigator, Bert, to send a suitable word of thanks to its skipper.

"Captain, we have a message from the Glasson."

"What is it?"

"Ta."

Joe was not one for wasting words.

By 0830 hours the job was done, and although a green cloud over Barrow was unusual, to say the least, it would take a bit more to excite the good folks of this town.

Cirrus gave the order to switch off the mixer and in a short time what was green was now white, and the Nimbus headed to a point over the Irish Sea near Liverpool to wait for dark. Darkness provided an opportunity to rain and lose the cloud that was now so famous, and the naked Nimbus made its way back to Wythenshawe Weather Centre.

Once Abigail, Puffy and Cirrus had disembarked, Mr Spite was waiting for them, newspaper in hand.

"Welcome to Earth", said Mr Spite, handing the paper to Cirrus, and the three of them looked at him in bewilderment.

They looked at the heading on the front page.

Martians Greet Manx People in Green Space Ship!

THE BIG FREEZE-UP

Wick in the Winter

On a winter's morning in Slaidburn, with frost-sprinkled fields glistening in the sunshine of a cold golden sky, the view from the Cumulus home was England at its very best. The river Hodder, winding its way past the village, with green banks and trees was a delight to look out on, and the sheep, as busy as ever, nibbling at the grass, gave a final touch to the scene. Captain Cumulus counted his blessings that he was so fortunate to live in such a tranquil place as this, and the smell of one of Puffy's bacon butties added an additional source of enrichment to his morning.

Cirrus Cumulus was, for the moment, at peace with the world, and instead of contemplating about the problems the world was facing and that of his beloved England, he was thinking about the features of his adopted village. The church, the school, the pub, the post office, the narrow streets and houses, they all contributed to his love affair with the place. Talking about love affairs, he had begun to cherish his relationship with Abigail. He didn't see her very often since both of them were very busy, and things had not developed into full scale embraces, for that was not something he could enter into very easily as he was intensely shy. It was however, clear, that they had mutual feelings that time would foster.

Puffy was most pleased that his Captain was of such a pleasant demeanour this morning and was anxious that it would stay that way. He had already been to the post office and purchased a copy of the Daily Gloom, but was not overly keen to take it into the lounge with the morning coffee. He knew the effect that reading the paper had on him. In spite of all this, Puffy was happy. His relationship with Carol was fully blossomed. Their infrequent meetings were made up by bouts of unbridled passion, verging on lust. Puffy didn't like to waste time and Carol wouldn't let him. All in all, these two middle aged men were not doing too badly on the relationship front, but whether things would develop in the future remained to be seen.

Reading the latest news, Cirrus fell into his usual trap of questioning the wisdom of the Government's decision-making. Cutting back on the country's ability to defend itself, at a time when so many potential enemies were developing such frightening means of waging war, just didn't make sense to him. The European Union, and cutting back on the welfare state, all weighed heavily on his mind, but it always did after picking up the Daily Gloom.

If only the editors would run the country we wouldn't have these problems; at least that's the impression they gave, he thought.

Puffy sussed the way things were developing and stepped in to try and diffuse any passions developing in his Captain.

"What do you think our next job will be, Captain?"

"I haven't the foggiest, Puffy."

"Foggiest, that's good, maybe that could be it, making fog."

Both men had a chuckle at this, but it had been done. Wally Lenticular could say a thing or two on that subject.

Goldilocks was busy on her computer as Cirrus and Puffy entered her office at Wythenshawe Weather Centre. She stopped work and looked up at them.

"Well look who we have here then, the crew of The Guiding Cloud."

"Go on with you Goldilocks," replied Puffy.

"You can take me out and guide me anytime Percival White."

Cirrus was keen to get down to business.

"What's new on the job front?"

"Go and take a look at the job board, there's quite a bit on it at present."

With that the crew of the Nimbus went off to the room that was devoted to displaying jobs on offer.

After a considerable period of time scanning the numerous boards for something that took his fancy, Cirrus studied the card that gave details of a task in Scotland. Loch Hempriggs was located just south of Wick, which was one of the most northerly places on the east coast of Scotland, and it had recently been drained in order that some work could be carried out. Now that the work was completed, it needed filling again. Cirrus had never been to Wick before, and on that basis, he thought it might be interesting and he took the card off its board and went to the office to make further enquiries.

Loch Hempriggs was not a large Loch and not very deep. It could be filled with one downpour from a Cumberland Grey, but the water quality was important. A match had been found with Lake Ullswater and permission had been given to take some of it up to Scotland. That seemed like a simple enough job to Cirrus, and he decided to take it.

Planning was not too involved: a night take off from Wythenshawe, fly to Ullswater and create a Cumberland Grey before daylight, and then a long flight up to Wick. On arrival they would loiter until it was dark, and then move to Loch Hempriggs to rain. Simple enough! Get back to Wythenshawe, collect the cheque, and hey presto, another job done.

Puffy was tasked to get the provisions together whilst Cirrus checked the Nimbus over in the large hangar. Later that evening, they would get airborne and get on with the job, in spite of high winds being forecast for the very northern part of Scotland. The Nimbus was restricted to working in winds that did not exceed 30 knots, and that limitation was listed in the Cloud Machine Operators Rules of Operation Manual, so they would have to keep an eye out.

A freeze-up in Wick

In due course the Nimbus got airborne in its usual fashion, and ascended into its natural habitat rapidly, to avoid any aircraft approaching to land at Manchester Airport.

Why on earth did the Authorities place the Weather Centre where they did? thought Cirrus.

Nevertheless the Nimbus reached a safe altitude of five thousand feet rapidly, and punching the appropriate co-ordinates into his soakometer/navaid, Cirrus got underway in the night sky.

The journey to Lake Ullswater was uneventful and, on arrival, Puffy started the process of atomisation. Before long a Cumberland Grey cloud was created, hiding the Nimbus from the whole of mankind in preparation for its forthcoming mission.

"Captain, do you remember that time when Wally Lenticular was up here, and he was forced to crash land?"

"No I don't remember that, what happened?"

"Well it was like this, he had just created a Westmorland White, just where we are now. He started to get on his way when a flock of geese flew into his cloud."

"What happened then?"

"Some of 'em got sucked into the port side fan duct motors and came out as minced goose. The two motors were damaged, and Wally had to make a crash landing at Glenridding. It took the engineers from Black, Black and Blackemore's a full week to get to them and replace the engines, and in all that time Glenridding was covered in Wally's Westmorland White. You can imagine how that went down with the locals, and what's more, the area was spattered with minced goose, but Wally played ignorance in respect of that.

"Did he get away with it?"

"Not only did he get away with it, he struck a deal with the local butcher, and they were selling goose mince pies for a fortnight after he left. The unfortunate thing though was the smell from the rotting goose they didn't find. It attracted dogs and vermin by the thousands, but Wally had disappeared by then."

Cirrus got the Nimbus underway again, hoping at the same time that he wouldn't suffer the same fate as Wally, but he wouldn't expect to meet geese at five thousand feet anyway, so how come his colleague had, he thought. The thought didn't last long, since there was work to be done, getting the Nimbus on course for Wick.

It had been the plan to make the long journey north in one long hop with Cirrus and his faithful engineer, Puffy, taking it in turns to catch some sleep. However, by the time they had reached the Firth of

Forth they were forced to stop. High winds further north exceeded their limits, and hence it was necessary to wait until it subsided. The Nimbus hovered for two days over the Firth of Forth, but the shipping coming and going down below, together with all the good folk on the mainland, were completely unaware of their presence. The constant flow of cloud on a westerly heading helped to protect their anonymity. It was also a chance to get some sleep, although their proximity to Edinburgh Airport was of some concern. At least their identification beacon was working, which should minimise the chance of any aircraft attempting to fly through them. It was a shame that geese didn't have ID beacon technology, thought Cirrus.

When the conditions had sufficiently changed, the Nimbus proceeded on its journey to Wick but, soon after they left the Firth of Forth, it was buzzed by two Typhoon jet fighters from RAF Leuchars, which was pretty scary. But they must have picked up the ID signal the Nimbus was squawking and they buzzed off, showing their glowing afterburners in a spectacular show of power.

"What do you think of the jet jockeys, Captain?"

"They are the tops aren't they?" answered Cirrus. He had a great deal of respect for the RAF. His father had served in the RAF, and that's where Cirrus had acquired his interest in flying.

"Its getting damned cold," said Puffy and Cirrus agreed. He turned up the heating system on the craft but as time went on it started getting colder again. Each time it got colder Cirrus turned up the heating, and this action was repeated several times.

"Blimey Captain, look at the temperature, its well below freezing."

"We are over the Cairngorms Puffy, so we may pass through this cold air."

The Cairngorms were left behind, and the Nimbus crossed the coastline to fly over the Moray Firth and up the east coast of Scotland to reach Wick. The temperature did not rise; it stayed at an incredible -30° Centigrade. The heater on board the Nimbus was working flat out, but both crew members were still cold, and they donned what coats and sweaters they had brought with them. Clad with woolly hats and gloves, they flew on to Wick with the odd shiver here and there.

Puffy's dentures had a tendency to rattle now and again, and it was not altogether a pleasant experience.

Cirrus spotted Loch Hempriggs, their destination, to the south of Wick, but since it was still light, he decided to carry on to a point north of the town, where he would hover until it was dark, and then return to rain. Why he had chosen this particular spot to hover he had forgotten, but it was of some significance to him, and he continued onwards.

A heavy cloud

As the Nimbus approached Wick, Cirrus noticed that it had lost some height and he advanced the throttles to take it back up again. The Nimbus lost more height, and Cirrus advanced the throttles even further, and this process continued until a point was reached when the throttles were wide open. Even with the fan duct motors working flat out, the Nimbus continued to lose height. The only solution left to the Captain was to pull back on the control column; this had the effect of rotating the fan duct motors to provide vertical thrust that was normally used when in the hover. This didn't work either, and the Nimbus was uncontrollably descending to mother earth, slowly.

Cirrus peered at his Plan Position Indicator and the TV screen. During his attempts to alter the descent of the Nimbus, he had overshot Wick, and was now overhead a place on the coast called Noss Head and he could clearly see a lighthouse down below.

"Brace yourself Puffy, we are about to force land."

The landing was no great affair, but it was accompanied by a loud crunching noise which went on for some time. Cirrus shut down the motors and turned to Puffy.

"Well we have arrived, but I'm not sure in what state."

The lighthouse keeper had been watching a falling lump of ice for some time, and was amazed that it wasn't falling faster. The size of it was also frightening. It looked like a frozen planet was about to hit the surface of the Earth, and he shouted to his colleague, Angus, to take shelter in the lighthouse which had extremely thick walls. Ironically, the lighthouse keeper was called Mr McCloud.

"What ere do ya ken it is Mr McCloud?" asked Angus.

"Och, it's a large lump of ice lookin' for a large whisky glass no doot."

Much of the ice cloud that had hit the surface had fractured and broken away, but much was left to keep the Nimbus hidden and suspended a good hundred feet off the ground. The lighthouse and its grounds and outbuildings had not escaped damage. Two of the more fragile outbuildings had collapsed, and a couple of the lighthouse windows were shattered.

Mr McCloud and Angus stepped outside the lighthouse entry door to find that they were stepping underneath a ginormous block of ice that was sitting upon the tops of the remaining out buildings, leaving a gap below, large enough for them to walk under. They went back inside to check the lighthouse and found that the lump of ice had been pierced by its top in such a way that it was stuck in the lump like a thorn in a human finger. They both stepped outside again and walked for some time before reaching the edge of the lump and found that they had walked as far as Noss Farm, where they were greeted by Jock McGregor, who lived there.

"Whatcha maak of it then?" asked Jock.

The three men looked up at this massive lump of ice that must have covered several acres of land, including Noss Head. They couldn't make out the shape of a Westmorland White lump of ice cloud, but that's what they had got.

"It's a good job it nae landed on the groond. It wood a killed many a sheep."

"Ach ya naer spoke a truer word, Jock," and three Scottish Highlanders stood contemplating what they feasted their eyes upon.

Cirrus and Puffy witnessed what was going on outside on their TV screen, but still hadn't worked out either what had happened to them, or what they had landed on.

"Puffy, go and open the access door will you, and take a look outside."

"It won't open skipper."

"Let's try the new emergency exit then."

It wouldn't budge, and it appeared that they were cocooned in the Nimbus. That was not too bad a thing since they had provisions, but they would only last for a maximum of a week. But what was keeping the exits closed, they both wondered. The TV camera simply looked straight through the ice and did not make them aware of its presence.

"Puffy, we better break radio silence and contact Wythenshawe regarding our predicament."

By the time Puffy communicated with the Weather Centre Superintendant, Mr Spite, word had already reached him, and he in turn had set things in motion to rescue the crew of the Nimbus. Word soon got round the Weather Centre, and it was a source of amusement that the usual rescuers needed rescuing themselves.

The fire service in Wick dispatched its only tender and part time crew, and as they arrived at Noss Head, they all gazed at the amazing sight of the world's largest lump of ice. They knew that somewhere in the middle of it was the Nimbus, but where? They had portable radios and had been supplied with a frequency to use, to contact the crew.

Cirrus had observed the arrival of the fire tender on TV, but was still surprised when a very Scottish sounding voice blurted out on Puffy's radio set.

The conversation that ensued put the Captain and Puffy in the picture as to what their cloud had been turned into by the current cold weather, and now everything made sense, but the real question now was, "What should be done?"

What to do about ice?

The general consensus was that the two Sassenachs imprisoned in the lump of ice, could not be left there. They would need food and drink, and there was also the possibility that they could freeze to death if the heating system on the Nimbus should fail.

The Fire Chief, Stuart McSquirt, had a brainwave, which was not unusual for him. His crew put it down to the vast quantities of Scottish Mackerel he consumed each week.

"Bring me my ultrasonic searcher," shouted the Chief, and in double time one of his kilt-clad firemen returned with it.

"Donald where's ya troosers?" enquired the Chief.

"A didna haff the time to put them on. A came straight fer werk."

"An what kind of werk wood that be Donald?"

"Am a tourist attraction."

"Well Donald, noo you're a fireman, so get yer troosers on."

Chief McSquirt walked up to the ice lump and, reaching the side of it, he lifted the gun-like ultrasonic searcher to shoulder level, and aimed it towards the lump. He switched the device on, and then proceeded to move its aim in many directions. This process continued for several minutes, until a clicking noise could be heard.

"Am on tae something here," said the Chief.

The aim was refined a little until a spot was found that rendered the loudest clicking sound, rather like the noise that you get from a Geiger counter.

"Thar wae have it, the Nimbus is foond."

A cheer went up from the small gathering, but this was only the start of the job. The Chief was able to take a number of readings from the ultrasonic searcher that established exactly where in the lump the Nimbus was, and he then drew some sketches. He gathered his firefighters around him to show them what must be done. They would have to tunnel through the ice to reach the access door of the Nimbus. The ice tunnel would have to climb one hundred and fifty feet, and proceed over one hundred feet horizontally. There would be a considerable slope to the tunnel and to avoid slipping inside it, they would need to cut steps into the floor of it. A double precaution would be taken by providing crampons for those cutting the tunnel.

A message was sent back to the fire station in Wick to bring up cutting equipment, and crampons, and in due course they arrived with several volunteers to help. Word gets around pretty quick around these parts.

Cirrus and Puffy were informed about how they were to be released from their ice prison, and although relieved, they felt a little indifferent, thinking that it would be just as easy to wait for nature to bring its own solution. For the moment it was just a question of waiting, and passing the time as best they could.

Placing a farm cart to stand on under the huge lump of ice, the rescuers worked vigorously to cut the staircase to the Nimbus, and whilst the cutters worked particularly well, it was still a time-consuming job, and made longer when it got dark and everyone went home until the following day.

The ice tunnel was large enough to allow one person at a time to ascend or descend using the carefully cut steps, and its ceiling was high enough to allow an individual to stand up straight without having to bend over. The enormity of the task was borne out by the fact that it took a full five days to reach the Nimbus, and by a stroke of luck the tunnel ended at the exact position of the entry door.

A cheer rang out when the Nimbus was reached and Stuart McSquirt took it upon himself to be the first person to greet the crew. He carefully climbed the ice steps and as he did so he had the distinct feeling that he was ascending to the Pearly Gates of Heaven. It was a strange and eerie feeling ascending steps in a tunnel made of crystal- clear ice, and he got no relief when he reached the door of the craft. Who would he be greeted by when the door opened? He heard singing from within and suddenly he had a vision, – It's the Archangel Gabriel, – and he wished he had been to church more regularly.

Stuart couldn't find the button to press that would open the door and, finding no door knocker, he resorted to knocking on it. The door started to open and as it did so the light from within was dazzling, and in a moment of panic he lost his balance and fell. The extensive padding of his fireman's uniform saved him from injury, but landing on his back, he started to descend the tunnel at a much faster rate than he had climbed it, and he accelerated as he went.

The team of helpers gathered around the farm cart under the entrance to the escape tunnel had a sudden surprise as Stuart McSquirt shot out, feet first, coming to an upright abrupt stop on the cart. He was somewhat ashen-faced, but kept his composure, and did not reveal what he had just experienced, and his recovery was aided by a wee dram, care of the lighthouse keeper Mr McCloud.

When the door of the Nimbus opened and no-one was there, Puffy turned to his Captain and, shrugging his shoulders, he commented that he was sure he had heard someone knocking.

"Look at this though, there's an ice tunnel with steps."

"Well let's take a walk, but we better be careful."

The crew of the Nimbus made their way down the steps very carefully, and emerged onto the farm cart that was waiting for them under the solid cloud of ice. An anxious audience was waiting for them and one individual in particular was glad that they were not the Biblical figures he had been half expecting. After something of a pregnant pause the throng cheered, and shook the hands of the rescued crew, and threw in a few bear hugs for good measure before the measures changed to a traditional Scottish drink.

Cirrus and Puffy could now see what they had ended up bringing to Scotland, and it was quite impressive, but so was the wee dram they had been given, and as the drams came and went, the mystical scene began to lose its clarity. As they sat on the farm cart a deep sleep began to embrace the two of them, and several of those gathered for that matter, and Cirrus, with a smile on his face, couldn't help thinking what a Wick of a place this was. In truth he was just reaching his Wick's end.

The long freeze

There was no let up in the big freeze for seven days, and the newspapers and other media had a field day reporting on the downed cloud of ice. The Daily Clansman had a particularly eye-catching headline:

Aircrew Encapsulated in Ice Cloud Saved by Wick Fire-fighters

There was a sudden upsurge in tourism as people flocked to see Wick's latest attraction, but the interest it brought generated its own problems. Cirrus was concerned that looters could get aboard the Nimbus and, as a precaution, the farm cart that acted as a step up to the ice tunnel was removed, and a police constable stood on duty there, twenty-four hours a day. That was a particularly cold job, and every hour there had to be a change of officer, and that made a heavy demand on the police service that consequently had to draft in personnel from around the Highlands.

Graffiti began to appear on the ice cloud and whilst some of it was humorous, some of it was downright vulgar, and detracted from the overall beauty of this rare Scottish visitor. Cirrus particularly liked the one that said, 'Find me a glass to take this one', and 'Come freeze with me' also took his fancy.

The ice tunnel generated a lot of interest, especially since the media was giving the impression that there was an aircraft in the middle of the great ice lump, but no-one gained access. The entrance did, however, become a popular place to have a photograph taken and the Daily Clansmen made a point of photographing the Fire Chief, and his crew, the lighthouse keeper, and his colleague Angus, and Jock McGregor of Noss Farm, who all appeared in subsequent copies of the paper, telling the story of their part in the rescue.

Cirrus and Puffy were under strict instructions to avoid publicity, and kept well away from Noss Head until there was a chance to get away from the location.

Wick was heaving with people and what available accommodation there was, was fully taken up by the many visitors that had arrived. Cirrus and Puffy were taken in by Fire Chief Stuart and his wife Jeannie. The crew of the Nimbus were made to feel most comfortable in the McSquirt's home which was near the harbour, and Jeannie was a wonderfully homely person, and a splendid cook. Scottish Mackerel appeared on the menu quite regularly. Stuart had two teenage offspring who were both charming and intelligent, and they both took a great deal of interest in the work that the Nimbus performed. Rob and his sister Moira were given access to more information about the cloud machine fraternity than usual, but this was because Cirrus was drawn to the pair of them.

Abigail and Carol got in touch with the men that were currently flavour of the month, but couldn't get to visit them because of the jobs they were doing, but they were both greatly relieved to hear that they were ok. The newspaper reports they had both seen had made little reference to the Nimbus, or its crew. Abigail and Carol had been left to work out for themselves that the encapsulated aircrew that had been rescued were in fact Cirrus and Puffy, and Mr Spite at the Weather Centre had confirmed it.

The meltdown begins

"Captain Cumulus yae better gae back to the Nimbus; the meltdoon has started."

Cirrus looked at the Fire Chief who had hurriedly made his way home to break the news.

"If yae dunnoo make yae way back noo, yae ice clood will be a slush clood."

There was an element of urgency in his voice, which was not wasted on the Captain.

"Puffy, we better get back now, grab the bag of clothes we brought."

"Aye aye, skipper."

The three men headed back to Noss Head at great speed, and on their arrival, they could see the meltdown in action. Under the ice cloud it was just like standing under a shower. The farm cart had been wheeled under the tunnel entrance, and both Cirrus and Puffy hurriedly jumped onto it, and then stepped into the tunnel, one behind the other. Although there was a little slush on the top of each step, they still held their weight, and they made their way up to the Nimbus.

Once aboard the Nimbus, Puffy closed the entrance door, and both he and Cirrus headed for the cockpit.

"If this meltdown carries on, the Nimbus will crash down to earth and damage the motors. Try switching on the atomiser Puffy and we will try and turn the ice back again to cloud."

"Right away, Captain, but that won't stop the Nimbus from crashing down; the cloud won't support our weight."

"No, you're right Puffy. I'll start the motors. They were left frozen in the hover position, so that should help."

Cirrus started the four fan duct motors without any trouble, and Puffy switched on the atomiser.

To those present outside, to their astonishment, the shower under the ice cloud gradually ran dry, and around the outside of the lump a mist started to appear until the mass of ice was completely hidden from view. Nothing else appeared to happen for several hours and then, as the weight of the ice reduced, the power of the motors provided a slow lift off.

"It's moving," cried one of the spectators, and although at first it was an imperceptibly small movement, it got bigger, and more noticeable.

"It's awa, its awa!"

The new cloud steadily, but slowly, climbed higher into the sky, and after a couple more hours, had reached one thousand feet.

"What do we do next?" asked Puffy.

"Well we wait for dark, and then make our way back to Loch Hempriggs to rain."

"Can we do that Captain?"

"Not yet. We have to get rid of some more ice and slush first. At the moment our motors are still jammed in the hover position. I won't climb above a thousand feet; it's warmer at this height."

Puffy made a cup of coffee, and the crew sat and waited for dark, whilst at the same time, the ice continued to melt and was turned into cloud as it was evaporated by the atomiser.

Mr McCloud and his colleague, Angus, were only too happy for the lighthouse to reappear as the new cloud lifted off and into the sky, leaving a wet patch behind it. Their feelings were replicated in Jock McGregor who was cheered by the thought that he could get back to working his farm. Literally dozens of sheep shared Jock's relief, and a chorus of baas sounded across Noss Head, and a number of musically-minded Gulls joined in.

As darkness started to fall, and there being no further evidence of anything else potentially happening, the throng of spectators dispersed, and things appeared to be getting back to normal. Once the newly created cloud had been immersed in the night sky, the police and fire service personnel left the scene, leaving behind a story that would do the rounds in the bars of Wick for many years to come.

By about midnight, Cirrus found that he could push the control column of the Nimbus forward, which rotated the fan duct motors to the horizontal position that provided forward propulsion. Not long after the Nimbus had got going again, the crew could see the winking lights of Wick on the TV screen and waved goodbye as they made the short journey to Loch Hempriggs.

It didn't take long to fill the Loch with rainwater, leaving just a vestige of cloud to hide the Nimbus. The job was finally done, even though it was a few weeks or so overdue, but then no-one had suspected such a harsh freeze-up.

A Question Of Passion

Two undergraduates

John Davies was the eldest child of Brian and Joan Davies of Oswaldtwistle. Both of his parents were hard working and had spent their lifetime establishing a family home, and giving their three children the best start in life that they could. Both hoped that each of their children would go on to be more successful in life than they had been, and had encouraged them to make the best of their education. John was an undergraduate at the University of Central Lancashire in Preston, studying medicine. Brian and Joan were immensely proud of him getting into University.

John's younger brother, George, was in the final years of High School, and seemed to be coping well. George admired his brother and had his mind set on following him into University. Sadie was a couple of years younger than George, but was also doing ok at school. Mum and Dad had nothing to worry about in relation to their children. They had every reason to be proud of them and believed that their development had been greatly enhanced by their skilful guidance, which they found difficult to desist from. This could be a source of irritation to their children, particularly John, the eldest.

Sarah Whittle came from Burnley. She was tall and attractive, and the regular exercise she took kept her looking fit and slim. Sarah came from a similar background to John, but had no brothers or sisters. Sarah was also studying at the University of Central Lancashire, but was following the path of her Uncle Steve by doing law. Her parents had high hopes for her and hoped she would eventually have a career as a solicitor.

The changing face of Lancashire had left many good folk feeling like a square peg in a round hole. The industries which had sustained so many for so long had declined to such an extent, that they were either extinct or almost extinct. Gone were the coal mines and gone were the mills, or at least most had gone. In the new age, production was almost a dirty word, and the new world of employment left many, who had found the transition baffling, floundering. Information Technology is a fine thing but many of an older generation were struggling to comprehend it. These were folk who wished they could get a television set with an on/off switch, volume control, and channel selector. A television with a remote control and a couple of dozen function controls was simply too much. Remote controls and computers were a costly trap for the unwary.

John's and Sarah's parents were trapped between an old and a new generation, and the intellectual journey taxed them considerably. They found it amazing that their children could cope with the new technologies far better than they could, and at times felt foolish when they had to ask them to show them how to do what they thought should be simple. They had developed a mistrust in all things new, which they felt were designed to make them dependent on others, especially when that dependence has to be paid for. Judging by the way John and Sarah were coping at university, there was nothing for their parents to be concerned about. Both seemed to be at ease in this new, highly technological, age.

John and Sarah had met in Preston in a pub frequented by many of the students from the university. The venue had become a regular Wednesday evening haunt, and over a period of time, the two warmed to each other. During the week they tended to concentrate on their studies, leaving Wednesday evening for socialising. They both lived in cheap student digs, but went home at the weekends. After their first academic year, they began to meet at the weekends in either Burnley or Oswaldtwistle, and their relationship started to blossom.

John's parents had been suspicious for some time that he had been seeing a girl, but were still shocked when he brought Sarah home. They fell for her immediately and her looks and personality helped to foster a loveable bond. John's brother and sister had no trouble relating to Sarah, and she was one of the Davies family in no time at all.

Sarah's parents took to John in much the same way as his had taken to Sarah, and although they had not yet met, there was already a link between the Davies and the Whittle families.

Whilst both sets of parents were happy about the choice of partners their offspring had made, they couldn't help thinking that it would not be wise to rush into anything. It was important to get a career mapped out first. Too much had been invested in their futures to throw it away at this stage. Being typical parents, they found it difficult to confer on their son and daughter that level of maturity that would allow them to make the decisions that they thought were the appropriate ones.

Both sets of parents refrained from telling John and Sarah what they thought they should do or not do, which is just as well, since it would probably have been resented. On the other hand, acting as a bystander and leaving everything to luck was a bit frustrating, and with a long summer break looming, John's dad thought it would be prudent to meet Sarah's parents and chew things over.

Meeting for the first time at Sarah's home in Burnley, John's and Sarah's parents set about becoming acquainted, and conversation flowed easily between them. Sharing a similar heritage was a distinct advantage and they did not have to resort to talking about the weather or football. In due course they got round to talking about the romantic link-up that was being established between the Davies and the Whittle family. Each complimented the other on the virtues of each other's offspring.

Both families had the same feelings when it came to expressing the hope that passion might be kept in check until careers had been established, and both worried about what a long summer break might bring. The feeling was mutual about minimising opportunities for the break to develop into a romantic interlude.

An agreement was reached that the only practical thing to do, without making it obvious that a plan had been connived between them, was to try and find a summer job for the two undergraduates, and discussion moved on to what form this might take.

Frank Whittle mentioned that he knew a man called Wally Lenticular who owned a cloud machine, and if approached he might be able to offer something for the summer. Other alternatives were discussed but nothing with the same ring to it as working with a cloud machine. That could look good on a CV. The two families parted on good form, with Frank pledging to get in touch with Wally.

Work experience

Frank and Wally met to discuss the possibilities of his daughter, or her boyfriend, getting a job over the summer holidays.

"What is Sarah studying?" asked Wally.

"She's studying law."

"And what about John?"

"He's studying medicine."

"I can't provide them with experience in either field. If one or the other came aboard the Discovery, they would be limited to looking after the galley. I could get my flight engineer, Bert, to show them what he does, but off the top of my head, I don't know what else I could offer," said Wally.

"That would be fine, Wally. The most important thing is that they have less of an opportunity to study each other's anatomy, and if one of them is with you, then that would take care of that."

"You're being a bit mean aren't you?" enquired Wally.

"When they have got their studies out of the way, they can be as passionate as they like, but for now we need to put a damper on it."

"Well if that's what you want I'll take one of them, but what about a bit of a compromise. If I take one of them I could ask my colleague Cirrus if he will take the other. At least that might make them feel that they are both sharing in something."

"Wally, you're a real pal."

"There is one thing though," Wally went on. "I can't guarantee that we will have work."

"Wally, let's cross that bridge when we come to it."

Agreement was then reached that Wally and Cirrus would make the approach to the two undergraduates for help in the summer, so that any involvement on the part of their parents would not be made known.

"Captain, there's a call for you from Wally."

"Thanks', Puffy, I'll take it here," replied Cirrus.

The call had brought some relief to Puffy as his Captain had been reading the morning's Daily Gloom and had been building up a head of steam, which generally spelt trouble.

"Hello Wally, Cirrus here, what can I do for you?"

Wally gave the full story of his meeting with his pal, Frank, before posing a question.

"So Cirrus, can you help by taking one of them for the summer holidays?"

Cirrus paused whilst he thought about it, but remembering how Wally had stepped into the breach at Windermere to help him on a previous occasion, he decided he would agree.

"Ok Wally I'm in, but I take the girl."

"As you wish Cirrus, but that brings me to the final point."

Wally described how he had been asked to invite the pair individually to help with the cloud machines, since it was most important that they know nothing of their parents' involvement. Wally went on to tell Cirrus that it was their parents' desire to try and keep them apart over the summer holidays so that they did not become over amorous.

"That's a bit mean," commented Cirrus.

"I agree, but the two families do have the best interests of their offspring at heart," replied Wally.

"In that case, I suggest we write to them on Wythenshawe Weather Centre letter headings and invite them to a meeting, and meanwhile, I will get in touch with Mr Spite and see if he can let us have some suitable work."

"That's marvellous, Cirrus, and when you have drafted a letter for Frank's daughter, let me have a copy, and I will alter it for Mr Davies's son."

"Spite here."

"Hello, Mr Spite, this is Cirrus Cumulus."

"Morning Cumulus, what can I do for you?"

Cirrus went on to tell Mr Spite what Wally and himself had got themselves involved in. and asked if some suitable work could be aimed in their direction.

"Leave it with me, Cumulus, and I will see what I can do. By the way, it's a bit harsh on these young folk, don't you think?"

Cirrus was surprised Mr Spite should speak in that way. There was a human side to him after all, he thought, but it was not the first time that he had been surprised by Wythenshawe's Superintendant.

A week later, a letter dropped through the letter box of Sarah's home, and when she got back from university at the weekend it was waiting for her on her bed. She opened the letter and was most surprised at its contents.

To Miss S. Whittle	**From Captain C. Cumulus C.D.M.**
24, Chaucer Grove,	**Wythenshawe Weather Centre**
Burnley	**Wythenshawe**
BL10 000	**M95 0LR**
	June 8ᵗʰ

Re: Forthcoming Summer Holidays

Dear Miss Whittle,

In a few weeks time you will begin your summer break from the University of Central Lancashire where you are currently studying law. I am writing to you to appeal for your help during this break period.

At Wythenshawe Weather Centre, requests are received from around the world for our cloud machines to go out and perform a myriad of functions, although making rain and other things is our business.

My machine is called the Nimbus, and I am its Captain. I have a flight engineer called Percival White, and between the two of us, we perform many tasks that come our way, but a third crew member helps considerably when we can find one.

I am currently searching for an additional crew member over the summer break period and wonder if you would kindly consider helping me. The work is not demanding, and would be well within the capability

of someone like you. Training would be provided, and a suitable salary paid. Furthermore, the experience of flying with us may widen your horizons, and prove valuable in the future. It may also be advantageous to have this experience on your CV.

An interview will be held at Wythenshawe Weather Centre on the date shown on the reverse of this letter, and your confirmation of attendance is requested, using the telephone number shown overleaf.

I look forward with anticipation of your acceptance of this invitation to serve aboard the Nimbus.

Yours sincerely,
Capt. Cirrus Cumulus C.D.M.

Sarah couldn't believe what she had just read, but was thrilled by its contents. She rushed downstairs to tell her parents, who were equally thrilled, but not necessarily for the same reasons.

"I must give John a ring and tell him."

Her parents looked at each other, hoping that there would not be a hitch about to emerge in the plan.

"John, its Sarah here and I have some news for you."

"And I have some news for you," replied John, "but you first."

"I have been invited to an interview to join the crew of a cloud machine for the summer holidays."

"So have I," replied John, who went on, "Mine's called the Discovery, what's yours?"

"Mine is the Nimbus, and the Captain is Cirrus Cumulus, who's yours?"

"The Captain of the Discovery is Wally Lenticular."

"John, do you think this is a wind up, I've never heard of such a thing as a cloud machine?"

"Neither have I Sarah, but we have nothing to lose by going along for an interview. When all is said and done, we might get a paid job out of it. By the way, where is your interview?"

"At Wythenshawe Weather Centre."

"Same as me then."

"If we should get this summer job, John, we wouldn't get much chance to see each other."

"That's true, but I think it would be daft not to seize this opportunity. It should be exciting, we will be paid and it should look good on our CVs."

"I think you're right. Let's go for it and have some fun."

Calendar work

Sarah and John arrived at the Weather Centre and knocked on the office door.

"Come in."

Goldilocks welcomed the two interviewees and told them where their interviews were to be held. She then told them that they would both be interviewed together, which took them by surprise.

"Just make your way along the corridor to the interview room, and sit down outside it until you are both called."

They did what they were told, and once seated they shared their impressions.

"This place certainly looks authentic," said John.

"I agree. I can't see this being a send up," remarked Sarah.

After a time that seemed like an eternity, the door of the interview room opened, and they were invited in. On one side of a large table sat four men, and on the other side were two chairs which they were invited to sit on.

"I'm Captain Cumulus, the skipper of the Nimbus. Allow me to begin by introducing my colleagues, first my flight engineer, Percival White, and next, the skipper of the Discovery, Mr Lenticular, and his flight engineer, Bert Drummond."

John and Sarah then told everyone who they were.

"Can I assume that both of you are available, and willing, to become crew members of the Nimbus and the Discovery for the months of July and August?"

John looked at Sarah, and then replied on behalf of the two of them.

"I think we would like to know what you are doing, and how much you will pay us first."

"Let me answer your first point," said Cirrus.

"We have a modelling job over the summer. Let me explain. The Welsh Tourist Board is preparing a Calendar for next year, and they want to feature a number of resorts in the best possible light. The job of the Nimbus and the Discovery is to present a backdrop of two Westmorland White clouds against a blue sky, to give a photographer the best chance of catching each place in some sort of glory."

"That sounds different," said Sarah.

"Everything we do is different," commented Wally.

"As for pay, well we haven't worked a salary out yet, but I can assure you that you will both be pleased with what you receive."

"What exactly will John and I be expected to do?"

Wally responded to this question.

"You, Sarah, would be a member of the Nimbus crew, and John would be part of my crew on board the Discovery. You would both have the same duties. We are expecting to be away from Monday to Friday each week, and on each Monday, you would be expected to get the necessary provisions and bring them on board. You would be expected to run the galley, although our flight engineers would share that duty with you. Your other duty would be to stand in for our flight engineers when required, but you will receive training for that. Don't worry too much about the latter role. What it amounts to is just keeping a watch on things when we are getting some rest."

"Where will we live," asked John?

This time Cirrus answered.

"You will live on board our cloud machines, and that means you will eat and sleep aboard. In fact, except for weekends when you should get home, you will spend all of your time aboard the Nimbus and the Discovery. Each Monday, you need to bring enough clothing to keep you going for five days, and a sleeping bag."

John and Sarah were given an opportunity to discuss things before they made any commitment, but it was a foregone conclusion, and they both jumped at the opportunity.

"We are very pleased that you have both agreed to help us, and so all that remains is to show you the machines you will be flying in. When you have had a look around, just report back here at 10-00 hours on the first Monday in July, bringing with you enough gear for five days."

"Ok Sarah, you are now part of the Nimbus crew, and I'm known as Puffy. Come with me, and I will show you your cloud machine."

Puffy and Sarah made their way to Wythenshawe's huge hangar, as did Bert and John.

The vast hanger was a jaw dropper for a start, but when the Nimbus and the Discovery were observed, the new cloud aviators were overawed.

Reaching the Nimbus, Puffy pressed a button on the side of the fuselage and the entrance door automatically opened, followed by the deployment of the access ladder. Ascending the ladder, the dim internal lighting added to the mystique, and the short walk to the cockpit raised Sarah's level of expectancy. The pilot's position and his flightdeck looked very sophisticated, and the view out from the cockpit window was extremely good, although the panorama of the inside of the large hangar was nothing to write home about. Puffy showed her his work station which was also impressive, and then he introduced her to the galley, which she thought was particularly well-equipped.

"Do you cook all your meals in here?" enquired Sarah.

"No, not really. Most of the stuff we take with us is prepared for us here in the Centre, and we either heat it up, or we microwave it. It's a bit basic, but it is adequate."

The drop-down double bunk was dropped down to show Sarah the sleeping arrangements.

"You will have to share one of the bunks, but don't worry; you won't have to sleep with the Captain, or me. The Captain will probably give you a watch duty during the night when we sleep, and then you can choose whichever bunk you want, and the snores will be your own. You can see why you need to bring your own sleeping bag!

The tour of the Nimbus was completed by Puffy taking Sarah back down the corridor, to show her the toilet and washing facilities.

Before leaving the Nimbus, Puffy thought it would be prudent to point out the safety features, and in due course she was acquainted with the fire extinguishers, first aid kits, emergency exits, and the stowage points for the parachutes, life jackets, and oxygen masks. This was an awful amount to take in, in one short visit, but Puffy was most helpful and provided some printed information about the Nimbus, together with some layout diagrams of the machine, to help her get familiar with the whereabouts of everything.

Reunited with John, Sarah expressed her excitement at what the summer had in store for each of them, and John felt exactly the same.

Driving back to Slaidburn, Cirrus turned to Puffy, and asked him what he thought about Sarah coming on board for the summer.

"I think it will be good. She's enthusiastic enough and bright, and it's always nice to have another face on board. She's got a nice backside as well!"

"I think we should keep it to ourselves, Puffy. No point in alarming Abigail or Carol."

Puffy was not sure that he agreed with his Captain, but refrained from saying anything.

In Oswaldtwistle and Burnley, the parents of John and Sarah were well pleased by the reaction of their offspring to the interview at Wythenshawe. In fact, they had never stopped talking about it since they got back, and there would be more to come.

July arrives

The first Monday in July arrived, and John and Sarah travelled to Wythenshawe to join the crews of the Nimbus and the Discovery. Puffy and Bert were waiting to greet them, and took them into the large hangar.

"Right, Sarah, let me show you where to stow your clothes, then we can get started."

Now that the big day had finally arrived and it was all about to happen she found that she was experiencing an adrenalin rush, and she cherished it. It made her feel like a child again.

"Now here is a list of the provisions we need, so you go into the Weather Centre, to the provisions store, and get them. Here is our card to pay for them. Whilst you are doing that, I will check out the Nimbus."

Most of the day was spent getting the provisions, and this was the last opportunity for Sarah and John to see each other for a few days, but that did not seem too much of a burden to bear, with all that was taking place.

By 1700 hours, Sarah found herself in the galley of the Nimbus, making tea. Captain Cumulus had come aboard by this time, and soon the three of them were eating together, although it was a bit of a make-do affair, there being no dining table that they could sit around. It was at this point that Cirrus could outline what was about to happen.

"At 2300 hours, we will get airborne, along with the Discovery, and head out over the Irish Sea. When we get there, we will make a cloud, and at about 0100 hours, we will fly to Barry Island on the south coast of Wales. We should arrive at about 0700 hours, and then, we wait for the photographer to contact us."

"That was enough information to be going on with," thought Sarah, and she finished off in the galley before settling down to read one of the books she had brought with her.

At about 2230 hours, things started to happen. The Captain sat in his pilot's seat, whilst Puffy took up his station facing his cloud and rain controls and other stuff. Sarah was invited to stand in the observer's position to the right of the Captain, and she had a splendid view through the cockpit window, although there wasn't much to see in Wythenshawe's large hangar. She couldn't even see the Discovery, which was on their starboard side, but if she had been able to, she would have seen John standing in the same position.

Cirrus started the four fan duct motors, and as he did so, the internal lighting dimmed. The lights in the hangar slowly dimmed, and finally, as the hangar doors started to open, they went out. The outside darkness made the internal cockpit instruments look as if they were glowing, and Sarah suffered another adrenalin rush as the Nimbus started to move forward before turning to port to exit the hangar. Once out into the night air, the Nimbus was halted, and the Discovery came alongside. The darkness prevented her from getting a really good view of it, but she could make out the internal glow through its cockpit window, and she wished she could see John right now.

Puffy was in radio contact both with Bert, on board the Discovery, and Wythenshawe Control. Both machines got the same message at the same time, "clear for take off," and Cirrus advanced the throttles, and held back on the control column at the same time. The Nimbus ascended, accompanied by the Discovery. It was like being in a lift, but one that never seemed to stop, and one that travelled very fast, and there was no more noise than you would get with a normal lift. Sarah felt herself gripping the flightdeck handrail, and was somewhat relieved when the Nimbus stopped climbing. Cirrus pointed out the altimeter to her. She couldn't believe that they were now at five thousand feet. Outside was just an inky black, but down below, she could see the twinkling lights of Wythenshawe. The Discovery was difficult to pick out in the night sky, which was a bit of a disappointment.

Soon, the two cloud machines were heading west, on a heading of 270°, and the speed settled at twenty knots. Puffy introduced Sarah to the Plan Position Indicator which showed the ground below, and he plotted their flightpath for her on his chart, so that she could relate what she saw on the PPI to the chart. Cirrus activated the Identification Beacon and explained to her what it was for. The next hour or so seemed to pass in no time, and when Liverpool was left behind, the twinkling ground lights disappeared to leave a blackness that she was unfamiliar with, and she felt it was most eerie.

At a particular position, determined by the PPI, the Nimbus was brought into the hover, along with the Discovery. At this moment, the only evidence of the Discovery was the blip that represented it on the PPI, and that was down to its skipper, Wally, having switched on his ID Beacon. Puffy called Sarah over, so that she could see what was about to happen.

He switched on his atomiser, to atomise some of the Irish Sea. He set controls that determined how fast the process would take place, and how much of the sea he would take. Some of the sea would be stored on board the Nimbus in its water tanks, some would be converted to ice and stored in the onboard refrigerators, but the majority would be converted into cloud that they would be immersed in. Puffy showed her the cloud type selector controls, and she was fascinated when he selected, 'Westmorland White'.

The next hour passed fairly uneventfully, and it seemed strange that the process that was taking place was both unseen and unheard, but Sarah could see the needles on the water tank content meters rising, along with those displaying the refrigerator contents. Nothing could be seen through the cockpit window except blackness, and the image on the PPI was stationary.

At about 0130 hours, the atomisation process was complete, and over the radio, Bert, on board the Discovery, confirmed they were done too. Cirrus got Puffy to read off the PPI their current latitude and longitude, which he punched into the soakometer/navaid, and then he asked for the lat and long of their destination, Barry Island. Puffy read this off his chart, and once this had been punched in, the Nimbus, in formation with the Discovery, got under way. Puffy indicated the flightpath for Sarah and explained how the soakometer/navaid would now fly them to Barry Island, and being at a height of five thousand feet, they would clear any mountains along their route.

The TV screen popped up in front of Cirrus, and as he rotated his camera, the outline of the accompanying Westmorland White cloud could just be made out.

"That's the Discovery," remarked Cirrus, who went on, "our TV camera sees straight through our own cloud, but can't penetrate others. Its penetration range is limited, but that's what allows us to see all the other clouds, and we do know that the Discovery is inside that one, because we can see its blip on our PPI."

"What a remarkable world this is," thought Sarah.

"Right, you might as well get your head down. There's nothing happening for the next six or so hours as we fly south, and we won't start the roster until tomorrow night," said Puffy.

That was great news for Sarah who felt quite tired, after such a fantastic introduction to cloud-making. The thought of what comes next was uppermost in her mind, but for the time being it, would be nice to fall into the Land of Nod!

Barry Island

At 0730 hours, Sarah woke from a deep sleep, and had to pinch herself, to tell that what she was experiencing was not a dream, and then set about her duties. Breakfast was first on the agenda.

Sunshine was cascading through the cockpit window, but nothing could be seen through it; it was covered by a mist. Then Sarah realised that this was the Westmorland White she was currently living in.

"Morning Sarah, how are you on this bright Tuesday morning?"

"I'm very well thanks, Puffy. Have we arrived at Barry Island yet?"

"Yes we have, take a look at the TV screen."

Sarah looked and could see that the Nimbus was hovering a little distance offshore, and looking north, she could see the resort of Barry Island in great detail.

"Where's the Discovery, Puffy?"

"Just rotate the TV camera control and you will see it on the screen."

Sarah did this, and got a fabulous view of the most picturesque Westmorland White Cloud anyone could wish to see, and, set in the clear blue sky that they were blessed with today, it looked stunning.

"Is that what we look like, Puffy?"

"Yes, indeed it is. Lovely isn't it?"

Cirrus came into the cockpit just as Sarah was about to answer Puffy. He had been shaving in the craft's washroom.

"Look at those white-topped waves down there. I don't think we will be photographed today."

Why ever not?" asked Sarah.

"The photographer is travelling around the coast of Wales in an old pilot boat, but he's not the best of sailors and won't put to sea unless the conditions are calm."

"Give Elwyn a call, Puffy, and ask him what he wants us to do."

"Aye aye, skipper."

Word came back that the wind was in excess of thirty knots, and was not likely to drop before nightfall. There was nothing for it but to hang around until the following morning.

"You better contact the Discovery, Puffy, and put them in the picture."

This was all a bit of an anti-climax, thought Sarah, but Puffy assured her that in their line of work this was nothing unusual. They were always at the mercy of the weather. Nevertheless, the next twenty-four hours were a bit of a drag, although it did give Sarah a chance to be gently introduced to the night watch which she shared, partly with Cirrus, and partly with Puffy, and she got a couple of hours sleep into the bargain.

By 0800 hours on the Wednesday morning, the wind had dropped, and after a leisurely breakfast, Elwyn's voice bellowed out from the radio.

"Cirrus, can you hear me? This is Elwyn Williams. Are you ready to go boyo?"

"Morning Elwyn, Cirrus here! Yes, we are ready to go. Just tell us what you want us to do."

"Where is the photographer?" asked Sarah.

"Just look at the TV screen. See that boat there? That's Elwyn's, and he calls it the 'Wilted Daffodil'.

"Puffy, put the Discovery on a shared channel will you? It will save Elwyn making two calls every time he issues an instruction."

"Right o skipper!"

"Right boyos, I want you to move to the other side of the town."

The Nimbus and the Discovery, or the two Westmorland White clouds as far as those on the ground were concerned, headed slowly north. They crossed over the coast and then, Barry Island itself; until Elwyn cried out, "Stop!"

Elwyn, sitting on the deck of his Wilted Daffodil, was watching proceedings through the viewfinder of his camera. Today was going to yield some good photos.

"Right boyos, now I want you to drop down a bit."

Both clouds did as they were told to do, until Elwyn burst forth again.

"Stop where you are boyos. Now whoever is on the left, I want you to move further to the left."

The Nimbus slowly moved, until the instruction to stop was issued. A certain amount of juggling went on before Elwyn was satisfied, and then he took a number of photos before thanking the cloud boys for their assistance. The time had flown by, and it was now 1400 hours, and the heat of the day was starting to create a haze.

"What happens now?" asked Sarah.

"We push off west, along the coast to Porthcawl, and wait for the Wilted Daffodil to catch up, and then we do another photo shoot."

"Will that be later today?"

"Oh no, we will set off now, and hover off the coast overnight. At this time of the year, its best to take the photos in the morning and it gives Elwyn the chance to get into position."

The two scenic clouds ascended to five thousand feet, and then headed west, following the coastline until Porthcawl was reached, and then came to the hover for an overnight stop.

Sarah's initial anxiety about taking this summer job on had already dissipated, and she felt part of the crew, who, she thought, were treating her lovely. She wondered if John felt the same.

The night roster passed without event, and all the crew of the Nimbus got some sleep before enjoying the fruits of Sarah's cooking, the smells of which were permeating around the whole craft.

Elwyn called out instructions as soon as he was in place, having sailed the previous evening from Barry Island. The same cloud juggling took place as the day before, until he was satisfied. The clear blue sky had held for another day, and another fine collection of photos were in the bag.

"Great job boyos! Thanks for the pose. See you next week."

"Have we finished now, Captain?" asked Sarah.

"But it's only 1400 hours, and its only Thursday!"

"We are going to head back to Liverpool Bay, along with the Discovery, and we should get there at about 2000 hours. When we get there, we have to wait until its dark, and we rain to get rid of our cloud. When that's done, we will travel to Wythenshawe and land. It could be about 0200 hours by the time we land, so we get a bit of sleep, and then get off home for the weekend."

"Brilliant!" exclaimed Sarah.

John and Sarah arrived back at their respective homes at tea time on Friday, and judging by the stories they had to tell, they were certainly enthralled by it all.

More cloud posing

As in the previous week, Monday couldn't come soon enough, and the two new, intrepid, cloud machine crew members arrived at Wythenshawe Weather Centre, to board their respective craft. Provisioning was the first priority, and it wasn't until tea time that they got the chance to learn about what they would be doing this week.

"We're going back to South Wales to do some more photo shots," said Captain Cumulus, who then went on to tell Sarah that the venues this week would be Laugharne and Saundersfoot.

After tea, there was time to do a little reading before the evening take off, which was just as exciting as the week before. Once airborne, the Nimbus and the Discovery headed out to the Irish Sea and both made brand new, Westmorland White clouds for this week's photo shoot. Clouds made, it was time to head south, care of the soakometer/navaid, which had all the necessary co-ordinates punched into it. With the knowledge that the ID Beacon had been activated, the pressure was off the crew for a few hours, as the pair of posing clouds journeyed south through the night. Each crew member took it in turn to get a couple of hours sleep, and monitoring the progress of the Nimbus using the craft's chart, in conjunction with the PPI, was not a problem.

Over breakfast at 0800 hours, Puffy, looking at the TV screen, pointed out Laugharne to Sarah. The Nimbus was hovering at five thousand feet on the opposite side of the River Taff. They were directly over a place called Llansteffan, which nestled on the west bank of the River Towy. On the port side of the Nimbus, the two rivers converged as they flowed into Carmarthen Bay. The castle at Laugharne was clearly visible, and looked like a likely centre piece for any photo.

"Where's the Wilted Daffodil?" asked Cirrus.

Before Puffy could reply, a voice came bellowing from the radio.

"Its Elwyn yer. Listen boyos, it's a change of plan see. I can't get my boat up the Taff. Its too tricky see, so I'm off to Tenby. I'll get a car in Tenby, an tomorrow morning, I'll set up on the east bank of the Taff, opposite Laugharne, an we can do the shoot then."

"Ok Elwyn, we'll be waiting for you."

"If I was you boyos, I'd take the chance of getting down to the pub. They serve a good pint in Laugharne. See you tomorrow, boyos."

When the radio went dead, the sudden silence was deafening.

"He's quite a character, our Elwyn," commented Puffy.

The next twenty-four hours were spent hovering over Llansteffan watching all the real clouds go by, which was a strange phenomenon to observe, when you are one. Strangely, no-one down below took any notice of the two clouds up above that didn't move, but on a lovely sunny day like today, nobody cared.

Breakfast on board the Nimbus on Wednesday morning was rudely interrupted by the latest bulletin from Elwyn.

"Mornin boyos, its Elwyn yer. I want to get an early start see, cos I need to get back aboard the Wilted Daffodil in time to catch the tide, see."

The Nimbus and Discovery responded, and awaited instructions. In due course, they moved to a position west of Laugharne so that they would appear in the background of any of Elwyn's shots. The height of each cloud was carefully arrived at by following further instructions, and then things were fine-tuned by moving one relative to the other. Having one cloud slightly behind and to one side of the other created better results, and by having them at slightly different heights, gave the final touches to the tranquil scene. The clear blue sky helped considerably.

At 1100 hours, the photo shoot was complete, and the two Westmorland White clouds made their way a short distance along the Welsh coast to come to a hover opposite Saundersfoot, which was to be the location for the next photo shoot. There would be a wait until Thursday morning before this could happen, since Elwyn had to make his way back again to Tenby to board his boat, and get to sea before the tide went out. Sarah was glad she had brought a few books with her.

Thursday morning followed the usual pattern, with an early call from Elwyn, who was at sea opposite Saundersfoot, and ready to start. With a rising sun in the east, and air free from haze, this was the time to get the best results, and they got on with the job. The two Westmorland Whites hovered behind the resort, in positions dictated by Elwyn, and when he was satisfied with what he could see, he took his photos. The way things were going it looked as if a good start had been made to next year's calendars, but what all the good Welsh folk made of what they saw, was anybodies guess. The tourists, however, thought it was rather special, and commented so at the various Tourist Information Offices.

To make the return journey to Wythenshawe that bit more interesting, Cirrus took the Nimbus west to St. Davids Head, before heading north over Cardigan Bay. Sarah was fascinated by the scenery on the TV screen, but it would have been better, she thought, if it could have been seen through the mist-covered cockpit window. The Nimbus continued north over the LLeyn Peninsula and the Isle-of-Anglesey, to reach Liverpool Bay where they hovered until dark.

Sarah watched Puffy set the appropriate controls to make rain, and over the next hour, any unfortunate ship below got a good drenching, as first the Nimbus got rid of its stored ice, and then its stored water, and finally, the cloud that they had been hiding in all week. She watched the needles on the various dials wind down to zero, and then turned her head to the cockpit window. She could just make out the clearing of the mist, but in the inky darkness of the night, there was nothing to see. Even without its cloud, the Nimbus relied on its TV camera in the dark, and in its infra-red mode, the picture on the screen was not much different from that in the daylight.

The Nimbus, minus cloud, flew on with its partner, the Discovery, through the early hours of Friday, to their destination, Wythenshawe Weather Centre. On arrival they had to hover until cleared to descend. This authority could only be given if traffic into or out of Manchester International Airport allowed. The two cloud machines descended rapidly from five thousand feet when cleared to do so. Sarah had the feeling that she had left her stomach behind as the Nimbus came down so fast. On meeting mother earth, each machine taxied into the large hangar and the doors closed behind them. It was quite startling when the hangar lights came on, but it made it easier for Cirrus to taxi the Nimbus to its allocated position.

Once Sarah had exited the Nimbus, she spotted John, and ran to him. She had missed his company. Having embraced John, she exchanged experiences with him, and they both had a lot to talk about.

146

This was a most unusual way of spending a summer break, and it still had six weeks to go.

Cirrus and Puffy bade Sarah farewell until the following Monday, and everyone hit the road for a weekend at home. Back in Oswaldtwistle, John faced his brother George and sister Sadie across the family table as they had tea. He missed Sarah already, and was glad that he would be spending Saturday night at her home in Burnley. But for the moment, he faced a barrage of questions from two very enthusiastic listeners, who, with open mouths, were thrilled by what he was telling them.

"Get away John, you are making it up," said Sadie, who couldn't comprehend the reality of her elder brother's adventures. From this time onwards Sadie and George looked at the clouds in the sky in a different way, but they found it no easier to pick out one that could be hiding a cloud machine.

Just another week

By the beginning of week three, Sarah and John felt that they were managing their roles quite effectively, and it was cooking in the galley that was turning out to be the greatest challenge, in spite of most meals being pre-prepared, breakfast being the exception. The week began in the same fashion as the previous two. Having provisioned the two machines, it was the usual wait until darkness fell, before take off, and then off to the Irish Sea to steal some of it and turn it from murky grey brine to an attractive Westmorland White cloud that would, in the following year, grace thousands of homes and businesses on calendars. What could be better?

The journey through the night took the two splendid clouds to the South Wales resort of Tenby, which was only a short distance from where they had finished the previous week. Photographer Elwyn Williams was waiting for them offshore, on board his Wilted Daffodil and gave the two cloud crews his usual greeting.

"Mornin boyos. Glad to see you back, but we have a bit of a snag. There are a few errant, grey, puffy jobs drifting through. They're bloody cloudless, if you get my meaning. You'll just have to hover until these bloody rain jobs have buggered off, see."

It was almost 1145 hours, before the sky was clear of the stuff that Elwyn wanted rid of, and it was now getting close to the first haze of the day.

"Right boyos, we better get crackin before we lose the clear air."

Elwyn got the two Westmorland Whites just where he wanted them, and they posed obligingly whilst he took the shots that would help deliver next years 'Wonders of Wales' calendar.

Soon after dinner, the Nimbus and its companion cloud, the Discovery, headed for their next destination, Fishguard.

Fishguard is at the southern end of Cardigan Bay, and is sandwiched between Strumble Head, and Dinas Head. Being on the west coast of Wales, the sun would be in the wrong position for an early morning photo shoot and Sarah wondered what Elwyn would do. The journey from Tenby took the two clouds overland to Fishguard, and then they hovered over the sea, just west of the town.

"Captain, why do you hover over the sea?" asked Sarah.

"These are holiday resorts, and we don't want to put them in the shade too much. The British weather is ropey enough as it is," replied Cirrus.

Whilst the journey overland for the two clouds was not a great distance, it was considerably longer for the Wilted Daffodil, and during the night it got quite windy, and on two occasions, it had to seek coastal shelter. The wind tended to blow the two clouds about a bit, and Sarah started to feel motion sickness coming on. Fortunately, the Nimbus carried suitable medication for just this eventuality, although the seasoned crew tended not to use it much, preferring a bacon butty and a cup of tea. Tuesday night seemed like a very long one to Sarah, who wished the Nimbus would cease its constant movement. This was one aspect of cloud life she could live without.

On Wednesday, there was no sign of Elwyn's boat, and by lunch time, Cirrus was beginning to think that he ought to do something about it. The need for any action was however averted when from the radio came the recognisable taffy voice of the man himself.

"Hello, boyos! Sorry about the delay. Ran into some rough weather last night. Old Neptune must have had a bad temper see. Anyway boyos, we had a few drinks see, and we got to a point where we didn't know the sharp end from the blunt, see. When I get my head back I'll come an join you. See you in the morning, boyos. Cheerio."

So that was Wednesday!

Thursday morning dawned with a lovely blue sky, and the wind had subsided. Down below, the Wilted Daffodil was on station for the shoot, and Elwyn was raring to go. No sooner had Sarah made breakfast for her colleagues than a call came in, over the craft's radio.

"Mornin boyos, it's your favourite Welshman here. Conditions are ideal, so I want to get started right away."

The two clouds were carefully manoeuvred into position behind the town of Fishguard, and very cleverly, Elwyn got them to mask the sun's rays from his camera lens. It took a little time to get them just where he wanted them, but just like two good models, they did exactly what he told them to, and he got the best shots possible.

By noon, Elwyn had finished with them, and it was then a case of heading back to Liverpool Bay and waiting for darkness again before raining. With that process out of the way, the Nimbus and the Discovery, in their natural naked state, made their way back to Wythenshawe. A weekend at home was in store for the two crews, and they both looked forward to it.

The weather turns

On arrival back at Wythenshawe at the start of the fourth week, the weather looked distinctly wintry. Low level stratus cloud kept the sun and its warmth at bay, and Sarah and John wondered what happened when these conditions were encountered.

Cirrus and Wally got their heads together and decided that they would have to sit it out. The weather was not right for photography, but the final call was Elwyn's.

"Don't you worry about a thing, boyos. We can't take a good picture with all this clagg about see. Go an have a good pint till it gets better, see. An give me a call each day see, an we can take it from yer. Yachy daa!"

Cirrus turned to Wally, and after some discussion they agreed to sit it out in Ballyhalbert, and they both informed their respective crews. Puffy was over the moon with the idea, but Sarah was unsure what the plan meant.

"You and John, and the rest of the Discovery crew, are going to stay at our place in Ballyhalbert, in Northern Ireland, until the weather gets better, and that could be a good few days. Sarah's eyes lit up and her broad smile conveyed the pleasure she felt. It would be an opportunity to share some extra time with the young man she was beginning to fall in love with.

The two cloud machines were provisioned in the normal way, and there was still the customary wait until dark before getting airborne. They ascended to five thousand feet, passing through the layer of stratus that was hiding the moon and the stars, and as they emerged from it, Cirrus adjusted the TV camera so that the cloud top could be seen in the silvery light of the moon. In these conditions the stars looked animated, and the whole of the night sky was in a form not witnessed by Sarah before, and everything in her life started taking on a new perspective.

The rules contained in the Cloud Machine Operators Rules of Operation Manual, precluded the Nimbus and the Discovery from journeying across the sky naked, and hence both of them still had the mandatory job of heading for the Irish Sea, and hiding themselves in self-made cloud, before commencing their journey to Northern Ireland. Cirrus intended landing at Newtownards airfield, and Puffy contacted his skipper's friend there, to make the necessary arrangements.

Once covered in cloud, Cirrus punched the start and finish co-ordinates into his soakometer/navaid, and the Nimbus headed for their destination. Puffy calculated that with the current head wind, and throttle settings, it would take in the region of fourteen hours to make the journey, and on that basis, they should be overhead Newtownards airfield at about 1600 hours.

The Nimbus flew slowly but steadily on, over the layer of stratus that stretched out to the horizon in every direction.

I bet this is just what it's like on the surface of the moon, thought Sarah.

At 1600 hours, the two formating clouds came to the hover. The only clue that the airfield was below them was shown on the PPI.

"Let's have some tea Sarah. It's a long wait to dark," said the Captain.

"Allow me," said Puffy. "I'll make it for a change."

Not only Sarah was evidently looking forward to time in Ballyhalbert!

When night fell, the two clouds moved to a position over Strangford Lough, and rained. The emergent Nimbus and Discovery then moved back over the airfield and descended rapidly, leaving Sarah's stomach behind once more in the process, and touched down outside an isolated hangar that had its waiting doors open. After the slight bump that accompanied the touch down, each machine taxied inside and came to a stop. With the hangar doors shut, the lights came on, and Cirrus shut down the motors on the Nimbus.

"Grab all your clothes, Sarah, before you leave. We don't know how long we are going to be here."

Stepping outside the craft, a voice shouted across the hangar.

"Top o' the morning to you Cirrus, an welcome to the ole country."

It's not another photographer, thought Sarah.

"Hello, Joe! What are you doing here?" asked the Captain.

"I heard you wer comin over, an thought Oi would give you all a lift to Ballyhalbert."

"Thanks, Joe. That's very kind of you."

"Who is Joe?" asked Sarah,

"That's Joe Riley, from Portrush. We did a job for him last year," replied Puffy.

In the early hours of Wednesday morning, six cloud crew members boarded Joe's minibus for the short road journey to Ballyhalbert, and a welcome break from Welsh calendars. But how the devil did Joe find out they were coming?

"The mystique of the Irish would never be unfolded," thought Cirrus.

A break in Ballyhalbert

Wally, Bert, Puffy and Cirrus spent the next few days catching up on things, and many pleasant hours were spent reminiscing. The spacious home that the Nimbus crew had purchased in Ballyhalbert was an excellent place to be for a few days, and Wally was most interested to find out what had gone on here during World War Two. The house had been built on an old airfield, and Wally was mad about aviation history. Ballyhalbert airfield had opened as a Royal Air Force Station, in June 1941, and fighter aircraft had been based here to protect Northern Ireland. Royal Navy aircraft had operated from here from October 1943 onwards, and in July 1945, it had been taken over by the Royal Navy and commissioned as HMS Corncrake, but its life as an airfield was short lived, and it closed in November 1945.

Through the bedroom windows of the house, the old airfield control tower could be seen, and it stood out as a reminder of times past, when aircraft came and went, and sailors and airmen from around the world lived and worked here. Some never went back home, as there were many crashes in those days, when young inexperienced men struggled with the complexities of the aircraft of that time. The four cloud machine men had an affinity with those that had gone before them at this place, and took time out to pay them homage by visiting several local churchyards where some of them had been laid to rest, in some cases thousands of miles from their homes.

Sarah and John left their four colleagues to their reminiscing and spent most of their time walking hand in hand. The village of Ballyhalbert is a very small place, and in ten minutes of stepping out of the front door, they were on the sea front. The Mull-of-Galloway and the Isle-of-Man can be clearly seen from there on a good day, and when the conditions are particularly good, the mountains in the Lake District can be spotted. The two young undergraduates grew closer by the day, and they journeyed further, by taking the bus to the fishing port of Portavogie, and further afield to Portaferry, which they took a distinct liking to.

A full week passed and there was no sign that the weather was about to change. A low layer of stratus continued to blight the country, and sunshine was in short supply. The low temperatures did nothing for the ice cream salesmen, and the only thing happening on the local beaches, was kite-flying. Cirrus and his long standing colleagues had just about exhausted what they could reminisce about, and his home was beginning to feel overcrowded. Nerves began to fray a little, and Puffy, who was well acquainted with the signs, took to gardening more frequently.

Each day a call would come in from Elwyn.

"Hello, boyos. No sign of any change see. This bloody cloud is still buggering things up. At this rate we'll still be bloody yer till Christmas."

It was the same message every day for twelve days, and by that time, even Sarah and John were getting a bit restless. A lack of privacy was a bit restrictive at times.

Exactly two weeks after their arrival in Ballyhalbert, the weather looked as if it was changing.

"Hello, boyos. We are back in the photo business. This damned cloud will have gone tomorrow, see. Get yourselves moving, and meet me at Newquay on Tuesday morning. And mind you are there sharpish, see. Cheerio boyos."

Sunday night would be the last in Ballyhalbert, and it came as a relief that they would be getting back to work again after their enforced layoff, due to the weather.

The photo shoot is back on

Monday morning, and the start of week six; it had come around so fast thought Sarah as she got in the taxi that Cirrus had organised to get the six cloud machine crew members to Newtownards. The journey was somewhat uncomfortable with six bodies squeezed into it, but at least it got them there. The taxi dropped John and Sarah in the town to get fresh provisions for the Nimbus and the Discovery. Cirrus, Puffy, Wally and Bert went on to the airfield, and made their way to the isolated hangar which had been home to their machines for two weeks.

By the time John and Sarah arrived, weighed down with lots of pre-prepared meals, both machines had been fully checked over.

When everything had been stowed aboard, it was time for tea, and then the inevitable wait until it was dark. In due course both machines started their motors and they began to taxi out of the hangar, the lights going out and the doors opening as they did so. As the two machines emerged from the blackness of the hangar onto a moonlit hard standing, something of a crowd was gathered to witness their departure.

"You can't keep a secret in Ireland," said Cirrus.

"I'll bet its Joe Riley that's behind this, and he's probably making a bob or two out of it," commented Puffy.

Cirrus gave the instruction to take off, and in the moonlight the Nimbus and the Discovery ascended vertically, until they reached five thousand feet. They disappeared from view well before they reached that altitude, but the congregation below were amazed and clapped to congratulate the crews. Shortly after, Joe Riley joined them to collect their contributions.

"It was well worth it Joe, Oi have never seen dat before," was a statement he heard several times.

Moving the short distance from the airfield to a position over Strangford Lough, Sarah was invited by Puffy to take his seat at his work station, and following his instructions she made her very first cloud, which she was immensely proud of. With two Westmorland White clouds freshly manufactured, the journey to their latest destination got underway. It was almost due south to Newquay, but that didn't really matter. Once the start and finish co-ordinates had been punched into the soakometer the Nimbus would fly itself to wherever Cirrus wanted it to go. With the ID Beacon activated, the crew could take it easy, simply monitoring the flightpath.

Newquay was just up the Cardigan Bay coast from Fishguard, the last location they had visited for a photo shoot. It was one hundred and forty-five nautical miles to Newquay, and flying at twenty knots meant that they would arrive at 0815 hours.

"Hello, boyos. Where the bloody hell are you? You should have been here by now."

Elwyn was clearly not pleased, but if he looked north, he would have seen them approaching, and Cirrus told him so in no uncertain terms.

"Ok boyo, ok boyo. Don't get your knickers in a twist. I can see you now, boyo."

The two clouds were only fifteen minutes late arriving, and Elwyn got to work immediately by issuing a stream of instructions to get them where he wanted. They were positioned just behind the resort, and they hid the sun's rays from Elwyn's camera lens. By noon the shoot was complete, and it was time to move on.

It was only a short distance up the coast from Newquay to the next destination at Aberystwyth, but there would be no more photo-taking today; the midday haze had arrived. It was going to be a case of hovering over the sea offshore for the night again, but at least it would give the Wilted Daffodil the chance to sail and join up with them.

The night passed without incident, and Wednesday morning breakfast was up to its usual high standard.

"Sarah, I think the Captain and I are really going to miss you when this job comes to an end."

"You mean you will miss my cooking, don't you?"

Whilst that was true, he could hardly tell her what else he would miss about her, he thought, as he looked over her slim figure and attractive face.

"Mornin, boyos. Hope you all slept well. The weather is good so we should get this job done fast today and you can get home early, see."

The pattern was all too familiar by this stage; just follow the instructions that bellowed out from the radio and pose: click, click and another click, and Elwyn would have all his shots in the bag.

"Well done, boyos. Get off home and enjoy a good pint. Cheerio and Yachy daa."

The two clouds headed for Liverpool Bay, and in the early hours of Thursday morning, they made rain and lost two clouds before heading for Wythenshawe in the dark. As usual, the fast descent from five thousand feet thrilled Sarah! She grabbed all her gear when the Nimbus had landed and headed home to Burnley for a long weekend.

Sarah's mother, Jane sat and knitted, whilst she listened to her daughters adventures. When Sarah described how she had made her first cloud, Jane remembered an old expression that folk sometimes used about knitting fog. She had never given it any credence in the past, but now she was not so sure. A lot can happen in three weeks, she thought.

John was confronted with the same awe as his girl friend, and his brother and sister, George and Sadie, sat and listened intently to his stories before bombarding him with questions.

"I wish I could have a go on the Discovery." said George.

"It's not all exciting, George. There are lots of times when you just wait around."

"Yeah, but it's not like waiting for a bus!"

It's all coming to an end

Week seven began in the same way as all the others, and Cardigan Bay was to be the location again for more calendar shots by Elwyn. By Tuesday morning, Barmouth was on the receiving end of the camera lens, but no-one knew which month of the year it would be. For that, everybody would have to wait and see.

From Barmouth the two clouds flew north to Criccieth, which was only a short distance away. Criccieth faces south over the expanse of Cardigan Bay and its castle makes it photogenic. The photo shoot was scheduled for Wednesday, but rain blew through, and it was Thursday before the job could be completed, and then it was time to push off to Liverpool Bay to dump some of their own rain. There then followed a weekend at home, before the last week of the summer break.

Sarah and John both felt somewhat sad arriving at Wythenshawe Weather Centre for the final week's work. It had certainly been an unusual, if not unique, experience, and they would not have missed it for the world. They had grown to like their colleagues immensely. They had been hosted with the utmost courtesy, but for now they had to get on with provisioning the two cloud machines.

"Back at the uni are you, next week, Sarah?" asked Puffy.

"Yes, back to studying law and it's going to be boring after this."

Eventually, the time arrived for their final lift off, and soon both the Nimbus and the Discovery were at five thousand feet, in the dark. They headed for Liverpool Bay to make clouds, and then set course for Caernarfon in the Menai Straits. This was the shortest overnight journey they had made, and their early arrival on the Tuesday morning enabled them to sleep a little longer, before having breakfast and then getting to work.

"Mornin, boyos. The last week eh! The weather might get a bit iffy tomorrow but we are ok today see, so let's get crackin."

Elwyn's unmistakable voice roused everyone aboard the two clouds, and with his guidance, they moved into their pose positions. Set behind Caernarfon's iconic castle, the Westmorland Whites added a special quality to the image in Elwyn's viewfinder, and he took several shots. Being a perfectionist, he issued instructions to adjust the position of his own clouds, and then took more shots, and he repeated this several times before he was finished.

"Well done, boyos. Now let's get off and I will see you at Llandudno tomorrow. Cheerio. Yacky Daa."

It didn't take long to cover the short distance to Llandudno, and in the hover, just east of Great Ormes Head, the view was most pleasant and the two crews settled for an overnight wait, whilst the Wilted Daffodil made its sea journey to join them.

As Wednesday morning arrived, it was obvious that the taking of photographs was most unlikely. The two clouds were being buffeted up and down, and sideways, by the strong wind, and even Cirrus and Puffy had resorted to taking medication, let alone poor Sarah. They all skipped breakfast and waited for the wind to abate.

"Well boyos, no pictures today. It's the bloody wind, see. I'll call you tomorrow, see."

Elwyn didn't sound like his usual self, but neither did anyone else.

It was much better on Thursday morning, and this, more than likely, would see the end of the calendar work.

"Mornin, boyos. Much better conditions today! One or two scraps of puffy white stuff blowing through but they shouldn't get in the way, see. So let's get crackin an finish this damn job so I can get home for a decent drink, see."

Like the obliging clouds that they were, they moved into the positions that Elwyn wanted them to be in, and posed, showing off their many curves and purity of white, which contrasted well with both the blue of the sky and the roughly shaped grey stuff blowing through on the breeze.

"Bloody good, see. A fine job, see. I'll send you all a calendar for Christmas, see! Boyos, with all those curves you've got, you should be in that Follies place in Paris.

Ta very much, boyos. Cheerio an Yacky Daa."

That was a voice that Sarah would remember for a very long time.

It was a real anti-climax arriving back at Wythenshawe, and the goodbyes brought a tear to Sarah's eyes, but before she left, Cirrus handed her two envelopes, one of which had a stiff cardboard backing.

"Now don't open these until you get home," said Cirrus, who then embraced her.

Well that's a turn up for the book, thought Puffy, but not to be outdone, he embraced her as well, and wished her good luck in her studies.

Sarah was glad to be heading home, with John for company, who also had two envelopes. They didn't speak much on the journey, but they did think a lot.

"Wally, I think that went very well," said Cirrus.

"I think it did too and they were nice young folk to have aboard," replied Wally, and he joined Cirrus and Bert and Puffy for a celebratory drink.

Back in Burnley

It was a great relief to both the Whittle and Davies families that the summer break had gone so well. Their son and daughter appeared to have had a brilliant time, and the separation had, hopefully, been worthwhile. The question of damping down passions, for that is what it had all been about, was another matter. The two had come back very much more in love with each other than before. It was almost a case of 'absence makes the heart grow fonder'. No doubt their return to university would keep them usefully employed in the near future.

Sarah opened the small envelope that Cirrus had given to her, and she took out a cheque which forced her to scream with joy when she saw it.

"What's the matter, Sarah?" asked her mother.

"Look how generous the Captain has been," she replied, with tears streaming down her face.

"My, that is generous. You must have struck a chord with them. But look, there's a note inside the envelope."

Sarah took the note out and read it.

"What does it say, Sarah?"

"Thank you for your kind help, Sarah. It was lovely to have your company over the summer. This cheque will hopefully help you to complete your studies without getting into debt, and you deserve it. When you have a degree, you can come back on board the Nimbus and lay the law down when we rain. Good Luck and Best Wishes, Cirrus and Puffy."

That's nice, Sarah. What's in the big envelope?"

Very carefully, Sarah opened the big envelope to find that it contained a very special certificate from The Guild of Cloud Owners in recognition of her work experience on board the Nimbus, and it made special reference to the fact that she had made a cloud.

The certificate was framed the next day and had a pride of place location on the wall in the front room of her family home.

"So what did you and John do over the summer hols then?" asked Sarah's university friends, but they didn't bargain for the answer.

"I did work experience in a cloud machine."

She got rather odd looks, and the conversation rapidly changed to football, but John gave her a very special look!

THE NAVY NEEDS HELP

Everything needs testing

There didn't seem to be any end to the work coming their way these days, and today, in the Cumulus home in Slaidburn, was not about to experience any change in that direction.

Captain Cirrus Cumulus CDM, was taking his morning cup of coffee and a bacon butty, care of his faithful engineer, Percival White, who was known around the cloud world as Puffy. Cirrus had just put his feet up as he sat in his spacious lounge and was about to read his copy of the Daily Gloom. Puffy couldn't understand why his Captain would want to do that on such a beautiful day. Why on earth spoil it, he thought.

Strangely, Cirrus skipped all the news and gossip stuff, and headed straight for the stars. He read carefully what was written under his sign, and then paused for a moment, before getting up and strolling across the room to a photograph of Abigail Windrush. He looked at Abigail's photo for a little while and then strode out of the room. Puffy had discreetly been observing his Captain. There was a strong link between the newspaper's contents, and the Captains mood, and he wanted to be prepared.

The newspaper had been left open at the page Cirrus had been looking at, and Puffy scanned it to see what had stirred him. Observing nothing of any significance, Puffy looked at the stars as a last resort, and the Sign of Cirrus in particular.

'You will be drawn to the Seven Seas to perform service of importance. Don't be over cautious, when all said and done, all the nice girls love a sailor'.

Now of what significance was that, thought Puffy, but he did not have to wait long to find out.

Cirrus returned with a copy of The Monthly Downpour and studied its contents carefully before he picked up the phone and rang Wythenshawe Weather Centre.

"Captain Cumulus here, can you put me through to Mr Spite please?"

"Spite here! What can I do for you Cumulus, not another young couple on heat is it by any chance?"

"Nothing like that, Mr Spite! I have just read the advert by the Navy in the latest edition of The Monthly Downpour."

"Now look here, Cumulus, take my advice: don't join up. You're too old for all that stuff, and you see enough of the sea already."

"I'm not thinking of joining up, but I am interested in helping with some new tests they are going to carry out."

"Oh that! You had me worried for a moment. I remember that now. The details only came in a few days ago. I'll send you the information and an application form."

An application form! That was most unusual in the line of business that Cirrus was involved with.

A couple of days later, a letter arrived from Wythenshawe Weather Centre, and in it there was a form to complete and a description of the work for successful applicants. The form was most forbidding; it had no less than twenty four sections. Many details were required if an applicant wanted to be in with a chance of being taken on by the Navy. Most of the details were pretty straightforward like your name, date of birth, place of birth, and so on. Some information was clearly to do with security: what political party do you support, what organisations are you a member of, etcetera. Other information asked for was a bit more obscure, such as, where do you usually holiday, and what languages do you speak? The most important bit for Cirrus however, was the section dealing with employment and experience. If anything was going to attract the Navy, this would be it, and he spent considerable time giving a good account of himself and his flight engineer, Puffy White.

The job description which accompanied the application form was a little vague, but the general idea seemed to involve monitoring an area of sea in which the Navy would be carrying out trials. Shipping and fishing vessels in particular, needed to be prevented from straying into any trials area for fear of getting damaged. Cirrus was shrewd enough to know that there was also another reason for wanting to monitor any portion of the sea in which trials were being conducted. He had read many times about how the Russians tended to keep a watch on all the things the Navy did. This was a bit more sinister, but at this stage there was no point in jumping to any conclusions.

In due course the application form was signed and posted, and for the moment, that was that, and Cirrus went into the garden to do some work. Cirrus was a man of fixed habits, and gave his lawn a weekly 'short back and sides'. That was usually followed by hoeing the borders, and checking that the Daffodils, or Tulips, were all on parade in straight lines, and saluting in true military order. He did not like things out of place. It was Puffy that had a true affinity with nature, and the truly skilful jobs, such as pruning and weeding, fell into his domain.

It was a couple of weeks later that the postman delivered a letter from the Navy, and whilst it was gratefully received, it did not prevent Cirrus from bellowing at him to shut the garden gate as he departed. Puffy joined Cirrus in the lounge to witness the opening of the envelope. The contents amounted to no more than a short letter inviting the crew of the Nimbus to an interview.

"Where is it?" asked Puffy.

"At the Navy Station at Inskip," replied Cirrus.

Inskip was not that far from Slaidburn, lying between Preston and Blackpool.

"When is it?"

"In two days time."

The two intrepid cloud fliers then began to wonder what they had let themselves in for.

A Navy interview

Arriving at Inskip, which was a former World War Two Navy airfield, the Nimbus crew where met by a panorama of radio aerials, which gave away the current purpose of the establishment.

"Drive down this road, past the junction, and take your first right," was the instruction given by the guard at the Station entrance.

"You will see the building you have to report to. Just go to reception."

"I'm Captain Cumulus, and this is my Flight Engineer, Percival White. We are here for an interview."

The Petty Officer behind the reception desk looked at them in a suspicious way before checking their documentation. With that out of the way, a clip board hanging on the wall was consulted and then he finally spoke.

"Wait over there until you are called."

"Not exactly very welcoming are they," remarked Puffy.

A full ten minutes passed before the Petty Officer came over to them.

"Follow me."

Soon they were ushered through the door of an office, and entered a Navy World. The office was huge, but the thing that struck them first was the various ship's crests and pictures adorning the walls, and several stunning models of ships in display cases. At the far end of the office was a large desk, behind which sat a Naval Officer they recognised. The last time they had met him was at Wythenshawe Weather Centre, when he was organising a search party for Abigail Windrush.

"Good morning, Cumulus. Good morning, Mr White."

Cirrus was immediately rankled by the way Commander T. Chaos had addressed him, but was not going to jeopardise his chance of working for the Navy, and said nothing.

From the outset, it was made clear that anything they were told in the interview was strictly confidential, and was to be revealed to no-one. Commander Chaos then went on to describe the job at hand.

"We have a new ship-to-air missile that we want to test in a variety of weather conditions, and that's where you come in. We want you to provide heavy rain, thunder and lightning on demand, so that we can see how the thing performs in those conditions."

That was not quite what Cirrus was expecting to hear. It all sounded pretty straightforward. The Commander went on. "We will be doing the trials in an area of sea just west of the Hebrides, and you will need to locate yourselves at Stornoway in order to be on hand when we need you."

"Does that mean that we are being appointed to assist you?" asked Cirrus.

"After Operation Windpower, and the successful recovery of Abigail Windrush, it's a foregone conclusion."

Cirrus looked at Puffy, and a great smile of pride gave away their pleasure at being appointed.

"I want you to base the Nimbus at the airfield at Stornoway. There is a hangar there that can be devoted to you, and we have plenty of accommodation."

How long will you need us?" enquired Puffy.

"I can't give you a straightforward answer to that. It could be one week, or a month; it will depend on how well the trials go."

With the interview over, an envelope with the details of Stornoway inside it, was handed to Cirrus, and they left.

"We better let Abigail and Carol know that we are going to be away for some time."

"Let's ask them over to our place," suggested Puffy and they did.

"You're working for the Navy! Come off it Puffy, pull the other one," and he tried, but she had a firm grip on his hands.

"I tell you, we have this top secret job with the Navy."

"Go on with you," and so he did, and they forgot all about the Navy.

"You may get to see St. Kilda again," remarked Abigail.

"I suppose it is possible," said Cirrus, who was wilting under the spell of the adorable Abigail, and he realised that he wanted to surrender his lips to hers. He fumbled whilst aiming with his eyes closed, and kissed the wrong part of her anatomy, and received an unexpected reward. The pain did not die away for several minutes and it took longer to find his composure, which he had left behind on the sofa. There was a lot more to learn about this romance business, thought Cirrus. God knows what Abigail thought, but she still seemed to retain feelings for him.

Testing times

The journey to Stornoway was no different from any other cloud journey, but it was handy that the airfield was next to the sea. In the darkness of the night, the Nimbus rained over the sea to lose its cloud, and then landed outside the single large hangar on the airfield before taxiing into its interior. The doors closed behind it and the lights came on. Cirrus parked the Nimbus, and Puffy opened the craft's entry door and deployed the access ladder. As the two crew stepped out, the base commander was there to greet them.

"Commander Percil here and I assume you are Captain Cumulus?"

"Yes I am, Commander."

"Had a good trip?"

"Not bad, but I must confess that I'm a bit tired."

"I'll get you both over to your accommodation right away."

Soon, the crew of the Nimbus arrived at the accommodation that had been allocated to them. A self-contained billet had been laid on for them and although basic, it was adequate. Apart from bedrooms, toilet, and bathroom, it also had a kitchen and dining room cum lounge.

"I'll have you picked up about 1130 hours tomorrow, and we can go over the Operation details."

With that, the Commander left, and it was time to get some kip.

The following morning, Cirrus was greeted by the smell of bacon, which was a sure sign that Puffy was already up and at work.

What a great colleague to have, thought the Captain.

With breakfast out of the way, there was a knock on the billet door. A Navy rating had called to pick them up.

"I have to take you to Commander Whitewash."

"Commander who?"

"Sorry, it's Commander Percil to you, Whitewash to the matelots."

It was only a short journey to the Commander's office and they could just as easily have walked, and judging by the competency of the driver, it might have been safer to do so.

Commander Percil wasted no time in introducing the pair of them to 'Operation Hitme', which was the name given to the trials about to take place. He moved to a large wall-mounted map, and started by indicating the sea area in which it was all about to happen. A Navy frigate was in the area, and had on board, the ship-to-air missile to be tested. A pilotless drone would get airborne from Benbecula airfield on the Hebridean Island of Uist, and it would tow a target into the trials area for the missile to be fired at. So far the trials had been successful. The missile had been tested both during the day and during the night, but not in inclement weather conditions.

"What we need the Nimbus to do to begin with, is to go out into the trials area as a Manchester Black, create a downpour, and thunder and lightning, and we can see what happens."

"When do you want us to do it?"

"Tomorrow morning."

The briefing was short and sweet and the two crew members opted to walk back to their billet to carry out the necessary planning.

Operation Hitme

In the early evening, Cirrus and Puffy checked the Nimbus over, taking particular care to check the Van de Graaf generator that produced lightning. It was not often that the Nimbus was called upon to produce this weather feature. As far as thunder was concerned, it was prudent to check the onboard loudspeakers, and the recording they used to blast out over the air waves. The thunder equipment was cleverly linked to the lightning generator to ensure that they were properly co-ordinated. Puffy inadvertently switched the thunder making device on without muting the loudspeakers, and the noise, when amplified by the huge empty expanse of the hangar, brought fear to all those working in the various add-on outer buildings. The simultaneous speedy exit of some fifty or so persons was well worth watching, and they took some persuading to go back in and resume working.

When darkness had fallen, the access ladders of the Nimbus were retracted, and the entry door closed. The crew took up their positions in the cockpit and soon the four fan duct motors were started. The lights in the hangar were extinguished and the doors opened and out into the darkness the Nimbus taxied. After a quick cockpit check, the cloud machine ascended into the blackness and rapidly vanished from view, to the astonishment of the hangar workers.

Coming to the hover at three thousand feet, the ID beacon was activated before a short flight was made over the adjacent sea. Whilst hovering over an area of sea known as The Minch, Puffy set the craft's atomiser and for the next hour an all-embracing Manchester Black was created, with the Nimbus in the middle. This type of cloud looks menacing in daylight and is spectacular in the way it extends upwards. If desired, it can be set to reach up many thousands of feet, but for the job the Nimbus would be performing tomorrow, it was not necessary to go beyond twenty thousand. The base of the cloud covered many acres and its dark texture allowed little light to permeate through. Wherever this Manchester Black travelled, it would be sure to cast darkness not far short of the black of night.

Once turned into a Manchester Black, the Nimbus headed over the Hebridean Island of Lewis to the trials area between St. Kilda and the Island of Uist. The darkness of the night kept the flight of the Nimbus obscured from any prying eyes below, but out here there were not many eyes that could pry anyway, for the Isle of Lewis is scantily populated. At least the fearsome vision of a large black cloud, travelling into wind, was not going to induce any panic in these remote parts.

In the early hours of the morning, the Nimbus automatically came to a hover at three thousand feet at the co-ordinates given in the Operation Hitme Order. These had been punched into the soakometer/navaid back at Stornoway and, as usual, the Nimbus had navigated itself to its current location and here it would remain until the trial was completed. Now there was a chance to get some shut-eye, before things started to liven up.

Cirrus was woken by Puffy, who welcomed his Captain to the new dawn with a celebratory cup of tea, and a bacon butty. Within a few moments of consuming Puffy's gastronomical bacon wonder, the radio blurted out!

"Uist Control to Nimbus! Come in Nimbus."

"Nimbus here. Go ahead Uist Control."

"Make heavy rain, and thunder and lightning, for fifteen minutes starting at 1030 hours, and watch out for the action."

"Message understood."

"What's the action we must watch out for, skipper," enquired Puffy.

"I'm not exactly sure, but I suppose we need to watch the TV."

Scanning the scene three thousand feet below, and scanning the horizon, St. Kilda appeared on their starboard side and Uist to port. Just forard of the Manchester Black, and plying a slow westerly course, was a Navy frigate.

At 1030 hours precisely, a downpour was started, and thunder and lightning played its part. The frigate appeared to be just on the edge of the drenching rain, and shortly after the downpour had begun, a pilotless drone flew by, towing a target a couple of miles behind it. The drone was being heavily rained on, as was its target. Suddenly a flash of light on board the frigate marked the firing of a missile which rapidly sped toward the target and blew it apart on impact.

"That firing was a success," said Cirrus.

On instruction, the rain and other features were switched off, but the whole process was repeated three more times before the day's work was over. The Nimbus was ordered to remain on station overnight in preparation for the morrow's work, which took the crew a little by surprise.

"Have we any rations aboard, Puffy?"

"I brought an emergency pack aboard Skipper, and the emergency kit bag as well."

Even though this was standard procedure, Cirrus was still impressed with his flight engineer. Now there was a long evening to endure before the trials got under way again, but in the meantime a bit of atomising would not go amiss, and the glory of a Manchester Black, if that's what it can be called, was restored.

The next day followed a similar pattern, and gave the weapons specialists the chance to see if their new missile worked ok in bad weather, and things were going fine until the time came for the third firing. Over the radio a single word bellowed out, "Stop."

This was followed by a more lengthy message.

"A fishing boat has strayed into the trials zone. Escorts take over, and remove the offending boat. The exercise will not continue until the trials zone is clear."

Two rigid inflatable boats were lowered into the sea by the Navy frigate, and they both sped off towards the fishing boat.

"This is going to slow everything down, skipper," commented Puffy.

The fishing boat arrived under the edge of the base of the Manchester Black, and that was not advisable when its human crew had been annoyed. A deluge of immense proportions fell on the poor fishermen crewing their small boat, and, for a few moments, they did not know if they were above water or below it, but soon reached the conclusion that they were very much below it. The thunderous noise, and flashes of lightning, accelerated the boats departure, and the high speed Navy RIBs had a job catching up. Witnessing the race below, the rain was switched off, and the Navy was left to do its escorting job, but it ruined the rest of the day's schedule. There would be no more testing today.

Sneaky Russians

After an exceedingly long evening with little to do on board the Nimbus, except top up the Manchester Black with Scottish brine, it was good to get back to another day of testing. This job was not half as exciting as the Captain had expected and he was already looking forward to its completion.

The pattern was to be the same as yesterday: just hover, rain, and thunder and lightning on demand, whilst the frigate fired off its new missiles at towed targets. The tests did not get far again before another halt to proceedings was called. Another fishing vessel had strayed into the trials zone, but had it? This was no ordinary fishing boat. The many antennae attached to the vessel gave it away. This was a Russian spy boat come to see what was going on, and then report back to its Kremlin headquarters. This would have to be dealt with differently.

"Uist Control to Nimbus. Come in Nimbus."

"Nimbus here. Go ahead Uist Control."

"Go and sit on that bloody Russian, and stay there until told otherwise!"

Cirrus looked at Puffy, but had no option but to carry out the order. The Manchester Black was manoeuvred over the Russian spy boat, and then slowly descended through three thousand feet of sky until its base met the ocean. The descending Black mass of cloud took the Russian crew by surprise, and when day became night again, and a swirling black mist obscured everything, there was nothing for it but to break out the Vodka, and shortly after, the little spy boat began the first of many hundreds of orbits around a wave, and the crew didn't know it.

Testing was cancelled for another day and the Nimbus spent the night obscuring a drunken fishing boat crew from the rest of humanity. It was just before the following dawn that the Nimbus ascended into the early morning sky, leaving the Russian crew wondering what a strange place they were in. Somehow the little boat with a jungle of antennaes, got up a head of steam, and slowly zig zagged out of the trials area, leaving a trail of empty vodka bottles on the ocean surface. By 1000 hours, the trials area was clear again, and it was all systems go!

"Uist Control to Nimbus. Come in Nimbus."

"Nimbus here. Go ahead Uist Control."

"The test today will be a little different. We want you to descend to one thousand feet and rain very heavily whilst thundering and lightning. The drone will fly through you, towing its target, and when the frigate fires its missile, it will fly straight through you to hit the target."

"Crikey, that's a bit risky! Suppose it hits the Nimbus instead," remarked Puffy.

"Those Navy boys know what they are doing, don't worry Puffy."

At the appropriate time, Puffy, sitting at his flight engineer's position, activated various controls, and a deluge began over a small area of the Atlantic Ocean just west of the Island of Uist, and it began to thunder ferociously whilst streaks of lightning shot between the

Manchester Black and the expanse of water below. From the frigate, the scene must have been frightening, even to a hardened sailor.

Looking at the flight deck mounted TV screen, Cirrus and Puffy could see the red and yellow painted pilotless drone approaching from their stern, and they followed it with their TV camera as it entered their cloud and passed dangerously close underneath them before flying on ahead and exiting their black swirling mist. The towed target followed, but the wire attaching it to the drone was too fine to be seen. Shortly they expected to see a missile and then, suddenly, it was there! It was literally only seconds between the missile entering the black swirling mass of cloud and then there was a loud bang.

"Christ, we've been hit, Captain!"

"Don't panic, Puffy. Let's just see if anything has stopped working."

The fan duct motors were ok, and the Nimbus continued to hover. They carried on raining, making thunder and lightning and so, to all intents and purposes, nothing was wrong, but the crew were aware of a distinctly cold draught.

"Puffy take a look around will you and see if you can find out where that draught is coming from."

"Aye aye, skipper."

Puffy walked back from the cockpit, and down the corridor past the various refrigerators and the mixer. The source of the draught was obvious as soon as he entered the corridor. There was a gaping hole in the stern of the Nimbus, and it was raining in heavily.

"Skipper, we have been hit in the stern, and it's raining in very heavily."

"Ok Puffy, you better switch off the condensers and the thunder and lightning."

Puffy returned to his station and stopped everything. Down below, it must have been a relief to be out of the rain and not subject to anymore thunderous noise and bolts of lightning. The crew of the frigate had heard the loud bang but were unaware of what had happened up there inside the large Manchester Black.

Within a few moments, a black swirling mist began to enter the cockpit, and Puffy was forced to rush off and cover the hole in the stern of the Nimbus with a copy of his Captain's Daily Gloom. Getting rid of what had already entered the craft was another matter. Cirrus turned up the heaters and soon, condensation covered everything, including the crew but eventually it all dried out, but not before a number of layers of clothing had been discarded.

"We better get back to Stornoway and get the engineers from Black, Black & Blackemore's out," said Cirrus.

"Contact Uist Control and tell them what we are doing."

"The radio transmitter is not working skipper. That missile must have damaged the antennae."

"Well try the sat phone."

"That's not working either."

"You better try your mobile phone then."

"There's no signal."

"Ok, we better start heading for Uist. I'm sure that as we get nearer, we will get a signal."

The Manchester Black headed toward the Island of Uist, and in due course, Puffy got a signal. A message was forwarded to the cloud machine manufacturers in deeper Salford, and Stornoway was tipped off about their impending return. In their present mode, there would not be a problem landing at Stornoway in daylight, but once on the ground, all other flying activity would be brought to a halt. A Manchester Black sitting on the ground renders visibility practically nil.

Commander Percil had been walking around in circles inside the Manchester Black for some time and was almost about to give up trying to find the Nimbus when he bumped into its crew.

"Now look here, Cumulus, you can't park this thing here. You are preventing all flights in and out, and I can't allow that. Why don't you shove off and rain somewhere."

What a greeting! Even though Cirrus went to great lengths to explain the situation, he could not placate the Commander, but the Nimbus remained where it was until repairs had been completed, and that took some five days, by which time the Commander had steam coming out of his ears.

News gets out

"It's Carol here. Have you seen that report in the paper about the thunderstorm in Scotland?"

Abigail replied that she knew nothing about it, but why should she. Why should it be of any interest to her? Carol exhorted her to take a look and ring her back.

Picking up the paper, Abigail scanned through it looking for an eye-catching heading that may have some relevance for her. Her eyes came to rest on something on page five.

Navy Missile Extinguishes Thunderstorm

She read the article with interest. Evidently a huge thunderstorm off the west coast of Scotland had been stopped by hitting it with a new kind of missile. The thunder, lightning and rain ended after the missile entered the cloud and created a loud bang.

Meteorologists were on their way to the area to study the latest phenomenon, which may have far-reaching implications. The possibility that this could have been weather that the Nimbus was providing, brought a realisation that the crew could have been injured, and she got back to Carol fast.

"I thought you might think the same as me. I'm going to ring Puffy."

Lengthy phone conversations took place over the next hour, between the crew and their female admirers, but for the moment that was the nearest they got to each other. The more pressing matter was getting Commander Percil off their backs or any other part of their anatomy for that matter.

After five long days at Stornoway, the time finally arrived when Cirrus and Puffy could make good their escape from Commander Percil, who was an absolute pain in the neck. Engineers from Black, Black & Blackemore's had completed the repairs to the Nimbus and it was fit to make weather again. Boarding the cloud machine, the crew couldn't wait to get the fan duct motors running again, and with clearance, and good riddance, from the airfield control tower, they ascended vertically to a position five thousand feet above the huge solitary hanger. The

Commander was standing outside the hangar doors making something in the form of a gesture towards them as they climbed to the heavens, but it didn't look like a kindly gesture.

"Shall we leave him something?" asked Cirrus.

A sudden deluge engulfed the gesticulating Commander, and the act was committed to history by a host of digital cameras, the results of which were distributed around the world within hours on a multitude of computers, using headings like: 'Whitewash gets a Washing Down'!

The locals living close to Stornoway airfield were greatly relieved to see daylight again, after such a prolonged period of darkness, and many held celebrations that evening, bringing out the best malt whiskies that they normally held over for Hogmanay.

Once airborne, the Nimbus flew a short distance east and then hovered off the coast. Contact was made with Uist Control and they discovered that the trials had been concluded, and the Nimbus was no longer needed. Their testing days were over, and it was time to go back home and spend some time with those glamorous admirers, and that's exactly what they proceeded to do, complete with a new stern.

The Death of a Colleague

The news breaks

After the rigours of missile testing, it was nice to be back at home in Slaidburn, and the sun shining through the lounge window brought a degree of tranquillity to what would otherwise be an ordinary Wednesday morning. Puffy was out in the garden, whilst Cirrus was sitting in his favourite chair, with a cup of coffee and the latest edition of The Monthly Downpour.

Cirrus was one of those individuals that read every single page of any magazine he subscribed to, and it was inevitable that he would eventually reach the page that described the death of one of his Wythenshawe colleagues. He was somewhat taken aback by the page heading: **Cloud Machine Owner Dies Suspended from Blackpool Tower.** Was it a case of suicide, and who was it? he thought. He read on to find the answers to his questions.

The report went on to describe what happened. The cloud machine Greystuff, crewed by Al Blighty and Flight Engineer Henry Black, had been raining in the dark, over the Irish Sea, at a point opposite Blackpool. The Greystuff had just completed a job and its skipper was getting rid of what was left of a Cumberland Grey, before making the journey back to Wythenshawe Weather Centre. They had almost rained off, when, it is assumed, a multiple motor failure occurred. The Greystuff plunged towards earth, but the crew managed to deploy the craft's emergency parachutes which helped to break their fall. The prevailing westerly wind blew the machine towards the shore, and the parachutes caught on the top of Blackpool Tower. Having hooked on to the top of the tower, the descent was halted rather rapidly, and Al, not having fastened his seat belt, was thrown up against the craft's internal cabin ceiling, breaking his neck in the process. Henry faired a little better, having strapped himself in.

The parachute straps had held the weight of the hanging Greystuff, and it had come to rest about a third of the way down the tower. Recovery was going to be a tricky business, and emergency engineers from Black, Black & Blackemore's were called in. Whilst waiting for the engineers, the local Fire Service managed to ascend the tower to the point at which the Greystuff was impacting with it. Following instructions given to them over the phone, they managed to reach the exit door button, and pressing it, they gained access. The Firemen, acting with great bravery, entered the machine with much care. Their additional weight, or undue movement, could cause the parachute restraining straps to break, and that could result in a catastrophic fall of over three hundred feet, down to the tower building roof. They did, however, succeed in rescuing Henry, and recovered Al's body.

When the crew had been extricated from the Greystuff, there was then the small problem of recovering the cloud machine hanging from the tower, but that was a headache for the engineers. The recovery process was intriguing. The Royal Air Force was called in for help, and a Chinook helicopter arrived with an under-slung strop, which had a rope attached to it. The Chinook could not get too near the tower for fear of its rotor blades hitting it, but it did manage to hover over a part of the tower building roof. An engineer, standing on the roof, caught a hold of the end of the rope attached to the strop, and walked with it to the base of the tower, to attach it to another rope hanging down from the Greystuff. At this point, the two ropes were then pulled up to the cloud machine by the engineers aboard it. This then enabled the strop, hanging from the Chinook, to be pulled across and attached to a hoist they had managed to get around the cloud machine. With the Chinook now attached to the hoist, it could start to take the weight of the craft, and as it was pulled away from the tower, the engineers held on to ropes attached to the hoist, to prevent it suddenly swinging away and generating a dangerous degree of instability for the helicopter to cope with. The parachute straps were cut, and the Greystuff was free from its temporary captivity. The crowds below, watching this spectacle, gave a huge roar of approval, before going back to the business of eating candy floss, and buying 'kiss me quick' hats.

The Greystuff was eventually taken back to Black, Black & Blackemore's factory in deeper Salford, where a full investigation would be held to establish what had happened.

What a fascinating story, thought Cirrus, but at the same time he was sad to hear of the death of Al, whom he had known for many years. They had first met when they had joined the Territorial Army. Both of them had arrived at the School of Electronic Engineering at Arborfield to train as Telecommunication Engineers. At that time, Cirrus was a radio and television engineer in civilian life, and had thought it would be interesting to work on transmitter/receivers, as it would widen his knowledge and experience. He was therefore surprised to find out that Al was an undertaker from Newcastle-on-Tyne. Why would an undertaker want to train as a Telecommunication Engineer? The only explanation he ever elicited from Al was something to do with 'contacting the other side', whatever that meant.

Cirrus had one lasting memory of his colleague, which stemmed back to their days in the Territorial Army. They, along with some fellow soldiers, had been having a beer in a pub near Arborfield. Each of them took it in turns to describe what they did for a living in civilian life, but it was Al that had them all spellbound. He gave a vivid account of how a crematorium worked. His captivated audience spread to those others out for a pleasant night's drinking, and a deathly silence descended on the congregation of boozers. The Landlord was not impressed, and asked the group of soldiers to leave, since they were depressing his regular clientele. Perhaps the conversation had been slightly sobering for an ageing band of half pint drinkers, but that didn't make the request for them to leave any less embarrassing, and it had stuck in his memory ever since.

Making arrangements

Al Blighty's parents had passed away many years ago, but he had a brother called Sean, and a sister called Maureen. They had both moved from the North East of England to run a hotel in Portaferry in Northern Ireland, which was not far from the second home of Cirrus Cumulus, but he had not been aware of that.

Al had never talked about his family, but evidently they were close. Sean and Maureen were proud of what their brother did, but were sworn to secrecy, and never talked about it to anyone. They made all the burial arrangements, and liaised with Wythenshawe Weather Centre. Funeral Directors in Portaferry High Street would arrange for Al to lie in state in their Chapel of Rest, from which the funeral cortege would depart. Al had always said that when his time came, he would like a service of remembrance to be held in Ardquin Parish Church. This little church is in a beautiful spot that looks out towards Strangford Lough, and is in a most peaceful location. Neither Sean nor Maureen knew of any particular reason why their brother chose this church, but somehow it felt most apt.

After the service, the funeral cortege would move off and make its way back to Portaferry via the Lough Shore Road, which was most picturesque. This section of the route would feature in his colleagues' tribute arrangements. On reaching the town, the cortege would make its way through the centre, and take the Kircubbin Road, until it reached Ballymarish Cemetery, where he would be buried with full cloud honours.

After the funeral, invited guests would return to the hotel on Portaferry Shore Road, run by Sean and his sister, for a farewell meal. 'The Blight on the Shore' was a name suggested for the hotel by Al, and it had gone down well with the locals who had a good sense of humour, but whether it brought business to the place was open to conjecture. Nevertheless, the name had stuck for the last ten years.

Mr Spite called a meeting at Wythenshawe to discuss things appertaining to the forthcoming funeral with all of Al's colleagues. First on the agenda was, who would represent his colleagues at the funeral? Al's brother and sister had expressed a wish that someone should be present from Wythenshawe, and it was unanimously decided that the Superintendant, Mr Spite, was the right man. Then there was the question of flowers, what would be appropriate, and after a lengthy debate, a decision was made.

The major point of discussions surrounded the most appropriate form of symbolic pageantry that they should embark on in connection with the church remembrance service, the funeral cortege, and finally, the burial. It all had to be choreographed carefully, and tastefully, to give Al the send off he would be proud of. It took an extraordinary amount of time to resolve this particular side of things, and at times, it felt as if it was insoluble. With all the experience the cloud machine owners had, it was inevitable that they would find a way of sending Al off with great ceremony, and one that his family would be proud of. With the main business dealt with, the congregation turned their attention to the subject of a headstone for Al's grave, and it didn't take long to come up with several ideas to put to his brother and sister, and then the meeting was concluded.

Lying in state

The Chapel of Rest in Portaferry High Street received the coffin of Al Blighty, and for a couple of days, that is where he lay in state, for those that wished to pay their last respects. That included Mr Spite, who represented his entire cloud machine operator colleagues from Wythenshawe. Mr Spite was the right man to do this. He had an air of great respectability about him, and both his deportment and manner were exemplary.

Earlier, back at Wythenshawe, there was a fever of activity to get everything ready for the funeral. Each machine owner had to carry out the mandatory checks required before flight, and then get airborne in the night sky to fly out over the Irish Sea and make clouds. Having reached this stage, the gaggle of newly-made clouds made their way past the Isle-of-Man to a point offshore, opposite the entrance to Strangford Lough, and there they split up. One cloud was designated to take up station over Ardquin Parish Church, and had certain things to practise. The greater majority would be on station as the funeral cortege made its way from church to Portaferry, and they had quite a lot of things to rehearse, and timing was particularly important in their case. Finally, two clouds had been allocated special duties at the cemetery interment, and this included the Nimbus.

The finale had fallen to Cirrus to perform, and he was anxious not to let anyone down. He had to work closely with Wally Lenticular to perform his designated role, and once again timing was of the utmost importance.

No less than five people were required on the ground to act as observers, and send signals to the clouds using mobile phones. The observers would have to be cloud machine operatives, for only they would be conversant with how they did things. Five volunteers came forward, and they were transported to Northern Ireland in a participating cloud, and were dropped off in the night, close to Portaferry. Joe Riley kindly met the five volunteers that emerged from the cloud sitting on the ground in the middle of the night, and escorted them all in his minibus to their respective positions around the town.

In Wythenshawe Weather Centre, Mr Spite's secretary, Goldilocks, had prepared a plan of action for all the participants, both on the ground, and in the clouds, to ensure everything would be well co-ordinated. The results of her work were e-mailed to everyone, and the scene was set.

Few guests had been invited to Al's funeral. His only family was his brother Sean and his sister Maureen. Neither of them had married, although they did have close friends. Al was only known to a small number of people in Portaferry. He was a rather private person, although in recent times, he had been seen socialising with a local lady that worked in a bakery, but neither Sean, nor Maureen, had heard their brother talking about her. But he wouldn't; he was that sort of person. Apart from a few locals, and Mr Spite, there would be few people to witness Al's send off, or so it seemed.

Goldilocks took it upon herself to contact the Guild of Cloud Owners with the details of the forthcoming funeral in Portaferry, and they in turn, sent out a bulletin to all its members. There was a tradition of giving a good send off to any member that passed away, and the response was very typical. Within twenty-four hours of notification, every available room in Portaferry was being reserved, and the town was filling rapidly with strangers, who were not here for a holiday. That much was obvious from their black armbands, but who was it they had come to see buried? No-one of any prominence in the town had died recently, but the locals were about to find out.

The funeral

Al's coffin was placed in the hearse parked outside the Chapel of Rest, in Portaferry High Street, whilst a throng of mourners watched on. The funeral cortege moved off on its journey to the church that Al had liked so much. On top of the hearse was a Westmorland White cloud made up of white Lilies, and the name **Greystuff**, in red roses down each side. Al was going out under his own cloud!

A couple of limousines followed the hearse and two minibuses carried the rest of the mourners. The last minibus had been a last minute arrangement, and the words running down the side of it – **Travel to another World and let Quinn's minibus help get you there** – added nothing to the serenity of the occasion. The adults watching the cortege pass by had no difficulty with this slightly undignified feature, but the younger ones couldn't help a snigger or two. As the cortege negotiated the town square to get onto the Kircubbin Road, a great awe was apparent. The huge Westmorland White wreath was centre stage, and people were anxious to know of its significance, and what did **Greystuff** mean?

"Dats a very strange ting ta have on anybody's hearse."

"I hope dat it doesn't rain on him, poor fellow."

The cortege left Portaferry, before making a left turn into a narrow country lane that would take it to Ardquin Parish Church. There was a slight hold up when a herd of cattle took precedence, accompanied by the contents of their bowels, and the usual swarm of blue bottles looking for a smelly banquet. An apologetic farmer did his best to get his livestock into a field, and off the road, but it was not without protest from his cattle, and they left a great deal of evidence of their travels on the country lane. The mourners couldn't open the windows of the limousines to help remove the stench for fear of invasion by a blue bottle army. It was with considerable relief that they all arrived outside the small church, and no-one noticed the Manchester Black, hovering in the distance.

The service

Six of Al Blighty's colleagues shouldered his coffin and conveyed it into the little church. It was a long time since such a large congregation had been gathered together in this place, and the few locals, that had kindly and carefully prepared the church, were a little staggered by the numbers that crammed inside, many of them standing. The service was simple, but sincere, and the hymns sung had been chosen well, by a vicar that never knew Al, but had been given some information about him by his brother and sister. The congregation was in good voice, which is more than could be said for the small church organ, which had seen better days, and those were a long time ago.

As the service was nearing its end, the congregation became aware of the decaying light of day, until a point was reached when it was almost dark. The vicar paused in his service, and the little church bell rang, and it was followed by a huge crash of thunder. Heavy raindrops fell on the church, and for a very short time nothing but rain could be heard, until the little church bell rang again. The rain suddenly stopped, and it began to get light again. The congregation began to clap, and the vicar commented that Al Blighty was letting us know that his spirit was still at work in his new place.

When everyone emerged into the sunshine, there was no evidence of the Manchester Black. It had done its job, and done it well, and was on its way home, or to another job, maybe even another funeral! The six cloud machine crew members representing Wythenshawe Weather Centre shouldered the coffin, and brought it out into the sunshine before placing it in the hearse for its final journey. Sean and Maureen, Al's brother and sister, both shed a tear. They shared their grief, but they also shared a feeling for their brother's comrades that were here with them, to help them through the grieving process. Company at this time was much valued.

One man who was finding all this particularly upsetting, was Henry Black. Henry had spent all his years as a Flight Engineer, working with Al aboard the Greystuff. They had done many things together, and been to many places. The years had created a bond between them, a bond borne out of trust and comradeship. He was going to miss Al. Henry was also concerned about the future. How was he going to earn a living? He was too young to retire, but for the moment, there were other things to dwell on.

The final journey

The cortege got under way again, but would return to Portaferry by a different route. A right turn on the small country lane would take it down to the shore line of Strangford Lough, and soon after making the turn, a line of miniature Pearly white Westmorland White clouds came into view. They were all beautifully formed and exquisitely pearl in form. They ran the length of the shore road to Portaferry. Behind the Westmorland Whites was an enormous Manchester Black which seemed to extend upwards, as far as heaven itself, and its presence magnified the whiteness of the others.

Reaching the coastline, a crash of thunder heralded their arrival, and the first Westmorland White changed to a Cumberland Grey, and rained to produce an angel ray, and as the cortege moved on, each Westmorland White did the same. A second crash of thunder occurred when it reached the halfway point, and another as they drew level with the Strangford ferry boarding jetty.

Along the coastline, cloud machine crew members had formed a guard of honour, with one person every two hundred yards. Henry recognised crew from the Flier, the Dismal, Spitting, Hurricane, Softly Blows, and the Astro, amongst others. This was a great tribute to the late Al Blighty, and clearly demonstrated the respect in which he was held.

The cortege left the coast road to make its way through the town of Portaferry to its destination, Ballymarish cemetery. The spectacle of

Al's funeral had attracted a great many people on to the streets of the town to witness his passing, and everyone wanted to know more about the deceased, who was someone, clearly, very special. To have somebody like this in the middle of your community and not know anything about him was distinctly odd, but it wouldn't be for long, for the media have a habit of honing in on these kinds of things.

Once out of the town, it was a short distance to Ballymarish Cemetery, and the cortege arrived for the burial. The mourners gathered around the open grave, and each one received an umbrella. It was at this point that the presence of Wally Lenticular's machine, the Discovery, posing as a Manchester Black, was noticed up above them. The coffin was taken from the hearse and lowered into the grave. The vicar said some final words, and then invited mourners to cast soil onto the coffin. Just at this point, there was a roar of thunder from above, and everyone recognised this as a signal to open their umbrellas, and they did so to avoid being drenched by the rain that suddenly came, but not in the usual heavy form one gets from a Manchester Black, more the steady, light stuff associated with a Cumberland Grey. Be that as it may, the rain stopped just as the last soil was cast, and the sky was illuminated by an enormous pearly white Westmorland White that emerged from behind Wally's Black thing, and as it did so, another clap of thunder announced its arrival. The mesmerised mourners watched the Manchester Black slip away, if Manchester Blacks can do that, leaving the Glory provided by the Nimbus, care of Cirrus Cumulus and Percival 'Puffy' White.

To bring the interment to a close, the glorious Westmorland White started to ascend, and steadily got smaller, and smaller, until it finally disappeared altogether. There was then a temporary loss amongst folk, as to what to do. After such a funeral, there was, inevitably, a feeling of anti-climax. There was nothing for it now, but to board the limousines and minibuses and set off for 'The Blight on the Shore' Hotel, where refreshments had been organised by Sean and Maureen. Apart from anything else, it would be a relief to get rid of Quinn's minibus, and let it get on with helping other folk to travel to another world.

The invited guests were extremely glad to get inside 'The Blight on the Shore'. It had been a trying day, but one which they all felt proud of. They had given Al a great send-off. Sean and Maureen collared Mr

Spite CDM to thank him for what he and his colleagues had done. Mr Spite was delighted, if that's allowed at a funeral reception, and gave them an assurance that he would pass on their gratitude to his colleagues at Wythenshawe Weather Centre. He was quietly impressed with both the contribution made by his colleagues, and the level of decorum they had displayed. Mr Spite thought his colleagues were more his employees and that made him even prouder. Even as employees, rather than professional partners, which is what they were in reality, he was still fond of them all, and had immense pride in what they did, at least most of what they did.

Henry had a chat with the Superintendant about his future, for this would soon be preying on his mind, and he got an invitation to discuss matters back at Wythenshawe, at his earliest convenience.

"I understand you are Mr Spite, the man that organised the spectacle today?"

The media had soon got in on the refreshments, but if Mr Spite could keep them occupied, then that would be ok by the rest of them, and they continued to eat, drink and talk, and then drink some more, to the memory of Al Blighty.

Dividing the estate

There was something rather sombre about handling the estate of their late brother, but it had to be done, and Sean, Maureen, and Henry Black, together with their solicitor, sat around a table to do just that. The view from the front room window across the water towards Strangford, and the ferry making one of its numerous daily sailings, was particularly nice and it helped to bring a kind of calm to the proceedings. Mr Chilwell had acted on behalf of the Blighty family many times before, and was on good terms with them.

Opening his briefcase, Mr Chilwell took out some papers and shuffled them into some kind of order, and then cleared his throat, before proceeding.

"This is the final will and testimony of Alistair Blighty, late of Green Pastures, Great Budworth, Cheshire, England."

Looking up at those around him and clearing his throat again, he continued.

"I hereby leave my cloud machine, the Greystuff, to my friend, and faithful engineer, Mr Henry Black."

After a further pause, he went on.

"I hereby leave my monetary estate to be divided in the following way - £80,000 to be shared equally, between my sister, Maureen Blighty, and my brother, Sean Blighty. £10,000 to Ardquin Parish Church, to go towards a new organ, and for the upkeep of the church. Finally, £10,000 to The Guild of Cloud Owners welfare home, at Grange-over-Sands."

"Is that the one called 'The Head in the Sky?" enquired Sean.

"Yes, but its generally known as The Half Way House," replied Henry.

Mr Chilwell cleared his throat again, but this time as a signal for everyone to shut up.

"My home, 'Green Pastures', in the village of Great Budworth, I leave to my engineer Henry Black, with the proviso that he never grows any more cauliflower in the vegetable plot."

Sean and Maureen looked at each other, but whether it was in response to the giving of the house, or the growing of cauliflower, is not known.

"Finally, I want to donate the following memorabilia to The Museum of Clouds in deeper Salford. First, the framed photograph of myself standing at the side of the Greystuff. Second my cloud machine pilot's licence. Third, the simulated galley in my garage. Fourth, the Plan Position Indicator also in my garage. Fifth, my model of the Greystuff. And finally, the model of Greystuff as a Westmorland White cloud."

Mr Chilwell put the papers down on the table and looked up to face the three beneficiaries before clearing his throat once again.

"Well, there you have it. That's the way the estate is to be divided. I know you will have things to talk about, so I will bid you all good day, and be on my way."

Mr Chilwell was thanked, and he left, and the three beneficiaries poured themselves a drink to celebrate their good fortune. They raised their glasses and made a toast.

"To Alistair Blighty!"

The findings of the enquiry

Back at home in Slaidburn, Cirrus was partaking of his usual morning coffee when Puffy brought him a copy of the latest edition of The Monthly Downpour.

"I think you will find this interesting, skipper."

"Why, what's in it?"

"It's the findings of the Board of Enquiry that sat to determine what happened to Al's machine."

Cirrus immediately turned to the pages that contained the Board's findings, and read on.

After intensive scrutiny, no defects had been found in any of the Greystuff's four fan duct motors, and there was no evidence that they had ingested anything that would cause them to stop. In the cockpit, the Board had found that the motors were switched on, and the throttles were still in the last position they had been set in, namely, maximum power. The fuel gauges were functioning ok, and there was no evidence of any fuel blockages. The fuel pumps had also been working fine.

The enquiry finally turned its attention to the fuel tanks. No leaks or punctures to the tanks had been found, but they were all bone dry. The only conclusion that could be reached was that the Greystuff had simply run out of fuel. Both the machine's fuel log, and that of Wythenshawe Weather Centre were checked, and it was evident that no fuel had been taken on board for some time. The crew must have forgotten to check their fuel levels before getting airborne. The Board had concluded that the accident that killed Alistair Blighty was caused by pilot error.

Sabotage At Work

An arrogant man

Arthur Treadmill was six feet tall, broad shouldered, and good looking, and he knew it. His tendency to think a lot about himself would have been acceptable if he had kept it to himself, but that was something he was most reluctant to do. If anyone engaged in conversation with Arthur, it was one way only. Anything you had done, so had he, but much better. Anywhere you had been, he had too, and other places as well. The wary would avoid engaging in conversation with Arthur, but the unwary did not, and they would come to regret it, for once Arthur had got going, there was no stopping him.

The cloud machine, Drip, was owned by Arthur, and it was a credit to him. He kept it in pristine condition, but that couldn't have been difficult, since he didn't use it very much. How Arthur did all the things he claimed he did, was a mystery to his cloud machine colleagues, when they considered how much time the Drip languished in Wythenshawe's huge hangar. Larry Oliver was the Flight Engineer on board the Drip, and had worked with, or endured, Arthur, for many years. The fact that they never did much work with the Drip was to his advantage. Larry played the euphonium in a Brass Band and used all of the time he was not on board the Drip, rehearsing and doing things for his Band, which, rumour had it, was the highly successful Leyland Band. To all accounts, Larry was an accomplished player, and had taken part in The Great Shin Dig on St. Kilda.

The relationship between Arthur and Larry had stood the test of time, but this had been put down to the fact that little conversation took place between them. When not working together, Larry would be practising playing his euphonium, and evidently that was fine with Arthur because he happened to love Brass Bands. It was what might be described as, a marriage in Brass. Apart from the lack of conversation between the crew of the Drip, they were, really, as different as chalk and cheese. Larry was down to earth and had no time for the air of authority that Arthur tended to put on, and strangely, Arthur loved him for it.

Women had always taken the fancy of Arthur, but that fancy had, on numerous occasions, proved to be his downfall from which, however, he always bounced back. Any mistakes that he made with the opposite sex, he was guaranteed to repeat, for mistakes or not, he always seemed to have some girl on his arm. Many a young woman had fallen for his looks and charm, or waffle, as Larry called it. It was little wonder that the Drip spent so much time in the hangar at Wythenshawe; Arthur had difficulty fitting any work in, between his amorous pursuits.

The latest victim to Arthur's charms had been a pretty, and petite, girl called Wendy. She came from Birmingham from which she had brought her strong accent to visit Manchester and the North. It was more of her physical attributes that had attracted Arthur, rather than her Brummie accent, but when he got talking there wouldn't be much chance of anyone hearing it anyway. And when he wasn't talking they were both pursuing a range of activities that only induced ooohs and aaahs. Wendy was a nice girl, just not very good at sussing out lecherous individuals like Arthur. The relationship was not destined to last, and came to an end abruptly one evening. Arthur had misguidedly accepted an invitation to go to Birmingham with Wendy for a weekend at her parents' home. On arrival, he was met by her mother Charlotte. She recognised him immediately as the man she had had a short relationship with on holiday in Jersey the year before, and her husband recognised him as well. Arthur's visit to Birmingham was cut short, and so was his relationship with Wendy, whom he had mentally confined to the transfer list!

Gwen, from Llandudno, was another female from a long line of girls who had fallen under the spell of Arthur's charms. Some girls had lucky escapes, like Wendy, some had given Arthur the push, and some, the unfortunate ones, suffered the ignominy of a relationship that lasted as long as Arthur's infatuation or lust, lasted, and then they got the push. Fortunately, the majority of women that came temporarily under his spell, did not fall into the latter category. Gwen realised what the score was at an early stage, and ended things before her dignity suffered a blow.

Most people would think that women would get to know about Arthur and steer clear, but Manchester is a big place, and it has a big pool of girls. The likelihood of them all knowing Arthur was exceedingly slim, and he was able to ply his charms with a degree of impunity. For the moment, however, there was no-one under the influence of his extensive repertoire of chat-up lines, although he was still trying.

"Haven't you pulled lately?" asked Larry.

"I'm taking a rest, Larry," replied Arthur.

"I'll bet the missus is wondering what's wrong."

There was no reply to this latter comment.

The Drip had just been washed down in Wythenshawe's hangar, and the crew sat inside to take a rest. Mr Spite ascended the entry ladders and, reaching the open door of the craft, he called out, "Treadmill, Treadmill, are you there?"

Arthur recognised the voice and replied, "Yes, come aboard."

"You keep the Drip in excellent condition."

"What do you expect? I'm a professional you know."

"That's so. I have a job you may be interested in."

"I don't think I can accommodate anything at the moment," replied Arthur.

Larry looked at his skipper, and wondered why he couldn't take a job on at the moment. It was ages since they had done anything.

"Anyway, Spite, you know I don't take anything on that doesn't pay over five thousand pounds."

"I'm surprised that you can afford that kind of attitude," said a disgruntled Mr Spite.

"You should know by now, that the Drip has a particular reputation to maintain, and that can't be done by taking on just any old cloud job."

"But this isn't just any old cloud job."

"Be that as it may, Spite, I'm too busy at present. Now if you could leave me, I have things to get on with."

Mr Spite left the Drip thinking what an arrogant person that womanising Treadmill could be. He strode out of the hangar and made his way back to his office.

First Acquaintance

Wythenshawe Weather Centre had a thriving Social Club, called 'The Silver Lining', and each month, held a Saturday night dance that was well supported by both the Centre Staff, and the many cloud machine crews that were not busy creating a storm somewhere. These occasions helped create the good morale that was so essential to a cohesive work force. They were a chance for people to let their hair down, and relieve themselves of some of the pressure of their weather work.

Arthur first cast his eyes on Abigail Windrush at one of the Social Club dances, and he was taken by what he saw. She was tall, slim, curvy and good looking, in fact, everything he desired from his victims. He noticed that she only used traces of make-up to enhance her best features; nothing was overdone. She dressed simply, but nicely and would not be out of place anywhere. She clearly had good taste. Not being able to take his gaze away from her, he noticed how at ease everyone that came into contact with her seemed to be. She had an easy-going nature with people, and those that got into conversation with her soon realised that she was quite an intelligent and informed person, although considering she was the owner and skipper of a cloud machine, that should have been no surprise.

Joy noticed that Arthur's eyes were wandering, and she had a pretty good idea where they were focused.

"Arthur, do you think we could have a dance," enquired Joy in an attempt to get him to focus on her.

"Not right now, dear. I'm looking at something."

"I can see that," replied Joy, and seeing that she was wasting her time, she slipped off to the ladies' room to powder something.

Wasting no time, Arthur made for the delectable Abigail, but was beaten to it by Sunny Blue, the skipper of the Flier.

191

Damn! thought Arthur. I'm going to have to wait this one out.

He then turned his mind to Sunny, and weighed up his prospects with Abigail.

No chance! he thought. With a set of teeth like his, if they were his, and a mop of hair that looked like an overgrown garden, there was not the slightest chance that a women like Abigail would take him seriously. Having said that, they looked happy together and Sunny appeared to be a good dancer.

Whilst waiting for the current dance to end, Joy reappeared on the scene, half-hoping that Arthur would turn his attention to her.

"Do you fancy a dance, Arthur," Joy asked, in anxious anticipation.

"No I don't, and you can bugger off," said an irritated Arthur.

"Well I know where I stand with you then Arthur Treadmill," and with that, Joy slunk off, but not before grabbing Bert Drummond around the waist and leading him onto the dance floor whilst he still had a pint in his hand. But he soon got rid of it, for his hand was needed for other things.

Arthur never noticed Joy's latest killing. He was mesmerised by the new woman in his dreams, Abigail Windrush, although at this stage he didn't really know much about her. He was developing a deep desire to know her better. That could have been a feeling that was building up inside him, or simply his lust coming to the forefront.

"Got your eyes on a victim tonight, Arthur," enquired his flight engineer, Larry.

"None of your business!"

"Oh, that means yes then."

"Mind your own!"

Larry decided it would be better to leave his lusting skipper to his own devices, and he meandered off to find more pleasant company.

The dance was coming to an end, and Arthur tried to work out where the new lady on his radar would step off the floor with Sunny. He would try and intercept them, and use Sunny as an alibi to meet her. He moved swiftly to meet them.

"Hello Sunny, glad you're here. I need to ask you something."

"Shove off, Arthur!" said Sunny, who excused himself to Abigail as he dashed off.

That was most opportune, for now Arthur was left in the company of Abigail, and he wasted no time in exploiting the situation.

"I'm sorry if I have interrupted things."

"No you haven't, Sunny had to leave. He has a big cloud to deliver tomorrow."

Her voice was music to Arthur's ears. She sounded cultured, but warm, and close up she smelled good.

"I'm Arthur Treadmill, skipper of the Drip."

"Hello, Arthur, I'm Abigail Windrush, the skipper of the Hurricane."

"So, she had status as well as all the other female attributes," thought Arthur, who was besotted. Conversation flowed between the two of them before she had to visit the ladies' room, and in her absence, Larry came across to speak to him.

"Skipper, you're not going to get far there."

"Why not?"

"She's got a thing going with Cirrus Cumulus."

"Cirrus! He's got to be more than ten years older than she is, and he's a boring fart."

Before the conversation had got any further, Abigail was spotted returning.

"Scarper, Larry! I don't want you cramping my style."

"Just remember what I told you."

Abigail arrived in Arthur's danger zone, and his desire to have her suddenly shot up his 'must have scale'.

"Did you hear about that nasty chap Cumulus?"

Abigail looked at Arthur slightly mystified, but decided to let him go on.

"No. Why do you say that?"

"Word is going around the Centre that he his two-timing a most beautiful woman, and she hasn't got a clue about it."

"Really!"

"I'm told he is a master of deception when it comes to women. He has a long list of conquests, and little in the way of conscience."

Abigail didn't believe a word of what Arthur was saying, but she did wonder if it was a rumour going around, and if so, who had started it.

"This is the first time I have heard of it, and why are you telling me anyway, we are strangers after all?"

"Oh, just making conversation."

"I'm afraid I must go now, I have a job on tomorrow."

"It was nice meeting you. Perhaps we can talk again sometime," replied Arthur.

Over my dead body, thought Abigail as she left.

Seeing Abigail leave, Larry came across to his skipper to see what had transpired.

"I gave her the run down on Cirrus."

"What do you mean, you gave her the run down on Cirrus?"

"I told her what a two-timing womaniser he is."

"That's rich coming from you, and considering Cirrus isn't here tonight to defend himself, it's a bit below the belt. You can be a nasty bugger at times skipper," and Larry hurriedly walked away before he did something violent.

A plan is hatched

Arthur was desperate to see Abigail again and wanted the chance to be alone with her. He needed to hatch some kind of a plan that would lure her on to his patch, so to speak. After careful deliberation, he worked out what he was going to do, and now it was a case of making contact again.

Entering Wythenshawe Weather Centre, Larry spotted a poster on the notice board.

"Hey, skipper, did you know that there is another dance on in The Silver Lining Club next Saturday?"

Arthur didn't know, but was glad to hear it. Before he got too excited he looked at the details of who was doing what currently, and he soon came down the list to the Nimbus. In black and white, it clearly listed the Nimbus as being away over the Faroe Islands next weekend, and that suited him down to the ground. With Cirrus Cumulus out of the picture, there was nothing to stop him from making a beeline for his current heart throb. He continued reading through the list to see if

Abigail was away or not, and to his good fortune, but not necessarily hers, she wasn't. So, Saturday it would be.

"That Sunny Blue bloke doesn't half spend some time dancing with Abigail," remarked Arthur.

"Not surprising really. They won a few competitions a couple of years ago."

"Oh, I see," said a relieved Arthur.

"You should leave her alone. She's spoken for."

Larry could see that his lecherous skipper had an eye for the glamorous Abigail, and didn't think it was right. For a start, Cirrus was a decent bloke, and didn't deserve one of his colleagues trying it on with the woman he never dreamed would be interested in him, but whom he was falling for, in a big way. There was a second reason, but it had never stopped his skipper from philandering in the past.

"I'm glad to have spotted you, Abigail. I want to discuss something with you."

Well if that's a 'come-on' it's a strange one, thought Abigail, but it wasn't going to stop her from letting him carry on.

"I have just purchased the latest technology in flying helmets, and wondered if you could give me your opinion of it?"

Technology and anything to do with it always turned Abigail on. She had an avid interest in all things aeronautical. This was something possibly interesting.

"What's special about the helmet?" she asked.

"Well, it's got a built-in all-round view finder. An image of what's outside a cloud is projected on to the helmet visor, and a small knob on the side of the helmet allows a 360° image to be moved past your eyes. All you have to do is plug a lead from the helmet into a socket on the flight deck."

"What's the big advantage? You have a TV screen."

"True, but whilst the TV screen is displaying the journey ahead, the helmet allows you to see everything that's going on around your cloud."

Now that made a lot of sense to Abigail, and Arthur could see that he had her hooked.

"Are you in the Weather Centre next week?"

"I'm there on Wednesday morning," replied Abigail.

"Good! I'm there as well on Wednesday. I will be on board the Drip, checking a few things out. Why not come and have a look then, and tell me what you think?"

This was not what Abigail had initially expected, and she was interested in the new helmet, so she thought why not, and agreed.

Arthur was jubilant that his plan was working and walked away smugly, thinking that this would help convince her that it was his new helmet that was the point of interest, and not his lustful desires.

There were only a handful of cloud machines in the huge hangar on the all important Wednesday morning, and not another soul in sight, which was quite convenient. Arthur pressed the button on the side of the Drip and the entry door automatically opened, followed by the deployment of the access ladder. He entered the machine, which was already dimly lit. He made his way to the cockpit and sat in the pilot's seat to patiently await the arrival of his female fancy. He had a good view of the hangar interior from the cockpit window, and he kept an eye out for her.

Almost an hour passed, and Arthur was getting a bit frustrated at the lack of activity, when, out of the corner of his eye, he spotted her entering the hangar through a small door built into one of the large hangar access doors. She sauntered across the hangar in the direction of the Drip, and his heart missed a beat. Bloody hell! The plan is working. He pulled himself back from the window in order not to be seen. Abigail ascended the ladders and paused as she entered the cloud machine.

"Hello, hello! Are you there, Arthur?" she called out.

"Come on up to the cockpit," cried Arthur.

Abigail walked down the machine's narrow corridor and into the Drip's cockpit. Arthur was standing waiting for her, and he simply couldn't contain himself. He had dreamt of this occasion many times and he wasn't going to waste a moment.

"Crikey Abigail, you're absolutely lovely!" And before she could respond, he had wrapped his arms around her and held her in a tight embrace, before attempting to get his lips impacting on hers. Abigail recoiled as best she could from the approaching lips, but the arms of steel embracing her restricted her freedom of movement.

"I came to try out your helmet not try you out!" she cried.

"Don't resist me, Abigail. I've waited for this moment for a long time and I'm not wasting it now."

Arthur made a second attempt at sharing the glory of his well-developed kissing talent with this delectable woman, but she didn't share his enthusiasm and aimed a deft blow with her shapely right leg at his nether regions. After an embarrassing struggle, Arthur's passion became subdued, and he became subservient to the pain in the region of his groin.

In true stateswoman mode, Abigail made it clear that the only man she was interested in was Cirrus Cumulus, and hence he, that is Arthur, was wasting his time. Arthur's powers of persuasion failed to have any impact, and he was left watching her shapely backside exiting the Drip, and Abigail expressing the opinion that he and his machine had something in common, they where both 'Drips'.

Ruining a reputation

After Arthur's disastrous Wednesday, it became clear to him that, unless he could destroy the reputation of a certain Cirrus Cumulus, there was no point in pursuing his obsession with the delightful Abigail Windrush, who, he was sure, would eventually succumb to his charms. The difficulty was how could he do it? He mused for some time before reaching the conclusion that the best approach would be to sabotage one of the jobs that Cirrus was contracted to do, and do it in such a way that it brought him into disrepute. But how?

A visit to Wythenshawe Weather Centre gave Arthur the opportunity to study what everybody was contracted to do, and when. Looking at the details of what the Nimbus was involved with, he noticed that, coming up shortly, the Nimbus had been contracted to provide overnight rain at the Chelsea Flower Show in the event of there being none of nature's making. That could provide the solution to the problem, he thought, and he rushed off to think about it.

The Nimbus was due to get airborne to pour rain on Chelsea late that evening, and therefore Arthur arrived at Wythenshawe Weather

197

Centre in the morning. Cirrus and his flight engineer, Puffy, would not be arriving to check the Nimbus over until the afternoon, and this would therefore be an opportune time to do the dirty deed. There didn't appear to be anyone about, and Arthur gained access to the Nimbus by pressing the button on the side of the craft that opened the door and lowered the access ladder, and went about his dirty business. It was possible to ensure that the button wouldn't work without keying in a number on an adjacent keyboard, but the fire regulations appertaining to the hangar prohibited that. When he had done his dastardly deed, he disposed of the evidence by putting it in the skip at the back of the hangar.

In the afternoon, Cirrus and Puffy arrived to check the Nimbus over. Once that was done, they checked that the fuel tanks for the four fan duct motors were topped up, and then took aboard several days' rations before taking a break and having a meal. When it got dark, the motors were started, and the Nimbus taxied out of the hangar and into the worldly darkness. After clearance from Wythenshawe Control, it ascended into the night sky until reaching five thousand feet, and then hovered. Cirrus activated the ID Beacon, and then moved off on a heading of 270° to reach the Irish Sea, where it could atomise the liquid below them, and create a Cumberland Grey around them. With that process out of the way, they could make the journey to Chelsea. All it required was the punching in of the co-ordinates of the start and end locations in the soakometer/navaid, and the rest should be all plain sailing, or at least, plane flying.

Early the following morning, the Nimbus arrived over Chelsea, and was put into the hover. No rain would be required until the following evening, and the crew could have breakfast before getting some sleep. This was a night shift job.

The following evening the Nimbus did its job whilst most good folks down below were tucked up in bed and getting a good night's sleep. The Nimbus slightly drizzled on the flower show for several hours. At least drizzle is not as noisy as a downpour and shouldn't disturb folks. With the drizzling done, there was nothing else to do until the next evening when they would do the same again, if required. The Cumberland Grey, and the stock of onboard water and ice, gave the Nimbus three nights' duration of drizzle, should it be needed, and the provisions aboard would sustain the crew.

Cirrus and Puffy had just slipped into a good night's coma, although it was, strictly speaking, a good day's coma, when a loud voice burst forth from the craft's radio.

"Cumulus, what the hell's going on in Chelsea? Cumulus, can you hear me?"

Both Cirrus and Puffy groped their way out of their bunks, and feeling slightly startled, tried to bring themselves back to the land of the living. Cirrus made his way over to the radio and replied to the voice he had just been woken by.

"It's Captain Cumulus here. What can I do for you?"

"It's Spite hear you blithering idiot! What the devil have you done at Chelsea?"

"We drizzled on it."

"But what did you drizzle on it? Look at your TV screen and you will see what I mean. They are going mad down there."

Cirrus, and Puffy, who had heard everything, looked at the TV screen on the flight deck, and what they saw was an enormous collection of soapy-looking bubbles over the whole of Chelsea.

"Bloody Hell, Captain, look at that!"

"Cumulus, you better get back here to Wythenshawe before they find a way of evaporating you big time, and rain whatever it is you are raining, before you get back."

The Nimbus left the scene of Chelsea bubbles, and headed back to the Irish Sea. Once darkness had descended, the Nimbus created a one hour deluge to rid itself of its Cumberland Grey, but they did take the precaution of letting Liverpool Coastguard Station know. A sea-going Fire Tender was dispatched to disperse the mountain of bubbles sitting on a large area of the Irish Sea, using a dispersant that had been successful with oil spills. The Fire Tender was successful in its mission, and discovered several boats, together with a Northern Ireland Ferry in the midst of it all, and they were all much cleaner.

Whilst it was still dark, and having disposed of its Cumberland Grey, the Nimbus headed back for Wythenshawe. The cloud machine grapevine had ensured that word had got around the cloud community regarding the Chelsea Bubble Show, and a sizeable crowd had gathered to jeer the Nimbus home. This was just about the worst return Cirrus could ever remember. Once taxied inside the huge hangar, the doors closed behind them and the lights came on. The crowd gathered around the craft as it was negotiated into its regular parking spot, and then came the humiliating bit! As the door of the Nimbus opened and the access ladders deployed, there was a deadly silence, but that changed as Cirrus emerged. A huge round of laughter and guffawing announced both their arrival, and their new found status as Wythenshawe's Clown Clouds, but they did have the cleanest cloud machine around, which now looked as if it was a fresh-from-factory delivery.

A clean repair job

"Now look here, Cumulus, there is no way you are going to get another job here until you have had the Nimbus fully inspected."

It was not an auspicious start to the meeting with Mr Spite CDM.

"I have no idea what went wrong, Mr Spite, but I have taken steps to get Black, Black & Blackemore's to carry out a full inspection, and I am awaiting the results," replied Cirrus.

"Well let me know the results as soon as you can. At the moment we are faced with a hefty bill."

Cirrus left Mr Spite's office feeling distinctly 'down in the mouth'!

It didn't take the engineers from Black, Black & Blackemore's too long to come up with any findings, and the results were quite surprising.

"We found traces of washing up liquid in the water storage tanks, the evaporator, and the dispensers. Whoever did this was certainly anxious to make sure that it worked," said the engineer from the Salford Works.

"Is it all cleaned out now?"

"Oh yes! You shouldn't have any more trouble now."

Puffy was glad to hear that the problem had been rectified, but like his captain, he was mystified at the thought of how it had all come about.

"What did you say happened? The engineers found washing up liquid in the water tanks, evaporator, and dispensers! We must have a saboteur at work. Does anyone have a grudge against you, Cumulus?"

"Not that I am aware of," replied Cirrus.

"In that case, we better convene an emergency meeting, and you better be there."

"Am I re-instated for work, Mr Spite?"

"Let's just see if we can get to the bottom of this first. Are you short of money?"

That was a pretty decent thing for Mr Spite to ask, thought Cirrus.

"No, I am ok at present, but thanks for asking."

"Don't mention it. Someone has done the dirty on you, and I intend finding out who."

It was about a week later that the emergency meeting was held in the conference hall at Wythenshawe Weather Centre, and it was very well attended. What few cloud machines owners that couldn't make it were all doing important jobs that couldn't be left. Mr Spite addressed the assembly and described what had happened at the Chelsea Flower Show, which brought forth considerable laughter, but it died down as he raised his hands.

"Ladies and gentlemen, I am sure you will agree that someone like Captain Cirrus Cumulus CDM is not likely to have committed such a blunder knowingly. You all know of him as a man who plans everything down to the last detail. He was just as surprised as you are about what happened. The truth is, ladies and gentlemen, this was a case of sabotage."

A momentary hush was followed by hurried whispers, accompanied by much gesticulating, and looking around. Mr Spite raised his hands again, and order was soon restored.

"Captain Cumulus has no idea who would do such a thing to make him a source of ridicule, but I am sure we have a saboteur at work, and that person, or persons, may well be among us."

There was an explosion of talking at this point and much turning and arm-waving as opinions were exchanged, and two people in particular were pretty confident that they knew the likely culprit. Mr Spite, raising his hands again, went on: "If any one of you has any information that may lead us to the culprit, I would urge you to come and see me. I assure you, that I will treat everything in confidence."

The meeting broke up, but the assembled cloud machine crews did not disperse so fast, and many stayed for some time discussing what they had been told. Others just filled in the time until the bar opened in the The Silver Lining Club.

It was not long after the meeting that Abigail decided it was time to go and talk to Mr Spite. She nervously knocked on his door, which was uncharacteristic of her, but this was a new experience, and it felt a bit like she was welshing on someone. She knew however, that this was the right thing to do.

"Come in. Ah, Abigail, how nice to see you. What can I do for you?"

Abigail related her experience with Arthur to Mr Spite, who sat and listened intently.

"That fellow Treadmill has always been a womaniser. I feel damn sorry for his wife."

Abigail was somewhat taken aback by the reference to Arthur's wife. She had no idea he was married, but that didn't change anything.

"He was lying about the helmet as well," Mr Spite went on. There is no such a thing. He was using that to lure you to his lair. Have you told Cirrus yet?"

"No I haven't."

"I think you better had, but in the meantime, I want a word with Arthur Treadmill."

Abigail left the office to go and find Cirrus, and as she left, she heard a message going out on the tannoy.

"Mr Arthur Treadmill to report to Mr Spite immediately. Mr Arthur Treadmill to report to Mr Spite's office immediately."

Fate takes a hand

Arthur Treadmill stood in front of Mr Spite's desk whilst he was given a severe dressing down. He was not asked if he had been the saboteur; it had already been decided that he was. And it was hard to challenge that assumption, since the amount of detail Mr Spite seemed to be knowledgeable of, regarding his ploy with Abigail, was most comprehensive. In the end, Arthur came clean, and admitted that he was responsible for everything that had happened.

"So you admit it then, Treadmill. It was pretty despicable that you should be trying it on with his female companion in the first place, but then, when you were rebuffed, you used your evil jealousy to try and make a fool of a very decent man."

Arthur coughed and spluttered, but didn't manage to say a word. He just waited for the crunch to come.

"Treadmill, you will pay the bill from Chelsea Flower Show, and in addition to that, I am suspending your cloud machine pilot's licence for six months."

Six months suspension and a bill to pay, it could have been worse, thought Arthur, and he turned to leave Mr Spite's office, but as he did so, the door was flung open and through it came his enraged wife, Lilly, with a large suitcase in her hand.

"I'm sorry for the intrusion Mr Spite, but I couldn't stop her from coming in," said a very nervous Goldilocks.

Lilly had been getting her breath back as Goldilocks was doing the talking, and then she started with a vengeance.

"I thought I might find you here, you great philanderer! Now I have news for you, Arthur Treadmill. I've been on your treadmill for long enough, and I'm through with it. Here's your suitcase with all your things in it. You can go and find somewhere else to live, and while I'm on with it, your place is being taken by someone else."

"What do you mean, Lilly?"

"It means I have another man, and that man is twice the man you are."

"And who is this other man, Lill?"

"It's one of your mates, Bert Drummond."

Bert was six foot three inches tall, and had shoulders to match. He had a flair for dancing, and boxing, and he was not someone Arthur felt he could face up to, and he mentally capitulated on the spot.

Lilly stormed out of Mr Spite's office followed by Arthur, at a slow and dejected pace. The Superintendent couldn't help smiling to himself and thinking, 'what goes around comes around', and Goldilocks felt relieved that all the excitement was over. Arthur had to face his colleagues as he left the Centre, and he learned first hand how it feels to be ridiculed and made a fool of.

Cirrus was humbled when he heard from Abigail what she had just told Mr Spite. His emotions boiled over and he embraced her, and kissed her, in a way he thought he had forgotten how to, and it was so good. A blossoming relationship might have implications for the future; only time would tell. In the meantime, she felt great!

Epilogue

Phew!

Who could blame the crew of the Nimbus from wanting to take a break at this point in the weather? When all is said and done, not many of us have such a demanding variety of things to do in a season. The expression 'it's all in a day's work', could hardly be regarded the same as, 'all in a week's weather', when one considers everything that the Nimbus might be called upon to do.

Fighting forest fires, delivering spies, guiding lost ships, keeping lovers apart, and attending funerals, may not be what you expected clouds to be involved with, but now you know, and it may be a bit of a shock. Talking of shocks, the Nimbus had its share, what with crashing on a delivery flight, freezing into a great lump of cloud ice, being hit by a missile, not to mention being sabotaged; it was all part of the itinerary.

Good training prepares everyone to cope with a wide variety of contingencies, and the crew of the Nimbus wisely fitted a course in to help them, and its value proved its worth in so many different circumstances. Having survived to this point, the future can be contemplated, and the past remembered, and who knows, Cirrus may even get that mysterious jug of 'Rob's tea' out for a celebratory drink.

I don't know about you, but I'm curious to find out if anything will come of the thread of romance that time has been developing in the world of clouds. Will there be a silver lining, a golden ray of sunshine, something at the end of a rainbow, or will it turn out to be a cloudy day, or a shower of tears? Whatever may happen, you can guarantee that it will have to fit in with the usual unusual weather.

ABOUT THE AUTHOR

Tony Smith, author of 'A Cloud's Life', is a retired Further Education Lecturer and former RAFVR(T) and SCC RNR Officer. He has a wealth of experience of young people and all things flying. As Bachelor-of-Education and former glider pilot he is suitably qualified to waffle on about a lot of things.

When Tony's head is not in the clouds, he builds model aircraft and helps a local Brass Band.

Tony is married and has two daughters, two granddaughters and a grandson. He lives in Atherton, a former mining and mill town in the north-west of England.

The author in his younger days chasing a cloud or was it a dream?

ILLUSTRATIONS

Cloud Machine – Nimbus – grade 1

SIDE ELEVATION

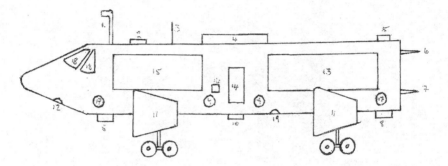

1. Periscope with tv camera which has infra-red capability to see through cloud or in the dark.
2. GPS antennae (Global Positioning System).
3. VSI antennae (Vertical Separation Indicator – used in cloud formation flying).
4. Emergency parachutes.
5. Identification Beacon (every cloud machine has its own ID code)
6. Telephone antennae.
7. Radio Transmitter/Receiver antennae.
8. Atomiser – converts water into cloud by a process of evaporation (some water is stored onboard, some as ice).
9. Dispenser – converts stored water and stored ice plus cloud vapour into rain by a process of melting and condensing.
10. SOAKometer – early form of navigation aid with built in water location system.
11. Fan Duct Motor – propels cloud. A cloud has its own natural buoyancy.
12. Porthole for winch cable.
13. Saddle type water storage tank.
14. Side entry door. -
15. Fuel tank for Fan Duct Motors.
16. Panel of buttons to open/close entry door and deploy/retract entry ladders.
17. Loudpeakers.
18. Cockpit window.
19. Fuel hose point.

Side elevation of the Nimbus

PLAN VIEW

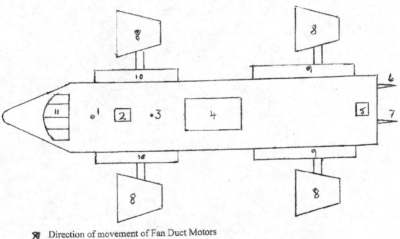

Direction of movement of Fan Duct Motors
to yaw the cloud left or right.
Movement made by cockpit rudder pedals.

1. Periscope with tv camera which has infra-red capability to see through cloud or in the dark.
2. GPS antennae (Global Positioning System).
3. VSI antennae (Vertical Separation Indicator – used in cloud formation flying).
4. Emergency parachutes.
5. Identification Beacon (every cloud machine has its own ID code)
6. Telephone antennae.
7. Radio Transmitter/Receiver antennae.
8. Fan Duct Motor – propels cloud. A cloud has its own natural buoyancy.
9. Saddle type water storage tank..
10. Fuel tank for Fan Duct Motors.
11. Cockpit window.

Plan view of the Nimbus

Manufacturers – Black, Black & Blackemore's, Salford

Cloud Machine – Nimbus – grade 1

FRONT VIEW

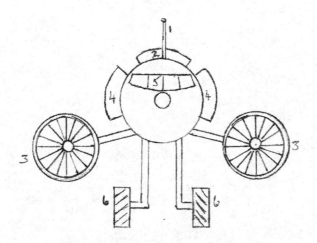

1. Periscope with tv camera which has infra-red capability to see through cloud or in the dark.
2. Emergency parachutes.
3. Fan Duct Motor – propels cloud. A cloud has its own natural buoyancy.
4. Fuel tank for Fan Duct Motors.
5. Cockpit window.
6. Rugged undercarriage.

Front view of the Nimbus

GENERAL ARRANGEMENTS

Fan Duct Motors (port side shown)

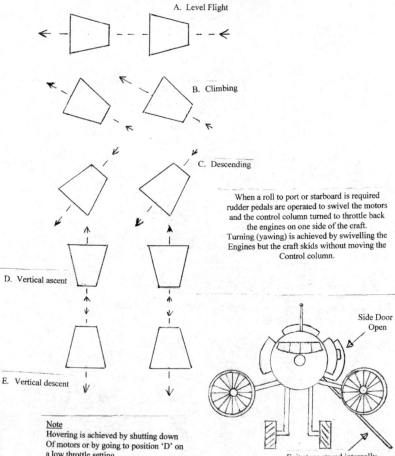

A. Level Flight

B. Climbing

C. Descending

When a roll to port or starboard is required
rudder pedals are operated to swivel the motors
and the control column turned to throttle back
the engines on one side of the craft.
Turning (yawing) is achieved by swivelling the
Engines but the craft skids without moving the
Control column.

D. Vertical ascent

E. Vertical descent

Side Door
Open

Note
Hovering is achieved by shutting down
Of motors or by going to position 'D' on
a low throttle setting.

Exit steps stored internally

General arrangements

<u>Manufacturers – Black, Black & Blackemore's, Salford</u>

<u>Cloud Machine – Nimbus – grade 1</u>

<u>INTERNAL LAYOUT and Emergency Features</u>

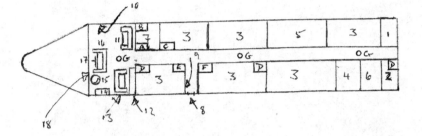

<u>Emergency features</u>

A = First Aid Kit
B + Fire Blanket
C + Oxygen Masks
D + Fire Extinguishers
E + Parachutes
F + Life Jackets
G + Smoke Detectors

1. Wash room.
2. Toilet
3. Refrigerator.
4. Mixer.
5. Sublimator.
6. Van de Graaf Generator.
7. Galley.
8. Side entry door.
9. Panel of buttons (includes door opening, access ladders & door jettison).
10. Drop down bunk location.
11. Passenger seat.
12. Flight Engineer's station.
13. Flight engineer's seat.
14. Winch winding mechanism.
15. Plan Position Indicater.
16. Pilot's seat.
17. Control column.
18. Flight deck instrument panel.

Internal layout of the Nimbus

PILOT'S COCKPIT ARRANGEMENTS

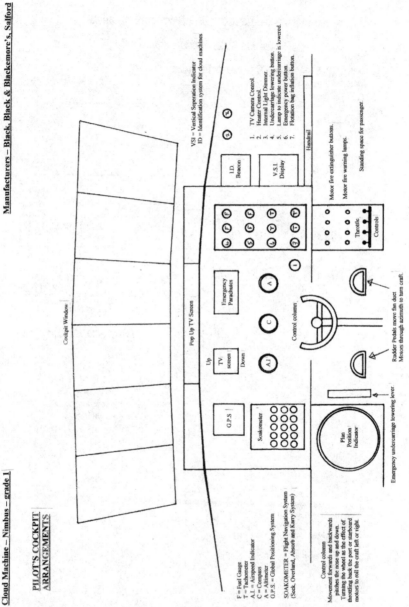

VSI = Vertical Seperation Indicator
ID = Identification system for cloud machines

1. TV Camera Control.
2. Heater Control.
3. Internal Light Dimmer.
4. Undercarriage lowering button.
5. Lamp to indicate undercarriage is lowered.
6. Emergency power button.
7. Flotation bag inflation button.

I.D. Beacon

V.S.I. Display

Handrail

Motor fire extinguisher buttons.

Motor fire warning lamps.

Standing space for passenger.

Cockpit Window

Pop Up TV Screen

Emergency Parachutes

Up
TV screen
Down

Control column

Rudder Pedals move fan duct
Motors through azimuth to turn craft.

G.P.S

Soakometer

Plan Position Indicator

Emergency undercarriage lowering lever.

Throttle
Controls

F = Fuel Gauge
T = Tachometer
A.I. = Airspeed Indicator
C = Compass
A = Altimeter
G.P.S. = Global Positioning System

SOAKOMETER = Flight Navigation System
(Soak, Overland, Absorb and Karry System)

Control column
Movement forwards and backwards
pitches the nose up and down.
Turning the wheel as the effect of
throttling back the port or starboard
motors to roll the craft left or right.

Pilot's cockpit arrangements aboard the Nimbus

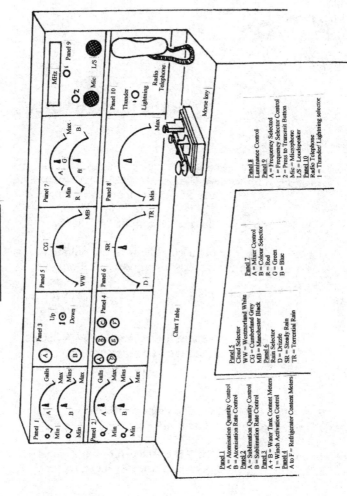

Flight Engineer's station aboard the Nimbus

The Guild of Cloud Owners

This Certificate is awarded to Sarah Whittle in recognition of her performing work experience on board the grade one cloud machine Nimbus.

Dates: – July 2nd – August 24th, 2013

As a member of the crew Miss Whittle enhanced her skills in the following areas: – 1. Cookery
2. Stores
3. Navigation
4. Weather

A special commendation is made in respect of manufacturing her first cloud.

Signed: – Captain Cirrus Cumulus C.D.M.
Flight Engineer: – Percival White

Superintendant: – Mr.I.N.Spite C.D.M.
Wythenshawe Weather Centre

Work Experience Certificate

MAPS

Route from Lücky in Slovakia to Perechyn in the Ukraine.

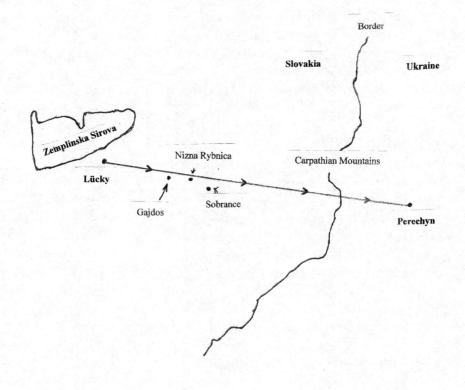

Location of landing site in Perechyn.

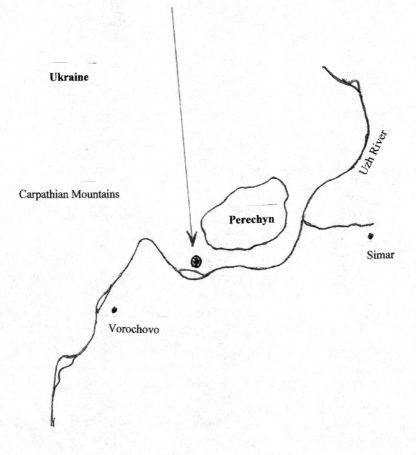

Route from Wythenshawe to Grantown-on-Spey
And Grantown-on-Spey to Peel on the Isle-of-Man.

Location on River Spey of atomising process.

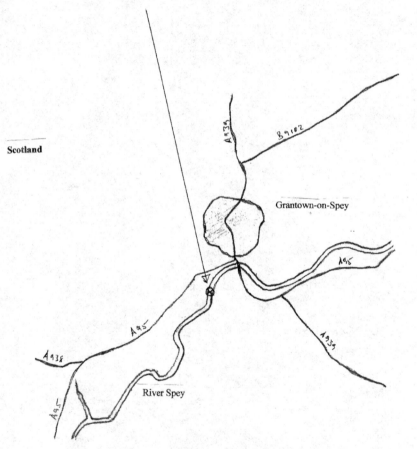

Scotland

Grantown-on-Spey

River Spey

Location of the crash site on the Isle-of-Man

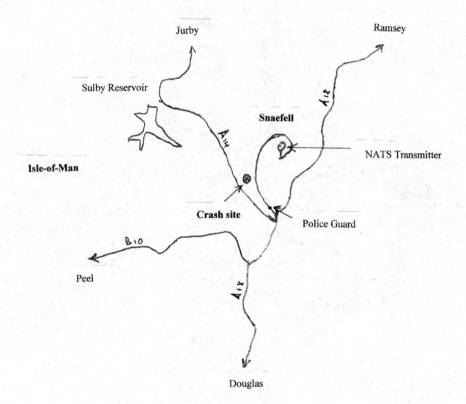

Route of Glasson Voyager and the Nimbus
from Mallin Head to Barrow in Furness.

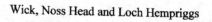
Wick, Noss Head and Loch Hempriggs

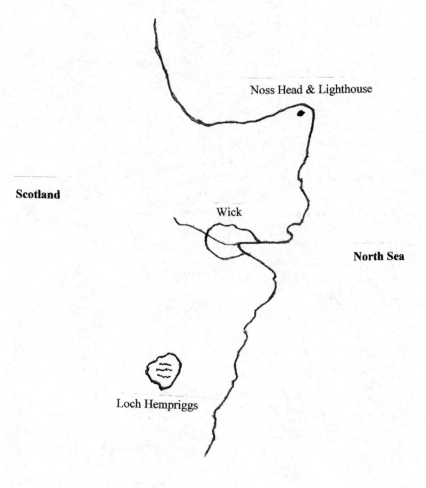

Noss Head & Lighthouse

Scotland

Wick

North Sea

Loch Hempriggs

227

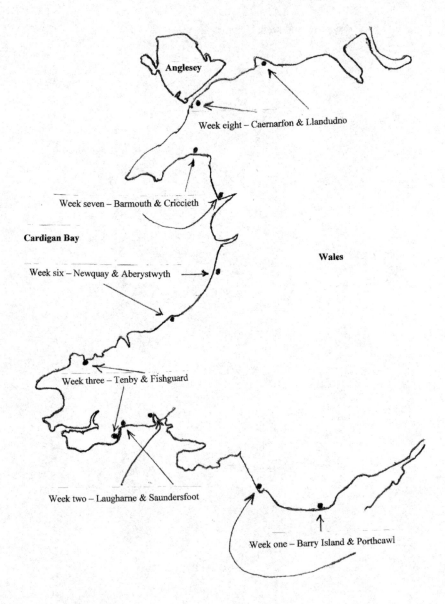

Locations for Welsh Tourism Calendar photo shoots.

Anglesey

Week eight – Caernarfon & Llandudno

Week seven – Barmouth & Criccieth

Cardigan Bay

Wales

Week six – Newquay & Aberystwyth

Week three – Tenby & Fishguard

Week two – Laugharne & Saundersfoot

Week one – Barry Island & Porthcawl

The Route of the Funeral Cortege

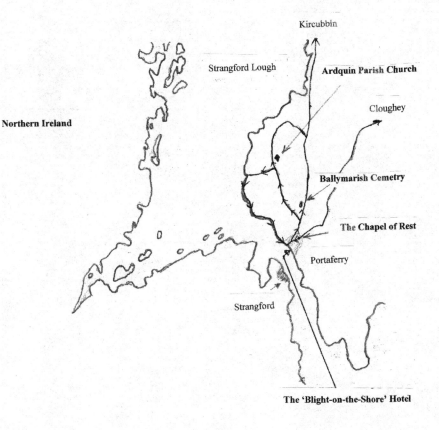

Kircubbin

Strangford Lough

Ardquin Parish Church

Cloughey

Northern Ireland

Ballymarish Cemetry

The Chapel of Rest

Portaferry

Strangford

The 'Blight-on-the-Shore' Hotel